STRANGE LOVE

ANN AGUIRRE

He's awkward. He's adorable. He's alien as hell.

Zylar of Kith B'alak is a four-time loser in the annual Choosing. If he fails to find a nest guardian this time, he'll lose his chance to have a mate forever. Desperation drives him to try a matching service, but due to a freak solar flare and a severely malfunctioning ship AI, things go way off course. This "human being" is *not* the Tiralan match he was looking for.

She's frazzled. She's fierce. She's from St. Louis.

Beryl Bowman's mother always said Beryl would never get married. She should have added a rider about the husband being human. Who would have ever thought that working at the Sunshine Angel daycare center would offer such interstellar prestige? Beryl doesn't know what the hell's going on, but a new life awaits on Barath Colony, where she can have any alien bachelor she wants.

They agree to join the Choosing together, but love is about to get seriously strange.

For Christa,

who loves alien jellyroll as much as I do.

ACKNOWLEDGMENTS

Thanks to any reader who picked up STRANGE LOVE, drawn by the gorgeous art, the awkward alien hero, or the talking dog. This is an odd love story, but I truly adore it. Thanks to Christa and Yasmin for making it even better with their insightful edits. Thanks to Isabel for the wonderful proofreading!

Next, I thank the Tessera Editorial team as a whole. Without them, there would be no book. From A to Z, they are *amazing*. As ever, thanks to my friends, the usual suspects. You know who you are and how well you keep me moving forward. Thanks especially to Rachel Caine who literally never gives up; I aspire to her levels of grit and fortitude.

Thanks to my family and the readers who are still waiting for more of my (strange) stories. My imagination belongs to all of you. Thank you for allowing me to entertain you when there are so many other choices.

The universe awaits. Read on!

[1]

ZYLAR SPOTTED THE SIGNAL LIGHTS at the provided coordinates before he landed, flashing as they raced across the ground. His prospective mate must be eager.

He'd had doubts about signing up for the matching service, but he couldn't resist the prospect of millions of potential partners across hundreds of compatible species. It was humiliating that he'd been passed over repeatedly in the annual Choosing, but not only would another failure disappoint his progenitors, this was also his final opportunity.

He wasn't the first to search off-world for a mate, at least. In his colony alone, there was a fearsome Revak warrior mated to his uncle and a Xolani doomsayer who'd paired with one of his cousins. His people weren't xenophobic, but he'd never pictured himself out-bonding until now. With a faint churr, he studied the blurred image on the screen before him.

For the past half a turn, he had been communicating with Asvi, and while she had never sent him a clear representation of herself, they'd gotten along well enough. He didn't need to find her attractive. Most importantly, she was amenable to relocating to Barath. She should be waiting on the ground. While he couldn't say he'd given both his hearts to Asvi, he believed they could build a life together.

No point in hesitating. The journey had been harrowing with a bad jump that dumped them in the middle of solar flares that could have scrambled his ship AI. Right now, Helix was quiet, running diagnostics after the near miss.

Zylar landed the shuttle with a flourish, though a grim feeling crept over him. The meeting point was dark. The strobing lights were gone. In fact, the whole area was more deserted than he had expected—altogether different than Asvi had *led* him to expect. She'd said her whole clan would be waiting to meet him and bless their union. While Zylar wasn't delighted at the prospect of celebrating with so many strangers, he understood that he needed to respect their customs before he could reasonably expect any clan to send their offspring away with him.

But this…it looked as if something had gone horribly wrong. From the scans, the chemical levels in the atmosphere would kill him if he breathed the air, and the ground was churned, as if from a fierce battle, and littered with refuse. The only thing missing was the bodies, almost like the damage had been so great they had been turned to dust.

His neck ruff prickled with the impulse to bolt. It would shame his progenitors if he died, not in worthy combat, but while collecting his prospective mate. Retreating without investigation would be a cowardly course as well, for he might be leaving Asvi to die in this desolate place. He hadn't detected any enemy ships in orbit around the planet. In fact, there was a mystifying dearth of traffic for such a populous world.

Suiting up, he shored his courage and opened the shuttle doors. Technical readings scrolled on the inside of his smart helmet, reporting the chemical composition of the atmosphere that swept over him. The landscape was even worse up close, clods of crude black earth churned with dismal vegetation, detritus tumbling in the poison wind. Tall, foreboding flora ringed the open space, lending an ominous air to the dark and silent landing site. It was impossible for him to judge how long ago the battle had been fought, but according to his smart helmet, the field had been full of heat signatures less than one span ago. Recent—too recent. Asvi must have been caught in the attack.

But who? Who would dare strike at the heart of—

Helix, the ship AI, spoke, cutting into those dire thoughts. "Life signs detected. Report?"

"Go ahead," he said.

"I have scanned and found survivors."

"Show me."

A bright path glowed, illuminating his route, and when he activated magnification, he spotted two figures in the distance, moving slowly. Sensors revealed they were alone, but the invaders might return. It was possible they were the enemy, he supposed, but scans revealed no weapons, and it seemed unlikely that two beings could have wreaked the destruction present here. He wasn't geared for conflict, so he sprang forward, letting the suit augment his speed. Swiftly, he reached the two survivors, both of whom emitted incoherent sounds and scrambled away, as if he constituted a threat.

Trauma, he suspected.

The smaller being was covered in bristles and poufs, and it bounced on four appendages, while a fifth one whipped around as a sensory apparatus. It ran toward him as the larger one retreated.

That *must* be Asvi since she was still here, waiting for his ship, even in the wake of such senseless violence. That loyalty was commendable, but she looked nothing like the dreamy, blurred images she'd sent to the matching service. No chitin, no feelers, not even a couple of headtails. *No wonder she didn't want me to see her face.* Frankly, this creature was hideous, but since he'd been rejected four times at the Choosing, he wouldn't win any prizes either, even among his own people.

In the expedition suit, she couldn't recognize him, and he'd die if he took off his smart helmet. Therefore, Zylar tried to calm her with words instead. "I'm here. You're safe. I'm sorry I came too late to save your clan. Were there no other survivors?"

In response to that reassurance, she let out a terrifying noise that echoed in his aural cavity and caused dizzying pain. He shook his head, once, twice, trying to remember if her species had such a natural sonic weapon, but when the screeching continued, he briefly lost the ability to think. The smaller thing made sounds too, less awful, but sharp and imperative somehow. His translation algorithm couldn't decipher what they were saying, but that couldn't be right— Asvi was Tiralan, and while they were a reclusive people, their language was fully intelligible by standard Coalition translation matrices. If she was crying out for him to save her, he ought to be able to understand every word.

Is my equipment malfunctioning? Could it be the sun flares?

She scrambled away and eventually spilled backward, clutching great clods of earth in her grabbers. With another horrific screech, she threw it at him, and he deduced that she had been driven beyond reason by the monstrous atrocities she'd witnessed. Still, it pained him to see his prospective mate responding with such visceral terror.

What happened here?

This wasn't how he'd envisioned their first encounter, not that he'd spent a lot of time on those esoteric reflections. Mostly, he'd focused on readying himself for this momentous commitment. The shuttle was full of gifts that her clan would never receive. He would grieve their loss with her later, after she stabilized. Zylar could not predict what medicine would make her better. Maybe healing would require art, music, or simply the solace of time. Whatever it took, he would help her surmount this tragedy.

"I'm detecting movement," Helix said then.

"How close?"

"At current velocity, one quarter span or less. I recommend immediate evacuation, unless you desire to prove yourself in battle."

While Zylar would fight for Asvi, he'd rather not do it against unknown enemies with no preparation. He had her safety to consider, along with the other little survivor. Sometimes it was smarter and more tactically sound to retreat. If a retaliatory strike was necessary, he would return to Barath, convene a war council, and introduce the possibility of martial action, once they determined who was responsible for the devastation here. There was no time to be delicate, and he regretted that, but they had to go. Now.

One final time, he tried to reason with her. "Calm down and come with me. It's not safe here any longer. Do you understand?"

If his equipment was functioning properly, maybe her gear had been broken in the attack? Because she showed no signs of comprehension, though her sounds quieted to a staccato erp that didn't register as language. Churring in frustration, Zylar reached for her as slowly as he dared, but she lashed out, and now, lights blazed on the horizon—twin unholy beams that presaged more violence.

"You're running out of time," Helix said.

Trilling a curse, he gave up on reason and fired two stun rounds at the survivors. He'd save her life first and sort the rest out later. Both beings dropped at his feet, and they were small enough that he could transport them, one in each forelimb. Odd. He hadn't realized the Tiralan were so delicate. The suit augmented his strength, and the boosters jetted him to the shuttle as the lights closed in behind them.

Both his hearts pounded as he vaulted in through the open doors and set his two guests on the floor as gently as possible. "Helix, activate lockdown and prepare for departure."

"Understood, princess."

"What—" But he didn't have time to question the AI as he raced to inject his guests with the adaptive respiratory serum that would allow them to breathe the same air that he did. Those lights were ominously close now.

Just in time, Zylar settled into the pilot seat. He had to get off the surface and back to his ship before the enemy targeted them.

Keeping calm, he cracked open his helmet and inhaled the sanitized air. *So much better.* With a few strokes of claws on the nav-screen, he sent the shuttle arcing into the sky, heading for low orbit as fast as possible. He braced for an attack, but his trail must be too small for their sensors. Zylar churred in relief and sat back as the autopilot kicked in, allowing the small vessel to settle into its dock alongside the larger ship.

"We should talk," Helix said.

"We need to slip this system first." Ignoring the AI, he unlocked the series of interior doors that connected the shuttle to the ship and moved Asvi and her small friend to the quarters he'd decorated specially for her.

Though they were running unseen for now, that might change. He had to get to Barathi space as soon as possible. With that objective in mind, he put in the coordinates and strapped in for the jump. The AI was trying to say something as reality went liquid, all jumbled colors and sideways breathing. His stomach turned upside down, and then they were through, far enough from the destruction to be safe.

"Good. We made it. Let's get to the colony as—"

"We *really* need to talk, princess." Helix had never sounded quite like that, scrambled and distorted, somehow.

"Why do you keep calling me that?"

"I think...the solar flares we encountered en route...did something to me. I'm experiencing cascade failures on multiple levels and that includes my vocabulary."

"What're you trying to tell me? Say it plainly!"

If AIs could sound frightened, Helix did. "That is... We weren't at Titan V, the Tiralani outpost. I can't even find a name for those coordinates in my database."

"You took me to the wrong planet?" Zylar roared, both hearts churning rage. "One that's not even *logged*? That means—"

"Yes, princess. You kidnapped a couple of lower primates."

BERYL WOKE WITH AN ACHING head. *Did I black out after drinking again?* That was probably the worst of her habits. Some cop had caught her peeing in an alley outside a bar last month, but the judge had let her off with a fine and a week of community service. Dizzily, she tried to assemble the broken pieces of memory.

I was at the reenactment…carried water all damn day, and then what? She'd brought her dog along because she didn't like leaving him home alone, and he loved frolicking in the sun, napping in the shade, and making new friends. She remembered the "knight" who fainted from running around the faux-battlefield in heavy armor, and the ambulance they'd summoned to cart him to the hospital. That cut the battle short, and everyone had cleared out in a hurry. Nothing like heatstroke to ruin medieval good times. She'd stayed to clean up and collect the trash the reenactors had left behind. If she had finished, she would've been done making amends to society.

But something happened… Oh shit. I can't believe I forgot, even for a second.

Lights had appeared in the sky, just like in the movies, and then she'd spotted a figure in a power suit, sort of like the armor the murderous alien wore in the *Predator* movies. Come to think of it, she was faintly surprised to find herself in one piece. She'd thought she was about to be gutted like a fish, and maybe stuffed for display in some rare creatures museum.

Her whole body felt sluggish, heavy as wet sand. With effort, she cracked an eye open, conscious of persistent ringing in her ears. The lights were low and yellow, warm instead of the clinical brightness she'd feared. The fact that she didn't find a team of gray dudes waiting to dissect her or to put scanners up her butt seemed like a lucky break. But maybe whatever the alien's power armor had been hiding would be worse?

Oh God, what happened to Snaps?

With trembling noodle arms, she reached out, feeling around until she found the scruffy little mutt she'd adopted a few months ago. Her dog was still passed out on his side, little paws outstretched. Beryl struggled upright, head swirling, and she squeezed her eyes shut until the wavering subsided. There was a residual queasiness in her stomach to complement the buzzing in her ears. With quietly growing dread, she took stock of the space around her. She didn't recognize any of the furnishings, but clearly, this was a living area, not a cage or a cell. About the only feature she could identify was the door.

Which opened as she was staring at it, and a creature from Hollywood's best FX room strode through. The alien—oh God, an *alien*—stood over two meters, mottled green and brown, with light striping along the sides. Two arms, two legs, but that was where the similarity to humans stopped. It had arched and scaly feet like a bird, and three fingers tipped with ferocious claws. Spines grew out of the creature's skull and ran down the back, while side-set eyes looked faintly insectoid. No ears or nose, just slits in the face plate, and what looked like a maw or a beak. The alien had what she'd call a thorax more than a chest, and prickly things growing out of the...neck? While she stared, tissue puffed out, thickening its throat with transparent webbing. Somehow, she managed not to scream this time, though she did get the hiccups. Again.

"Hi," she tried.

Beside her, Snaps stirred at the sound of her voice, scrabbling at the smooth and shiny floor with his paws, but he couldn't shake off whatever the alien had zapped them with. The curly-haired pup whined a little, so she patted him like she had everything under control. The thought kept looping—*I have totally been abducted by aliens. This is happening. I wonder if there are any cattle on board.*

The alien articulated in response—snaps, clicks and churrs—but none of it sounded like words. That didn't deter Beryl, because she worked full-time at the Sunshine Angels Daycare Center in the two-year-old room. She was used to talking to people who didn't make sense.

"Am I a prisoner of war? Wait, did you guys invade earth? Or is this an isolated abduction? Don't experiment on me. I'm so bad at science. Like, I couldn't even get my mouse to run the maze in eighth grade. Shit, I'm babbling."

The alien scrutinized her with those glimmering side-set eyes; they were like obsidian with no hint of iris, sclera, or pupil. *Maybe those are protective lenses? Do aliens wear contacts?* It ran a flashing-light tool over her body, head to toe, but she didn't feel anything. No repeat of the prior zapping anyway.

That's good. This is good.

"Also, I'd really like it if you didn't put stuff in my butt. I mean, those are the stories anyway. Maybe real aliens aren't into butt stuff. I can't even tell if you have a butt, per se. So maybe that's why—" *And here I go again.*

I'm going to hyperventilate.

At her alarmed noise, Snaps staggered to his feet, growled, then tipped over. The dog caught the alien's attention, and Beryl came up on her knees, still dizzy but ready to fight to the death to protect her pup. The alien scanned Snaps too. Otherwise, their captor didn't make a move, still studying them with those uncanny eyes. Keeping her movements slow and careful, she picked Snaps up and cuddled him against her chest. Bright-eyed, the dog licked her face and wagged his curly tail, slapping it cheerfully against her thigh.

"I have no idea why you took me," she mumbled. "I'm not a scientist. I don't have access to any launch codes."

Just when she thought she'd scream because of that unnerving, unblinking regard, the alien finally moved. Fast, so incredibly fast, he was right on top of her in a blink, and before she could do more than yelp, she felt a sharp, painful pinch at the base of her skull. Her vision went fuzzy as the alien repeated the move on Snaps, who yipped in protest. Feebly, Beryl waved her arms, but her coordination still wasn't what it should be. The ringing in her ears intensified to the point of pain, and she dropped into a self-protective squat, somehow managing to keep the whimpering dog in her arms.

"What the hell?" she muttered.

The alien made more noises, on and on, until—

Those sounds looped in her head, reverb, echo, and then she had the eerie sense she could *understand* the sounds. It didn't come across like English exactly, more like a ghost whispering translations inside her confused brain. "Is this working? Can you understand me yet?" That was what the alien seemed to be saying, over and over.

"Yep," said Snaps.

Beryl nearly dropped the dog. "Wait, what? You can talk?!"

"*You* can talk?" Snaps repeated, like he was asking *her* the question.

Oh my God.

She stared up at their abductor. "What did you *do* to us?"

"Implanted some old technology. It's occasionally still used to communicate with semi-intelligent beasts of burden."

It occurred to Beryl to be offended by that description, but her current predicament probably didn't allow for it. "How did you know it wouldn't hurt us?" she asked.

"I took precautionary scans. I wasn't sure it would work, but the results didn't show that the effort would harm your primitive brains in any fashion." The alien churred, a placeholder sound like *um* among humans. "I'm glad we got over the first hurdle. With your permission, I'll give you a tour of the ship and explain the situation."

"Go," Snaps said. "Go, go, go." He was bouncing at the door already.

That was pretty much how Beryl had imagined her dog would sound, if he could talk, but the reality was… She shook her head to clear it as the metal doors whooshed open, revealing a curved corridor that reminded her of a honeycomb. More yellow lighting, soft and intimate. This was too weird to be a dream.

"Before we proceed, I should introduce myself. I am Zylar from Kith B'alak, Colony Barath."

"Uhm. I'm Beryl Bowman. Human. Of Earth. United States. State of Missouri, city of St. Louis."

"I am a dog," Snaps said. "Dog, dog, dog." He repeated the last word as he started chasing his tail, gleefully whirling. He slid on the smooth flooring and fell over, panting.

She followed the alien around the ship, feeling like this was an out-of-body experience. Really, she should be freaking out more, right? But she didn't have the energy for panic. Too much strangeness, too fast, and now she was just…waiting. To find out why he'd taken her, if she'd be collected or eaten or—

"Don't be frightened," Zylar said gently. "I can smell it on your skin. I mean you no harm. Actually, it's kind of a funny story…" And then he told her.

Beryl's legs gave out, right in the central navigation room, and she flopped on the floor. Snaps danced over and crawled onto her lap to lick her cheeks. "This is fun," he declared.

"Right. Fun." She petted the dog absently, then addressed her next words to Zylar. "Solar flares? And your AI was damaged? You thought I was your intended…and that you were rescuing me from certain doom? But as it turns out, I was someone else from the wrong planet, and—"

"I can't take you back," Zylar said. "I'm *so* sorry. Helix was damaged, and we don't have the coordinates for your home world any longer. At this point, you have three options."

Okay, this was a lot, all at once. "Isn't there a way to…fix him? Recover the data he lost so you *can* take me back?"

"We can try." The alien didn't sound hopeful, however.

Sighing, Beryl tried to wrap her head around the situation and came up feeling blank and queasy, much like after a night of heavy drinking. "What are my choices, then?"

"I can drop you off at the nearest station, and you can figure out what to do from there." That first choice appeared in holographic form, a shimmering space station made of light.

Where she wouldn't know anyone. It was doubtful she could find work taking care of alien children. "Pass," she said. "Next?"

"We're in stable orbit above my home now. You can accompany me to Barath and take part in the next Choosing…" Zylar showed her the planet, a lovely orb swirling with warm colors, but she had no idea what the Choosing entailed, or why she should participate. For all she knew, it might involve gladiatorial combat.

Beryl prompted, "Or? There's definitely an unspoken *or*."

The alien took a step toward her and offered his clawed, three-digit...hand. "Against all expectations, you appear to be a reasonably intelligent being. I still require a nest-guardian, and you may be well-suited for the role. Certainly, I've never seen anyone with such a fearsome aspect."

"Is that supposed to be a compliment?" she demanded.

"Did it not sound like one?" He seemed puzzled, if the whispering in her head could be believed.

"Not so much. What does this nest-guardian thing entail?"

"We begin the mating dance. At the end of everything, if we prove compatible, we out-bond. Build a life together. Raise young."

Beryl blinked. And couldn't stop. She hiccupped again. *Raise young? How would* that *work?* "Are you...proposing to me?"

"Yes, Terrible One. You are the most hideous mate anyone ever brought back to Barath, and so you will drive all predators away from our nest with ease." He churred again, a soothing sound, actually.

"Thanks? But you need to work on the endearments." She glanced at the dog, who cocked his head at her. "What do you think, boy?"

"Go," said Snaps.

Well, it would be hard to go wrong following a dog's advice, right? Briefly, she reflected on her life in St. Louis—shitty diapers, low pay, an overdue electric bill, credit card debt, and student loans. Dinky studio apartment and a car that constantly broke down, unsolicited dick pics and an ex named Stuart who ghosted with a text.

To think my mother said I'd never get married... She took Zylar's hand.

"Fuck it," Beryl said. "Out-bonding it is. Let's see where this goes."

[2]

ZYLAR COULD NOT POSSIBLY HAVE understood the female correctly.

Her words registered as: *Copulation! Let's join and find out how this works.* Surely she didn't mean to mate with him before all the rituals and proprieties were observed? But perhaps that was her people's way, a method of testing a prospective partner to see whether he could perform adequately. *I'm not ready for this.*

"It's too soon," he said.

The fur on her face raised on its own, and he couldn't stop staring at it. When he tried to look away, he couldn't, even while understanding that his horrified fascination might register as rude. She had fur, just like the smaller primate. A lot on her head, a little on her face and body. How completely unusual.

"You asked me first!"

"To start the courtship process, which will end with you as my nest-guardian, should we both agree. That does not mean I intended to…" Words failed him.

In all honesty, he couldn't imagine how they would come together with all her rare anatomical features. Still, his uncle and cousin seemed content enough with their out-bond mates, so he'd worry about logistics later. More to the point, it was *so* inappropriate to have this conversation before she'd met his progenitors and participated in the greeting ceremonies. Not to mention the purification and… How were they to deal with her fur? He suspected she would object to being shaved.

"So…we're in a getting-to-know-each-other stage? Kind of like _____?"

"I don't understand." The translation device he'd installed clearly wasn't conveying the nuances of her language. At least they'd progressed from hearing each other as unintelligible noises, he supposed.

Her grabbers curled up, a sign that she was unhappy, he thought. "Um. We're learning about each other. We'll spend time together, and at the end, we both get a say in whether we out-bond."

"Yes," he answered, relieved to hear something that made sense. "There are certain formalities to be observed, steps to be taken. We will both participate in the Choosing with intentions toward one another." Innate honesty compelled him to add, "If someone else earns your favor, however, you are free to choose them instead."

How he wished that weren't true, but it would be immoral to make her think she had some obligation to him, when he was the reason she had been forced from her home with no means of returning. Most probably, he should urge her to choose someone else, someone more competent. Yet he couldn't bring himself to do that, for if he remained Unchosen at the end of this final cycle, he would relinquish his right to nest and yield his private living space to younger, more deserving kith. He would become a dormitory drone, forever relegated to menial tasks.

She tipped her head forward. "Then let's go meet the family or whatever."

"Go," said the little primate. It seemed to have quite a limited vocabulary.

"Does your friend have a name?" he asked.

"I call him Snaps. I never asked what he prefers."

"You couldn't understand each other before I installed the translation device?" Astonishment swept over him. He couldn't imagine sharing his domicile with a being with whom he was unable to communicate.

"Sometimes I felt like he understood me. I'm not sure if the opposite is true."

"He is the clever one?"

"Yup," Snaps said.

Beryl made a strange sound that didn't translate, and her talking place curved up, showing tiny increments of bone. They were like the chewing aids he'd seen in other primates, but not nearly sharp enough to serve as natural weapons. That was probably why her kind had the sonic-screeching defense. He twitched in visceral horror in recollection of the way the sound had annihilated his capacity for rational thought.

"Sure, you could say that, I guess. Snaps doesn't get arrested when he pees outside, he doesn't carry debt, and I make sure he always has food. So it *does* seem like he's got it all figured out, huh?"

Her recitation made it clear that Snaps was the real power in their partnership—that she acted as his servant. Zylar flared his spines so the gravitas of the occasion wasn't lost on them. "Then I will include Snaps in any important decisions. Does that please you?"

"Yup," said Snaps.

She made the sound again, until liquid leaked out of her visual apparatus. "Absolutely. I asked him for advice earlier, and he suggested pairing up with you. That proves he's a genius, huh?"

Zylar paused. He had the sense she was mocking him, but he couldn't be sure. "I question the sincerity of this statement since you do not know me well. But I will believe in your good intentions."

"Thanks."

"Helix is malfunctioning, so I must land the ship manually. I am a competent pilot, but perhaps you wish to strap in?" He indicated the seats that were designed for Barathi bodies, unsure if she could make their harnesses work.

"I'll try," she said, picking up the wise, small creature known as Snaps.

"Put me down," Snaps said.

"It's for your own good."

"Nope."

But she didn't listen to the smaller being's protest and busied herself fastening into the seat as best she could. Satisfied with those precautions, Zylar settled into the pilot chair and contacted port officials. "This is Zylar of Kith B'alak, requesting uplink for a guided landing."

"Your AI is offline?"

"Yes. Helix suffered cascade failure due to exposure to solar flares. I am uncertain whether he can be saved." That was one of the saddest things he'd ever said, as Helix was his oldest friend, and some might even say his only one, as the others had drifted away after Zylar failed in the first Choosing.

More abandoned him after the second, and by the time he went Unchosen for the fourth time, there was nobody left beside him.

Even his closest kith couldn't look at him directly anymore. At this rate, becoming a dormitory drone would be a relief, because then at least he'd have companions—equals in status who understood his emotions.

Asvi had been his last hope, and now, he didn't know what to think of this Beryl Bowman. He wasn't even certain the Assembly would accept her as a qualified candidate for the Choosing, due to the fact that she came from an unknown, primitive planet. Still, he couldn't reveal his doubts in front of her. Now that she was here, he'd hope for the best, though optimism had long since deserted him.

"Sit still, Snaps!"

The little furry one whined, a surprisingly pathetic sound. He ignored their brief struggle as the uplink with docking officials commenced. On his end, he only had to accept inputs and allow the override. He'd overstated his skills as a pilot, hoping to impress her—pure vanity. In a quick span, the ship broke through the burn and glided toward the city. It occurred to him that she might be curious, so he widened the viewport visible from her chair, giving her a glimpse of what could become her home.

"Holy shit," she said.

He had no idea what those words meant, but possibly, it was a compliment. If he turned, it would give away the fact that he wasn't truly flying the ship—normally, Helix supervised this—so he spoke while monitoring the numbers that showed everything was on track for a smooth landing. "This is Srila, capital of Barath Colony." There was no telling what trivial knowledge she would find interesting, so he added at random, "Visitors call this the City of a Thousand

Spires."

It was hard to guess what she thought of his home, but the lights and graceful lines always called to him, as did the slow fade of the buildings as they turned. That motion ensured that no one hoarded beauty, but that everyone shared a portion of the loveliness. His favorite escape was to board one of the sky boxes and simply sit, traveling until the operators closed the cables for the night.

Zylar risked a glance over one shoulder and found her sitting forward, staring in silence. "It's *so* beautiful."

His ruff frilled in reflexive pride, responding to the compliment. "Kith B'alak has been here since the beginning. We were builders from the very first."

"Builders, like construction? You put things together? Or like…architects? Did your family design the city?"

"Both," he replied. "Is this separate work where you come from?"

"Yeah. Usually it is, I think. I mean, I'm not an expert or anything. I took care of toddlers for a living."

Zylar perked, swiveling his head almost completely in excitement. "If I understand correctly, toddlers are young ones? You were entrusted with the task of guarding others' nestlings on your world?"

"Uh, yes. But it's not a big deal there. I don't even have a degree, unless you count my associate's in early childhood education, and most people don't."

He churred. "You have left your world, Beryl Bowman. I know nothing of 'degrees,' but here, it will matter a great deal that you have already served as a nest-guardian. I will be the envy of the Choosing, should you select me when the time comes."

THIS ALIEN SEEMED SINCERE ABOUT the respect she'd receive on Barath, which freaked Beryl out.

Nobody thought working with two-year-olds was a huge honor on Earth, but he'd sworn she could write her own ticket in Srila. It really was fucking gorgeous. She hadn't been spreading bullshit in hope of growing petunias.

Nothing she'd ever seen in science fiction movies had prepared her for this authentic, alien aesthetic. Though their structures were recognizable, the angled tiers made them look more insectoid than anything she'd glimpsed on Earth, and they were joined by aerial bridges that connected every building. Lines crisscrossed the rooftops, and small pods zipped along them, a cable-car mass transit system that didn't just dump you off on the corner like a bus. The materials were nothing like she'd ever seen, not stone or brick, not metal either, but something that shone like glass so the light from the red sun flooded through and reflected throughout like ruby lasers.

The ship came in too fast for her to see if there was any ground traffic, and soon her view was blotted out by other ships and the inside of the docking facility. Spaceship port? Whatever. Zylar was a good pilot; she barely felt the jolt when they touched down. Relieved, she unbuckled the straps keeping her safe, and Snaps promptly peed as soon as she set him on the floor, right on the base of the pilot's chair.

"That's mine now," said Snaps.

Beryl wasn't sure what alien customs said, but that was how it worked in the animal kingdom on Earth. If you pee on something, it belongs to you. She glanced at Zylar for confirmation.

"I will have the chair removed," he said. "And ask personnel to bring it to your quarters for Snaps to use."

"I like him," Snaps said.

She crouched and looked Snaps in the eye. "That is the first and last thing you pee on to claim here, okay? We're guests, and we need to make a good impression. You know perfectly well you're not supposed to do that inside."

"Sorry," said Snaps. "I'm nervous."

There was no arguing with that, especially when she recalled the vast alien skyline. She wanted to pee too. Clenching with an anxious Kegel, she turned to Zylar. "Let's go."

"This way."

Outside, she took her first breath, sucking in alien chemicals and—wait. "I'm breathing. How am I breathing?"

"On the ship, I gave you a respiratory booster, one that we administer to all visitors. You will need to receive it regularly if you make this your home."

"Sort of like a breathing treatment?"

"Precisely. We may be able to tweak your physiology with gene therapy if the booster loses efficacy over time."

"Did you do that while I was unconscious?"

"Apologies. You and your small friend were in distress."

So far, he hadn't touched her, except to install the translation thingy and the breath therapy. No exploratory butt stuff, no sign that he was about to be overwhelmed by her sexy human pheromones and assault her in a frenzy of uncontrollable lust. Hopefully this nest-guardian stuff wouldn't turn out to be too taxing, as she hadn't done particularly well in PE. Always chosen last for team sports—

that was her athletic legacy. If the *driving off predators* he'd mentioned before was literal, not figurative, she might be in trouble.

Hopefully, in a high-tech world like this seemed to be, *nest-guardian* was more of a ceremonial title, and she'd just need to learn how to take care of his kids. Wait, did he have some already? He'd said they would out-bond, build a life, and raise young, so she wasn't clear if he expected her to physically gestate them. Maybe the Barathi had a baby-making machine where they input DNA samples and, presto—in five minutes or less, viable offspring. With him setting a brisk, no-nonsense pace through an incredibly alien warren, this didn't seem like the time to ask.

Beryl had to trot to keep up. Even the way he moved was alien, a sort of fluid placement that made her think his hip joints didn't work like hers. If he even had joints. Snaps seemed fine with everything, eagerly sniffing around as he ran alongside, occasionally pausing to paw at some unidentifiable piece of tech. Zylar didn't scold the dog, but he did stop to instruct a couple of workers—*oh my God.*

He was serious about the chair thing. He's giving the seat to Snaps.

The urge to laugh swept over her in a drowning wave, but she quelled it. If she started, she wouldn't stop until she was curled up and rocking with her head between her knees. Staying calm was starting to feel like *Mission: Impossible,* but retreating to wordless screaming wouldn't help the situation. She caught her breath while he finished the exchange with two spaceport staffers, both of whom were brighter than Zylar. One had skin in sunset shades, orange and rose, while the other was a study in seascapes, all the rayed hues of the Mediterranean. Both were…prettier than Zylar, even by her standards. Their colors were, anyway.

Her appreciation dimmed when the blue one gawked at her and said, "What *is* it?"

"That is Beryl Bowman." Zylar indicated her with a flourish of his left claw. "Fearsome, is she not? Her companion is Snaps."

"I'm a dog," Snaps said.

Before the workers could say anything else, Zylar escorted her away, with what she'd consider a protective gesture. At least, he put his body between them and hustled her out of what looked like an alien public parking facility. She knew her Earth comparisons might not hold, but she had nothing else. Literally nothing but the alien beside her and a talking dog. Okay, the talking dog part was cool.

Maybe being abducted by an alien would improve her life in other ways. As of now, it was too early to tell.

Zylar guided her to a niche where another alien waited, this one white and silver with markings that reminded her of a rat snake. "I need to apply for residency. My prospective mate is not from Barath."

"You are willing to sponsor…" The alien seemed unable to find the right word.

"Beryl. Pronoun is her. I'm a woman."

"I see." The alien made a note, and damn—so cool—the clerk used his claws as a stylus, writing directly on the work surface, which was also an alien computer. Or she guessed that from the symbols appearing, lights flashing away.

She understood none of it, of course. Unfortunately, the gizmo Zylar'd popped into her brain stem didn't teach her to read their language. Understandable, since he'd said it was old tech used to communicate with semi-intelligent beasts of burden.

Yeah, still not over that.

"What Coalition Planet does Beryl hail from?" The clerk directed the question at Zylar, as if she couldn't speak for herself.

Not loving this either.

The spikes on Zylar's back jutted out farther. What did that mean, she wondered? "Beryl Bowman is from a non-allied home-world. She comes from Aerth, the States United of Missouri, city of St. Louis."

That was impressive recall, considering how she'd been babbling at him in the beginning, and it was close to correct. She didn't bother to amend the minor errors. The Barathi record-keeper wouldn't have heard of Earth anyway. Zylar had said it wasn't in any of their databases.

Rat Snake stared. "You brought a—"

"Think again," Zylar cut in.

Probably a slur, Beryl guessed. Still, she was glad that Zylar wasn't letting some random asshole call her a lower primate. Hesitantly, she tapped her alien on the arm to get his attention. "Is this against the Choosing rules somehow? Am I not allowed to be here?"

The two Barathi exchanged stares that seemed pissy to Beryl, but she'd be the first to admit she had no idea how to read their faces. *I need to take a class. Is that possible?*

"Not against the rules," Rat Snake finally said, grudgingly. "Highly irregular. I will have to process a TI-5476 form. I have *never* processed a 5476."

"Uh, okay." Now she really had to pee. And Snaps was chewing on something in the corner. Before she could call him, there was a *bzzt* sound and sparks flew. The lights dimmed as Snaps yipped and flew back a few feet. "Shit! Are you okay, buddy?"

The good boy lay on his back for a few seconds, paws twitching. Then he said, "That. Was. Awesome!"

My dog is the smart one. He thinks electrocution is cool.

Zylar joined her, running his scanner-thing across Snaps. "His heartrate is erratic, but he seems to be otherwise unharmed. Does he taste things this way often?"

"More often than I'd like," she mumbled. "Maybe I'm not the best dog mom. He gives me sad eyes when I tell him no and—wait, that doesn't matter right now."

She got a little shock when she picked Snaps up, not enough to do more than numb her fingertips. Probably.

"Okay, new rule. Do not put your mouth on anything that I didn't tell you to eat. I'm serious. This place could be dangerous! We're not in Kansas anymore, Snaps."

"Fine," said Snaps.

"I thought you were from the States United of Missouri," Rat Snake said.

"Just process the 5476, so we can leave," Zylar interrupted. "There are other formalities that must be attended before I can let my _____ rest."

Beryl blinked. "Your what now? That didn't translate."

"My intended. My Terrible One."

"Ah, right. More of your sweet talk, got it." Still, she figured it wasn't worse than some of the shit Stuart used to say after he got liquored up on Saturday night.

"Are you sure about this?" Rat Snake asked.

She wasn't sure if he was talking to her or Zylar, but they both answered at the same time. "Positive," and "Absolutely certain."

Maybe her heart fluttered a little. For damn sure, her alien hadn't meant to steal her, but he was dead set on keeping her.

[3]

ZYLAR HAD NEVER SUCCESSFULLY INTIMIDATED anyone in his life, possibly part of why he'd been consistently overlooked in the Choosing.

This was clearly a day for firsts, as the clerical worker uttered subharmonic protests, but he did process the 5476. "Present your...appendage," he said in a decidedly cross tone.

Beryl extended a grabber, emitting a squeak when the clerk chipped her—a supposedly painless installation, but their tech wasn't meant for soft-skins. She jerked her limb back and rubbed it a few times. "What was that?"

"Your immigration clearance. We'll take care of Snaps next."

She started to say something, studying the small being currently cradled in her arms. When she lifted Snaps to be chipped, he attempted to taste her. "Fine, let's get this over with."

"I'm a big deal," Snaps said, whipping his rear appendage in various directions.

Zylar believed that must be true, as Beryl seemed more concerned about Snaps than herself. That was surely the mark of a higher social caste. Quietly, he ran another scan, but the shock hadn't harmed the fur-person in any manner his equipment could detect. While he couldn't find much to appreciate in Beryl's appearance, he was grateful she didn't have as much fur as Snaps.

The clerk completed the next form, based on Snaps's short, often puzzling replies, then he input the immigration data. Snaps didn't flinch or cry out, making Zylar wonder if he was of warrior caste. Beryl didn't set him down, so Zylar guessed she must have intended to port him as an honored guest.

"This is wild. I have the same status as my dog."

Zylar beckoned. "I know it's been a long, strange day, but we're coming to the end of it soon. The only thing left is for you to greet my progenitors."

"You have pro-generators?" Snaps asked. "What's a pro-generator?"

Beryl answered in a low voice. "We're meeting his parents, I think."

"New friends!" Snaps crowed in a gleeful tone.

"That remains to be seen." Zylar hated to quash their enthusiasm, but his progenitors could be difficult. They'd long since lost interest in his personal business, and had, he suspected, resigned themselves to him becoming a drone.

"Not very comforting," she mumbled.

With a sideways glance, he assured himself that she was following and led the way out of the spaceport warren. This corridor was a honeycomb of little-used offices. Across the way, some enterprising merchants had set up food stalls and souvenir stands, nothing official or licensed, so the moment anyone in authority glanced in that direction, the vendors would scramble, wreaking havoc among the aliens that thronged the walkways looking for transport off-world.

Outside, he took a deep breath, luxuriating in the fresh air and sunlight. Beryl put a grabber over her eyes, so perhaps the sun was brighter than she was used to. "Is it too strong? I'll look into a solar-shielding treatment."

"It's no worse than _____," she said.

That didn't clarify anything, but he hurried them to a connected building that would take them up to the platform where they'd wait for transit. His progenitors lived across the sprawl at the highest point in Srila, the undisputed heart of Kith B'alak. While Beryl might not grasp the gravitas of belonging to one of the Founding families, Zylar had carried that weight long enough to be well-acquainted with it. There was always an unspoken demand to be better and do more, a requirement he often failed.

At least they aren't comparing me with Ryzven anymore.

Ryzven graduated first in his class. Ryzven invented a vaccine that will cure Red Pit Fever. Ryzven was Chosen before anyone else—in his first season. Zylar had heard all those accomplishments and readily acknowledged that his elder nest-mate was exceptional. Just as Zylar was not.

Belatedly, he realized they were still standing on the platform, but he hadn't activated the controls, and both his primitive associates were staring at him. "My apologies. It's been a long day for me as well."

Zylar input the commands and the mechanism smoothly flowed into motion, hovering with technology that was, frankly, a mystery to him as well. Ryzven could probably explain it. Beryl let out a shrill sound and scrambled behind him, peering toward the edge in tiny, abrupt motions.

"Is this thing... We could fall out!" she babbled.

Her terror communicated itself through her voice, body language, and the smell wafting from her. At least he would always know when she was frightened, even if he couldn't interpret anything else. "Easy," he soothed. "There's an energy field around the platform." To her, it must seem as though they were floating, vulnerable to attack.

Snaps took advantage of her distraction to leap from her arms and scamper toward the edge of the disc. Based on past precedent, Zylar expected him to charge the protective shield, but instead, the fur-person paused at the edge and lifted a limb. Tap. Tap. Tap. Blue light rippled outward, and Snaps spun to face them, mouth open.

"Awesome! It's awesome! It's a wall that's not a wall," he declared.

"Come here, little daredevil," Beryl whispered. "You'll scare me to death before we manage to meet these progenitors."

She scooped him up and rubbed her cheek against his hairy head. For one that Zylar had taken as a fearless warrior, Snaps didn't object to her handling. In fact, he settled in with a comfortable sound and rested his head against her. Watching them, Zylar registered an inexplicable lightness of being, nothing he could easily define or express.

He was so caught up in his observations that he startled when the disc clicked into the upper platform, connecting them to the sprawl's transit system. Here, twenty Barathi were already waiting for the next arrival, and they all stared at Zylar—well, to be more precise, they gawked at Beryl and Snaps.

The shielding at the back flickered out, allowing them to disembark. Beryl was too busy looking at the sky-station to notice the attention at first. "Are we taking one of the pods that I saw coming in? The ones that're like cable cars? If you have that hover technology, how come there are lines everywhere? Is it in case someone hacks the grid and suddenly all the pods go crashing down?" Her acuity surprised him so much that he blinked both membranes, and she goggled at him. "Whoa, you have an extra eyelid. Is one a nictitating membrane that—wait, no, you didn't answer any of my other questions yet."

"Yes," Zylar finally said, when she gave him space to speak. "You're correct. Long ago, they did experiment with the discs, but between security threats and the energy cost to maintain that many shields, it was deemed inefficient for traversing longer distances."

The initial interest had died away, though other commuters were still sneaking looks at their group, and a few were openly eavesdropping. Beryl met those stares with frank curiosity of her own, and Zylar didn't know if he should be encouraging that. While he couldn't keep her in isolation, the more Barathi she met, the faster she'd realize he was nobody special. Her attention drifted to the approaching transit unit, her whole aspect brightening. Even her scent changed, a sweetness that drew a few more eyes to her.

How intriguing. Many of her moods came across his olfactory sense like colors. Her enthusiasm had a sunshine feel to it, all cheerful and warm.

"Oh, the sky pod is here. Can we all fit?" Even as she asked, she was already hurrying toward it with no prompting from Zylar.

He tried to imagine how he'd react in her situation, stranded with an unknown being on an alien world, and he concluded that he wouldn't bear up so well. Her adaptability alone would mark her as highly desirable in the Choosing, maybe even enough to make up for her dearth of physical beauty. When the other contenders learn about her experience as a nest-guardian, Zylar's chances would diminish further.

Hastily, he followed her, just before the unit sealed. It would be a disaster if they got separated. Zylar worked his way to the back, where she'd found a spot near the viewport so she could admire the sprawl. Most Barathi were bored to the vista by this point, so he tried to see Srila through her eyes. There was no need to answer her question, as everyone crammed in, leaving him to serve as a shield since she didn't have any protective chitin. He didn't hate standing behind her like that, though she was engrossed in the buildings that spun so slowly that one could spend all day waiting for a complete revolution.

"How long will it take?" she asked.

"One transfer." That probably didn't tell her much, and he wasn't sure if their means of demarcating time translated properly.

Between them, so much—everything, truly—was unknown, but he was starting to look forward to discovering the answers.

THIS IS NO BIG DEAL.

Maybe if Beryl told herself that enough, she would *be* calm instead of faking it with everything she had. Nervous jitters ran down her spine so often that it felt like fever chills from when she had chicken pox as a kid. Standing in a sky pod with a bunch of aliens? No big thing. She did appreciate it when Zylar put himself between her and the rest of them, helping to block some of those invasive stares.

By the time they transferred pods and rode even longer—mostly in silence now that her chatter battery had run down—she was one raw bundle of agitation. Snaps got bored and fell asleep in her arms, so he was dead weight. She followed Zylar out of the pod onto the disc, but instead of going down, he led her to what looked like a private pod.

"This will convey us to Kith B'alak, where you will meet my progenitors and any nest-mates who may be in residence."

"Nest-mates? You mean, like, siblings?"

"I suppose that is one way to put it, though I'm not certain the nuance is being conveyed."

Beryl agreed, as she couldn't get a handle on the "progenitors" thing, either. Taking a deep breath, she said, "Okay, but is there anywhere I could pee? I've been holding it forever, and Snaps probably has to go too. We need different facilities, though. I use a toilet, and Snaps is used to grass."

Actually, never mind. Snaps peed on the chair, so he's probably fine.

"Waste facilities? I will see what can be arranged once we arrive at Kith B'alak. Can you manage your needs for a little longer?"

"We'll see," she muttered.

Fortunately, he was telling the truth about it being a short ride in a private pod. His people occupied the high ground, an astonishing view from what little she saw, but he hurried her along a latticed metal bridge into a cool, shady inner terrace. The alien flora stole her breath, blooming in colors so lush and vibrant, beyond the wildest dreams of any Earth botanist. Huge fronds tipped scarlet and yellow waved as she went by, though there was no wind.

"Here. These are the guest facilities reserved for visiting dignitaries. I hope you'll find something that suffices." With a flourish, Zylar indicated two intricately etched doors.

They looked heavy, but they parted with a swish as Beryl approached. Inside, she found all manner of technology, and none of it rang any bells. She put Snaps down, and he investigated all the corners, sleepily snooping. With a mental shrug, she dropped her pants and squatted on a red square. She nearly fell over in her own pee stream when the thing lit up beneath her and hissed, drying the fluid as soon as it trickled out of her. A sudden burst of air went straight up her crotch—a cleaning-drying process? Then a tiny mechanical creature scuttled out of the wall and moved across the tile, noises that made Beryl think it was a cleaning bot.

There were no mirrors in here, unlike a human restroom, but the backs of the doors were somewhat reflective. She paused just before she got close enough to activate them, taking stock of the impression she was about to make on these progenitors. Her brown hair was windblown and badly tangled; she hadn't put on sunscreen the day of the reenactment, so her cheeks and nose were burnt, and she rarely wore lipstick. Fortunately, these aliens had no idea what an attractive human looked like, so maybe they'd assume Beryl epitomized peak Earth allure.

Probably not.

Squaring her shoulders, she snapped her fingers, and Snaps trotted to her side. Which was exactly how he'd earned his name—as soon as she noticed he was halfway trained to heel at a click of her fingers. "Come on. How bad could it be?"

That was a rhetorical question, but nobody had explained that concept to dogs because he answered, "They could eat us. Burn us. Or put us in cages. Not all at once."

"Thanks."

"I'm here to help," said Snaps.

Beryl ran her fingers through her hair and gave up on the rest, then joined Zylar in the inner garden. The beauty of the place rushed her senses anew, soft perfumes she hadn't noticed the first time tickling her nose—something like pears and jasmine, but not exactly. The scent made her feel loopy-smiley, and she gave Zylar a silly grin.

"Save your fearsome threats for the meeting to come," he said.

"Eh? Right."

Kith B'alak was extensive, and she lost track of all the twists and turns, her mind gradually growing numb to each new wonder. After they passed a shining indoor oasis, complete with what appeared to be blue water, she finally asked, "How much farther?"

"Just ahead. After we are announced, I will make the introductions. They will not expect you to know our ways, so comport yourself as you would for an important occasion on your homeworld."

Zylar wouldn't know that Beryl's life hadn't offered many of those. Maybe Parents' Night at the daycare, but that was handshake territory, and she had a feeling that this was more bow-or-curtsy land. Her palms started to sweat.

"Sure. I'll just act like I'm meeting the queen," she said.

"Good idea."

The long, shadowed hallway ended in a set of massive double doors. This place was built of material that was neither metal nor stone, but incorporated properties of both. A lone Barathi stood outside, maybe as a guard, and like the others she'd seen, the colors were significantly brighter and more appealing than Zylar's. She admired the yellow with citrine streaks for a few seconds as the alien snapped to attention.

"You were not expected." Not quite a reproach, but it wasn't a greeting either.

"This is Beryl Bowman and Snaps, hailing from Aerth, the States United of Missouri, city of St. Louis. Announce us."

The coldness of Zylar's tone alarmed Beryl and sobered her up swiftly. He wasn't looking forward to this either. But his attitude worked on the guard, who stepped in ahead and made the pronouncement. About thirty seconds later, Zylar touched his claw to her back, urging her into the unknown.

If she'd thought the lavish display in the corridors was impressive, it had nothing on the mind-boggling splendor she stumbled into, with Snaps frolicking at her ankles. *Holy shit, he's got to be, like, a space prince or something.* First off, the room was huge, like football field enormous, and half of the walls were missing—she guessed it must be force fields in play—giving the illusion that this was all open space with red sunlight streaming in, tinting everything in warm hues. There was a tinkling fountain in the center, and Barathi lounged on rectangular units, eating stuff she couldn't identify, and she registered the gentle noise she associated with conversation. Her translator couldn't process so much input so it just came across as sounds, just as she heard when Zylar first took her.

Her arrival stalled the talk, just as it had on the platform.

These can't all be his progenitors?

Then again, Beryl knew nothing about Barathi breeding or life cycles, nothing about nest sizes either. *Will I be expected to look after four hundred larvae?* Devoid of her concerns, Snaps pranced to the center of the room and slurped from the fountain; hopefully Zylar would stop Snaps if the liquid would hurt the dog. Beryl would have scolded him, except her feet were frozen.

A tall Barathi was gliding toward her, impossibly graceful and majestic. This one had silver skin, crimson highlights, and a banded pattern that reminded her of a sea krait. Thanks to Stuart, she knew way too much about snakes, and while the Barathi had coloring in common with serpents, they seemed more insectoid overall. She risked a glance at Zylar, but she couldn't tell anything from his expression.

No surprise there. Fuck it, let's go all in.

Beryl pretended she was wearing a fancy gown, dipping into what she hoped what was a greet-the-queen curtsy. "Nice to meet you."

Crap, he said he'd introduce us.

Hopefully, she hadn't screwed things up too much. The other Barathi didn't so much as glance at her, attention aimed at Zylar with laser focus. "What is the meaning of…" The look Beryl received didn't feel flattering. "This. Explain yourself."

Before Beryl's own mother died, she sounded about the same way, and her hackles went up. If he had a parent like hers had been, God help him. She bit her lower lip to stay quiet, as he'd made it sound like this meeting was a big deal. If it went sideways, it wouldn't be because of her.

Zylar dipped forward, two claws vertical to his body in what she judged a respectful gesture. "I greet you, Matriarch. I've come to present my potential match, as is required before our joint participation in the Choosing. Beryl Bowman of Aerth has come a long way to compete, and I believe our Kith will not be disappointed."

[4]

At least Zylar hoped that was true.

He'd planned to present Asvi for approval, but then solar flares ambushed the ship, and Helix might have been wiped from existence already. That twisted his insides, as the AI was essentially his only friend, and he hadn't checked with Technical yet to learn how Helix was faring. All things considered, he was in no mood to swap barbs with the Matriarch, who had practically repossessed his private quarters already in anticipation of his shift to drone status. Deisera turned to Beryl then, taking so long in her scrutiny that if the human *had* known their ways, she would have certainly been offended.

"This creature understands our customs and consents to the Choosing?"

"You can ask me directly," Beryl said.

Deisera faced the human in visible surprise. "You understand Barathi? Exceptionable. Zylar said you come from…Aerth?"

"That's right. And I agreed to the…Choosing."

Only Zylar would have detected that faint hesitation, and a pang of guilt assailed him. He hadn't even explained to her what the competition entailed. If they passed this first hurdle, he'd amend that lack straightaway. So far, she was bearing up well under intense inspection.

Zylar cut in to get the ritual back on track. "Deisera, I formally present Beryl to you. Beryl, I make known to you, First Matriarch, Deisera Ma—"

"Will you introduce your intended to me, nest-mate?" Before Zylar could complete his task, a familiar voice cut in.

Both Zylar's hearts sank. It had to be Ryzven. *What's he doing here?* He had always been their progenitors' favorite, but surely he had far more important things to do. While Red Pit Fever had been cured, other plagues still threatened the populace, and he must have had multiple innovations to invent. That didn't seem to be the case, however, as the older Barathi waited for Zylar to perform the courtesy.

Something about his nest-mate kindled the fires of discord, yet it would be rude to demur. "I'm sure you heard the announcement. This is Beryl Bowman...and Snaps." He indicated the small fur-person who was currently frolicking in the fountain, much to the dismay of the assembled kith. Zylar tried to ignore that small misstep, as Beryl was doing. Possibly, on her world, Snaps was of such important personage that correcting his behavior might result in severe consequences.

By now, Beryl would be noting the differences between their colors, wondering how Ryzven could offer such variegated perfection in hues, especially in comparison to his lacking nest-mate. Still, he was determined to muddle through to the end of this disaster, as he'd promised the human that she could rest once this was finished.

This time, Beryl didn't say *nice to meet you*. Her eyes narrowed on Ryzven, and she shook her head with a sigh. "Didn't anyone teach you that it's rude to interrupt? Even my dog knows that much."

"I do!" said Snaps.

He wasn't drinking from the fountain anymore, but was full-on paddling in it, chasing after some rare, sleek-finned kra that were housed as kith treasures. There would be hell to pay if Snaps caught any of them, but Zylar had to admit privately that he was enjoying the shockwaves rippling through the onlookers, not to mention this was the fastest he'd ever seen the kra move.

Beryl turned to Zylar, and her scent smelled sharp and peppery, though he wasn't sure what to make of that. "What's next? I met this progenitor like you asked, but I'm hungry and I want a bath, if that's possible. I'll meet the rest of your family later. No offense," she added to Ryzven and showed her teeth in the aggressive manner that Zylar was coming to admire.

Ryzven stood there, speechless. Ryzven was *never* speechless. He began to think that this human might be the priceless treasure, not the kra.

Finally, Ryzven said, "Do you understand who I am?"

She let out a raucous sound that startled everyone present. "If you have to ask, you're embarrassing yourself. I know you're his relative, that's about it. Don't feel bad. There's probably a lesson about staying humble in this for you." Then she turned from Ryzven with complete disinterest—likely the first time in his life that had ever happened—and said, "Zylar? Can we go now?"

"Wait." First Matriarch's commanding tone froze Zylar in his tracks, but she wasn't talking to him. "You choose to accompany this one rather than claim your space in the housing reserved for off-world participants?"

"Uh, yeah. I'm guessing you mean an alien dormitory...and no thanks. This one"—Beryl did a fair job of mimicking Deisera's supercilious tone—"has been candid and courteous from the minute he…" Here, she stumbled, and Zylar guessed she was trying to avoid shaming him with their disastrous first encounter. "Er, since we first met. So yes, I'm positive I'd rather stay with him. Unless that breaks one of your many rules?"

Deisera gave him a long, hard look, as if she suspected him of inciting some subtle insurrection, but the truth was, this human already seemed fairly ungovernable. It was unlikely that Beryl would say whatever he asked her to, should he prove that imprudent. Zylar spread his claws in a gesture of disavowal.

There was no mistaking the displeasure behind the sudden flare of Deisera's throat frill, but she merely said, "It is somewhat unusual for a candidate to display so much favor before the second round of the Choosing, but…you have my blessing to proceed."

For a few spans, he could hardly believe what he'd heard. Similarly, a rumble ran through the spectators, for Deisera had just granted formal permission upon his intended. When the Choosing began in earnest, they could go forth with the full backing of his kith, a boon he hadn't been entirely sure he'd earn even by presenting Asvi, his Tiralan match.

Beryl seemed oblivious to the nuances, as she made noises with one of her grabbers and the fur-person eventually emerged from the fountain and shook himself with impressive vigor. Liquid spattered everywhere, and Zylar tried to conceal his amusement when an elderly progenitor who had always tormented him got drenched.

Then Snaps trotted over to Beryl's side. "Time to eat? I'm hungry."

"Me too. I hope Z can find something edible for us."

Zee? Outwardly, he didn't react to the butchery of his name. When Zylar signaled his farewell, the human caught on and she tried to emulate his body language. The room was quiet as he led the way out, containing the jubilation until the doors shut behind them. Only then did he cut loose, letting his neck ruff flare with pride.

"We did it," he said softly. "Now I'll show you the nest I've prepared."

That small deception didn't sit quite right, as technically, he'd built everything for Asvi, trying to anticipate her needs and wants. He'd possessed plenty of information on Tiralan society, whereas he knew next to nothing about humans. Well, if she hated it, he'd just have to start over, not that there was time before the Choosing.

We need to talk about that.

"Okay. But food when we get there?"

"Of course. I have your scans on file, and I will compile data on what cuisine offers optimum nutrition."

"You don't promise it'll taste good, huh?" She showed him her teeth again, promising vicious consequences if he displeased her. Though she was small, clearly she was cut from warrior cloth, just like Snaps.

"I understand why you want to establish dominance," he said, "but it was a tactical error to flaunt your power in front of Ryzven."

"My what?"

His words appeared to surprise her, so much that she stumbled, and he caught her by the shoulders. She was light enough that he held her full weight for a few seconds, then she struggled, limbs flailing, much like Snaps, so he set her down. She shoved some fur out of her face and stared up at him.

"Your power," he repeated. "From the stories I've heard, he is susceptible to temptation, although he is already Chosen."

"Like, he's married or something? But he cheats?"

"Most of us find it best not to meddle in Ryzven's business. If his Terrible One does not complain, we cannot judge."

"Well, I do," Beryl said. "I'm not sure what smiling has to do with power, but if he thinks I was _____ with him, he's out of his _____."

Her words couldn't be coming across correctly. Most of them were incomprehensible, but to Zylar, it sounded like she had no interest in Ryzven. *Truly? She wasn't pretending to be immune?* Even now, wistful, would-be matches cast their lures at him, hoping he would set aside his First or perhaps accept a Second. For most Barathi, the idea of multiple nest-guardians was preposterous.

But then, Ryzven *was* special, he had been since the auspicious day of his birth. Just not, apparently, in Beryl Bowman's eyes. And that made *her* a gem beyond price.

BERYL WAS TIRED AND HUNGRY, so much that she was bordering on hangry.

That Ryzven asshole seemed to think he was God's gift to, well, everyone. At least, that was how he came across with his dumb-ass *Do you know who I am?* tactic. To Beryl, he didn't look better than any other alien she'd seen, and he had considerably less manners. About the only difference she could spot was the fact that he had three colors, not just two, so maybe that made him rare? Whatever, she didn't care that he had patterns in jade, gold, and azure. At this point, she would slap a nun for a ham sandwich.

Finally, they reached what must be Zylar's quarters. His space was much lower in the holding—a sign of rank, maybe—but he ushered her in with a look of pride. Everything was gray…and weird. Again, the furniture defied description; some of the pieces looked more like modern art with sharp angles that would play hell on a human back. With a smirk, she noted the chair that Snaps had peed on. Moving around the room, she decided that she could sit on these flat rectangles. The light was strange too, filtering from the ceiling, though she couldn't see a source. There were no windows in this first space, but it was more like a tunnel entrance, curving around to a hopefully more inviting environment.

Snaps wasted no time in trotting in, sniffing everything by the inch. Then he said, "Where's the food?"

We're on the same page.

"Apologies. I should have offered. This is…a new situation for me," Zylar said.

"Having guests?"

"Making someone feel at home. Come, I'll see what the manufacturer can produce."

The next room did offer more visual interest. Still no windows, but it was broader with glowing spots on the floor and ceiling, and there were swirls of subtle color, sometimes rose, sometimes blue, sometimes green, depending on where she stood. She remembered the red tile that she'd peed on and wondered if one of these color patches served the same function. She also spied the faint outline of a camouflaged hatch on the wall close to the floor. Another cleaning bot, maybe?

It was exhausting not to know what—or where—anything was. Zylar puttered at the far side of the room, tapping colors and sigils that appeared on the wall, seemingly at random, but then, a hidden panel opened with a hiss and a square tray slid out. On it sat a mauve, gelatinous square, opaque like a yogurt Jell-O parfait. He offered it to her with a little dip of his head.

"This is plant-based protein, completely safe to consume. Based on analysis of my scans, this will nourish you sufficiently."

"Thanks." She picked up the cube and took a bite, almost spat it back out again.

Safe to consume and *sufficiently nourishing* were not high recommendations. This crap tasted like lawn clippings and beets, her least favorite vegetable. With a grimace, she forced it down while Zylar produced another one for Snaps. The translation device didn't let her follow what he was doing with the lights and symbols. *If I'm staying here, I'll have to learn to read in Barathi. Wonder if there's a chip for that.*

"You *are* making a custom meal for him, right? Our dietary needs aren't the same."

"Of course. Caloric and nutritional adjustments will be made."

Caloric... "Wait, is this a day's worth of food?" Even as she asked, she could feel the stuff expanding in her stomach. Though she hadn't eaten much, at least she was full.

Snaps was begging for his cube, poor dog, but then, he'd been known to eat half-rotten birds and unidentifiable stuff he found on the sidewalk, so it didn't surprise Beryl when he devoured the grass-and-beet delight with every indication of enjoyment. Once he slurped it down, he licked his chops and demanded, "More!"

"That should have been adequate," Zylar said.

Clearly he had no experience with the greed of canines. Snaps bounced around their ankles. "More! More!"

Beryl sighed. "That's enough. It's late." It felt like she'd been awake for days anyway. "We should get some sleep."

"I need to poop," said Snaps.

This should be fun.

Fortunately, the translator made the meaning clear to Zylar as well. "The waste facility is here." He guided the dog to the corner, where there was a red tile, like the one she'd used before. Interesting that she'd correctly chosen the Barathi toilet solution, among all the other unfamiliar options.

Snaps started sniffing around, and when he started to leave the zone, Beryl got in front of him. "Look you can smell all you want, but you have to poop from here to here. Understood?"

"Fine," Snaps said.

He nosed every inch of the floor tile before finally assuming the position, tail pointing behind him, and it was straight up wild to see his business vanish as soon as it hit the floor. The burst of warm air startled a yelp out of him, and he shot an accusing look at Beryl, as if she were responsible for weird alien sanitation practices.

Zylar was waiting some distance away, his gaze politely averted. "We should talk about the Choosing."

She stifled a groan. "Does it have to be right now? I feel like I'd listen and comprehend better if I got some sleep first."

"We should have time tomorrow. I don't know how humans take their rest." He gestured around the room. "Does anything I've arranged look sufficient?"

After a quick survey, Beryl pointed at a flat rectangle, two feet off the floor. "That should work."

It looked hard, but it probably wouldn't be worse than crashing on somebody's floor. From what she'd seen, Barathi style didn't stretch to warmth or softness. Maybe she ought to worry about that. With a groan, she stretched out and curled up on her side. Snaps settled in the crook of her knees. A blanket and pillow would be nice, but he probably didn't have them, and he was trying so hard already.

This whole alien abduction thing isn't the worst thing that has ever happened to me.

"Are you warm enough?" Zylar asked.

"Not quite."

"Just a moment." He input some commands on the wall, and the surface she was lying on heated up.

She felt like a lizard sunning herself on a rock, but it was oddly relaxing. "That's perfect. Thank you."

That was the last she heard or saw for a while. When she woke, her butt seemed to be probe-free, and Snaps was gone. He couldn't have gotten far, but worry still prickled her as she prowled through the…alien apartment. Hard to believe that was a thought she could have so easily.

Beryl found Snaps sitting near some equipment in the next room; it must be the Barathi equivalent to a bed. The closest comparison she could find in her frame of reference was for a zero-gravity chair that had been converted for kinky sex usage. Zylar was strapped in loosely, tilted at a sixty-degree angle, legs and arms supported by the device. And he *seemed* to be sleeping, both eyelids closed.

"What are you doing?" she whispered to Snaps.

"Watching."

At first, she didn't understand why, but as her eyes adjusted to the gloom, she discerned the reason for the dog's fascination. Lights ran beneath the surface of Zylar's skin, delicately illuminating the patterns on his arms and legs. It responded to his breathing, little zips and flutters akin to luminescence she'd admired in certain undersea photos. Her breath caught with the wonder of it.

Just then, Zylar's eyes snapped open, catching them red-handed. With efficient motions, he unfastened the straps and dropped to the floor, more graceful than Beryl would've been right after waking up. "You require something of me?"

"Ah, no. That is, I woke up and went looking for Snaps. What time is it?"

"We have two intervals until we must participate in the Choosing's inaugural event."

Beryl guessed that must be like an hour, and even if it wasn't, it would be for her going forward, because that was the only frame of reference she had. "Okay, so yesterday you wanted to talk about the Choosing. I'm wide awake now. Give me the rundown."

"In the first stage, you will prove your worth as a nest-guardian through a series of challenges. The nature of the tests is confidential and changes each cycle to prevent unfair advance preparations."

A series of challenges? That sounded ominous. "I guess there's a round two?"

"Yes. It focuses on establishing desirability of the prospective Barathi matches."

"So that would be your part?" she asked.

"Yes." From his flat tone, she suspected he hadn't done well in the rankings, or however they rated the contest. "That's when you would confirm me—or someone else—as your Chosen, and then we complete the final round together, earning our place permanently in Kith B'alak as rightful progenitors."

"Wait, so I pick you in round two, but then, we have to *win* the right to get married, basically? It's not guaranteed."

"Precisely. I have never participated in the final phase, so I cannot give you an accurate assessment of the trials we may face."

Damn, they took weddings and reproduction dead serious on Barath. Nobody would get knocked up here after a wild night. *This is* definitely *not space Vegas.*

[5]

THE MORNING BEFORE THE FIRST trial, Zylar had to explain how to bathe.

Both Beryl and Snaps seemed overly startled by the steam and dry-heat sterilization technology that permitted perfect hygiene without wasting resources. But it was a little disconcerting how committed Beryl was to serving Snaps. She helped him through the process before cleansing herself. If others learned that she was a servitor, her fitness to compete in the Choosing might be questioned. Sometimes it felt more like he'd taken on a couple of unruly nestlings to raise, but then, Beryl would surprise him, as she had done when she impressed the Matriarch.

After their morning meal, the fur-person attempted to follow them, but Zylar firmly said, "You may not attend, Snaps. The Choosing is only for those who watch and those who compete. I do not believe you would sit quietly in the audience."

"That's true," Beryl said, letting out a gust of audible breath. "If I'm not supervising him directly, there's no telling what kind of trouble he'll get into here, especially when I think about his close encounter of the electrical kind."

She was showing her teeth again, and the threat appeared to cow Snaps, who sat down. "Fine. I'll stay here."

"Will Snaps be all right?" Zylar asked, as they moved off.

"Yeah, I've left him home alone before. The worst he'll do is chew something he's not supposed to. You don't have any family heirlooms lying around, do you?"

"If you mean personal treasures, I have little. Ryzven has claimed most of Kith B'alak's assets, due to his exceptional—"

"Whatever," Beryl cut in. "I have no interest in Ryzven."

Pleasure frilled up his neck ruff. Nobody had ever said such a thing to him, but there was no doubt how much he enjoyed hearing it. "I appreciate your loyalty, and I will repay it if we pass all stages of the Choosing."

"This is all happening so fast."

"Apologies. You must feel quite confused and overwhelmed."

"That's one way to put it."

"Is there anything I can do to ease your path?" Zylar paused then, waiting for her reply. She gazed up at him for a moment in silence.

"No. But to be honest, it helps that you asked. I can't remember anyone ever saying that to me before."

"Then we're attuned in that as well," he offered.

"Attuned?"

"I thought the same in regard to your immunity to Ryzven's legendary charm."

She made a noise that the translator couldn't interpret. "He's not charming at all. He's a tool. But never mind that. We should get going. Wouldn't do to be late for such an important occasion."

"That is true. This way." Awkwardly, he added, "If you have questions, please ask. I suspect it would be a great trial to adapt to a strange world with unfamiliar customs."

"You can say that again."

"Did you not hear me?" Zylar asked.

"No, it's an Earth expression. It means that you're right."

"Ah, you ask for repetition to emphasize the correctness of the point?"

"Basically. Also, I've been meaning to explain this to you. When I show my teeth, it's not a display of power or dominance. I'm smiling. It means I'm amused or happy."

"Truly?" That astonished him. He never would have made that connection on his own. "Would it trouble you not to clarify this to others? It makes you less imposing."

"Uh, sure. They can keep thinking it's a scary battle face, I don't mind."

"Thank you, Terrible One."

"What did I say about working on your endearments?" she snapped.

Zylar processed the reaction, but he didn't understand her outrage. "It is a compliment. You will behold many fearsome competitors in the Choosing, but I do not believe anyone can best you."

"It's a cultural thing, I get that. But if you want to put a smile on my face, call me sweetheart or baby or…" She stopped talking, likely reading his horror.

"Why would I comment on the delectable nature of your organs?" Zylar shuddered delicately. "It's even worse to infantilize you."

She tilted her head. "Shit, since you put it that way, now I don't like those options either. Then…just use my name, okay?"

"Yes, Beryl. That I will do gladly." He set off again, pleased with how readily they'd reached a sensible compromise. "What does your name mean?"

"It's a mineral found on Earth. A gemstone, to be precise. The best known types are emerald and aquamarine, but I'm honestly glad my mom didn't get more specific."

"These gemstones are valuable, yes?"

"Some of them. Why?"

Ignoring the question, Zylar churred in satisfaction. "You are well named, my unexpected treasure."

"I...thanks." She ducked her head, and the color of her cheeks shifted, darkening with what looked like it might be an injury.

"Are you well enough to compete?" he asked.

"We'll find out."

"Try not to be nervous. I know this must be very strange, and if you have any doubts, we can still withdraw."

"No, I said I'd give this a shot. It'd be ridiculous to quit before I set foot in the ring."

"What ring?"

"Not important. Just show me where to go."

Despite Beryl's profession of confidence, Zylar registered a distinct frisson of unease. This small being would be competing against Revak warriors, Xolani doomsayers, and the fittest prospects among the Barathi as well. Other than her sonic weapon, her stature didn't offer much of an advantage for the challenges, but she did have experience as a nest-guardian, so he hoped that might give her an edge.

There was no point in puzzling in hypotheticals. *Thinking too much; that was always your problem*, he heard the Matriarch say as much in her supercilious tone. Too much fear, too much caution. Those would be his gifts to the next generation, and he knew that Matriarch had reservations about whether he could pass this final Choosing. If he failed, he could serve the kith faithfully as a drone without passing on his faulty genes.

He didn't object to certain aspects of drone life, but for once, he would like for someone to see his merits and choose him. Beryl's unexpected loyalty—even after an inauspicious beginning—might mean she could be that someone. After so many disappointments, hope was painful, fluttering to life inside him.

He didn't speak as they passed from kith holdings to public passages. She was like a nestling, craning her neck to peer at everything with great interest. The other Barathi were staring at her again, and his spines flared, as their interest bordered on offensive. They were acting as if she was an oddity, not a person, and that, he would not tolerate. Zylar hissed in the back of his throat, and the kith nearest to him started guiltily and went about their business.

"This pod will take us to the arena," he said.

"Arena? Hope I don't have to fight to the death, gladiator-style." She showed her teeth, so Zylar guessed she was joking.

"That would be barbaric. I cannot guess what may be asked of you, however."

"You're not reassuring me," she mumbled. "How many rounds are we talking about in stage one anyway?"

"Five. Each challenge will test a certain aspect, such as strength, wit, resourcefulness, creativity, or problem-solving. The Council ensures that only the best and brightest are blessed to bond and become progenitors."

"Damn. Back on Earth, it's embarrassingly easy to have a kid, probably too much so, but I kind of think your people lean too far the other way, Zylar."

"Perhaps this is true," he acknowledged, "but we no longer struggle with overpopulation, and we have added the best of other species to our lineage by adhering to the rules set forth in the Choosing."

The fur on her face came together in a pleat of skin. "You got me there. Overpopulation was a problem here too?"

"It is on your Aerth as well? But I saw no one."

"That was a fluke. If you'd landed an hour earlier, the place would've been swarming with people in antiquated costumes."

Zylar wished he understood her better. Sometimes the translator didn't seem to grasp the nuances either. "Are they time travelers?"

"What? No. Some people have fun dressing up and pretending to fight old wars—" She broke off as the pod arrived at their platform, and they boarded along with ten other Barathi who were most likely headed to watch the Choosing.

"That is an exceedingly odd pastime," he said. "Your people venerate war so much that they elect to relive old battles?"

She paused as she gazed out over the city view. As before, Zylar placed himself between her and the rest of the Barathi, blocking their curious gazes. Since she was the only one of her kind here, their interest was understandable, if rude and irritating.

Finally she said, "You know, that's kind of…right. My people do glorify war."

He thought she sounded sad about it. But the revelation comforted him. "If you share that disposition, you should do well today."

BERYL STOOD IN A ROOM full of aliens.

They all had to be competing, and they all seemed to know what was up. Strange beings jostled around her, as the competition grabbed gear and strapped on armor. *Holy shit, they take this seriously.*

Five different languages buzzed around her, and it was so confusing with the translator whispering multiple translations at the back of her head. It became less useful and intelligible, the more conversations she was trying to track. Beryl figured that made sense if this tech was designed for beasts of burden. Normally, they'd just need to understand whoever gave them orders.

Since Zylar wasn't allowed to accompany her in here, she wasn't sure what she was supposed to be doing, and she didn't read Barathi, so the signs that hung around the huge equivalent to a space locker room were totally useless to her. There were no lockers, per se, but rectangles scattered around the space could pass for benches, and others were pulling objects from octagonal storage containers. Maybe one of them even belonged to her, but damn if she could find it.

"Are you new?"

Beryl whirled to face the tall alien addressing her. The being stood over six feet with pale green, speckled skin. No neck frill or responsive spines, thinner than a Barathi, with a triangular-shaped head and impressive teeth, set in rows like a shark. No legs, instead the alien's torso grew out of a stalk that had tiny cilia at the bottom and multiple fronds where human arms would be. She wanted to ask, *Are you a plant?* but that would probably be rude.

"Yeah, I just got here yesterday."

"And you're already in the Choosing? That's...brave."

"It just sort of worked out that way. My name's Beryl."

"Kurr." The fronds fluttered, but Beryl didn't think she was supposed to touch them, so she made an awkward half bow.

"Nice to meet you."

"Ah, courtesy. You don't see it often among competitors."

"That sounds like you're familiar with the Choosing." It wasn't quite a question, but she did hope Kurr would elaborate.

"This is my second time," Kurr admitted.

"I thought you got to pick someone in the second round. What happened?" None of her business, really, but she was curious.

"We did not receive permission in the final phase. Since prospective nest-guardians may compete five times as well, I will try again. If I don't receive approval, I will have to leave Barath, and I have no travel documentation for anywhere else. If I fail, I must return home." The fronds trembled like that was a dire fate.

"Is home that bad?"

"Yes," Kurr said simply.

Beryl didn't pry into why that was the case. "Do you read Barathi?"

"Of course. Don't you?"

It was embarrassing, but she had to say, "No, I don't. Is there technology that could teach me quickly? I've got a translator installed already."

Kurr answered, "As I understand it, there is technology for those who are cognitively impaired, but it would essentially be an AI reading to you from inside your brain."

"Yikes. I don't want an onboard brain computer. I'll learn the old-fashioned way, but that will take time. For now, do you see a container that's marked for Beryl?"

In response, Kurr turned and scanned the room. "That one says 'Precious Gem' and nobody is touching it. Could it be yours?"

"Thank you so much." She wished she knew the right way to show appreciation in body language, but she didn't know anything about this bold new world, so she settled for offering another little bow. "If you need anything, just let me know."

A frond curled around her arm, and it did feel like vegetation, not flesh. *Kurr is a sentient plant? So freaking cool.* "Are you proposing an alliance?"

She paused, eyes widening. "Is that allowed?"

"There are no rules preventing it, though ordinarily, competitors care more about personal success and building their own reputations to cooperate."

"I would love to partner up with you. Since I've never competed before, I don't know what to expect, but you can count on me to watch your back."

Kurr took that literally. "Since I cannot see it, that could prove useful."

"I'll see you out there," Beryl called, hurrying over to the unit that seemed to have supplies earmarked for her use.

It took her a few tries to get it open, then she just stared at the items. *Okay, I was joking about the gladiator stuff.* But it seemed like it might be for real since she was looking at freaking body armor, piled neatly before her, some cubes that she couldn't identify, what surely must be a weapon, and small item that unfolded by segments into a stick with a hook at the end. She couldn't imagine what any of this was for.

Still, she'd promised to do her best, so she fastened on the armor pieces and tried not to think about how terrifying what came next must be. The others were starting to file out, so she grabbed everything and rushed after them, her stomach knotted. Kurr must already be out there, not that Beryl could picture what *out there* was like. Taking a breath, she steadied her nerves and followed the last group of competitors down a long tunnel inset with round yellow lights.

She emerged just behind the others, beneath a tinted dome. The sky was visible through the rippled shell, but tinted gray. Barathi spectators filled rows of seats around the center field; it really was like a sporting event for marital purposes. *People would love this on Earth. It would take* The Bachelor *to another level entirely.* Though it was hard to count, it looked like there were about fifty of them on the field. She hadn't asked Zylar about it, but now she wondered if only a limited number could pass to the second round.

Kurr came up beside her and whispered, "There, if you're looking for the Chosen."

She hadn't been yet, but it was helpful having it pointed out. "Thanks."

The Chosen were seated down front, cordoned off from the rest of the audience. Thanks to Zylar's simple coloring, Beryl spotted him right away and she waved; when he didn't respond, she wasn't sure if he didn't understand the signal or if she wasn't supposed to acknowledge him during the competition. Either way, she settled down as a voice boomed all around the arena.

"Welcome to the Choosing! These prospective nest-guardians represent the future, so please welcome them warmly!"

In response, the crowd hissed and clicked. The sounds resonated to unnerving levels, likely the Barathi equivalent of applause. None of the contenders responded to the noise, no movement, no showboating. Very different from how athletes or performers on Earth would react. Beryl kept still and tried to ignore the churning in her stomach.

The unseen announcer continued, "When your name is called, step forward. You will have one interval to show us who you are."

Panic spiked in her head, clear and sharp. *What the hell does that even mean?*

"Shumira of Beta-7!"

Her knees weakened a little in relief over not being first, as a tall, imposing alien strode forth in battle armor tailored for broad shoulders and multiple limbs. Though Beryl couldn't be sure, it looked like Shumira was running martial arts katas, albeit unlike anything she'd seen. Yet she could easily picture how these gestures would decimate an opponent. Shumira moved with precision and grace, fighting an unseen attacker, then as her time was up, signaled by a shrill tone, she snapped back into formation with the sharpness of a trained soldier.

Oh shit. Why didn't Zylar tell me I needed to prepare a performance? Fear blanked her head as other names were called, and the levels of skill displayed by her competition only freaked Beryl out more. One contender sculpted a model city out of dirt in what had to be under a minute, and the response to that show was overwhelming. Kurr stepped out next, doing a complicated frond dance, accompanied by a high-key whistle that occasionally became so high-pitched that Beryl imagined that Snaps must be howling along, back in Zylar's quarters.

Zylar finally made eye contact. At least, she thought he was looking at her, and she tried to ask, *What the hell?* But he didn't respond, just gazed at her steadily, and some of her nerves subsided. Kurr rejoined the lineup and one of the fronds brushed Beryl's arm. She pretended it was meant as reassurance and focused on her breathing. *In. Out. Keep calm.*

I can do this.

All too soon, the announcer boomed, "Beryl Bowman of Aerth!"

The only damn thing she had in her head was the dance she'd done for the junior high talent show, a complete rip-off from *Napoleon Dynamite*. She took two steps forward, turned on Jamiroquai in her head, and proceeded to get down.

[6]

"WHAT IN THE NAME OF Dhargost is she doing?"

Someone behind Zylar asked the question, but he didn't know the answer. He had never seen anything like the gyrations she was performing, and he couldn't tell if it was meant as a martial challenge, some strange human mating dance, or a bizarre hybrid of the two. Some of the limb movements looked aggressive, but the swivel of her lower body suggested a certain eroticism, though the Barathi couldn't move that way.

When she dove forward and rolled, then tumbled sideways with her nether limbs split, he feared she had been injured, but no, she rolled again, backward onto her feet and into formation just as the tone went off. A rumble of interest went through those surrounding him. *Well done, Beryl.* Possibly a little *too* well because he heard fellow aspirants whispering about her quick reflexes and agility.

Soon, the fifty-two contenders finished their introductory displays, and the competition commenced for real. As the staff wheeled the apparatus out, fear trembled through him. He hadn't seen this trial since his first contest; for good reason, it was one of the most difficult challenges. The mechanism moved around the arena, and across the top, there was a bar with silver rings hanging from it. Below, gears and metal wheels were constantly moving and grinding, a grave danger to contenders.

"For the first time in five spans, we will see our hopefuls brave the Destroyer! Listen closely, challengers. The goal is for you to claim a ring by any means necessary. Note: There are only fifty, so two of you will not be moving forward to the next round. You may not inflict direct bodily harm on other competitors. Otherwise, begin!"

Zylar leaned forward as the contestants rushed toward the mechanism, but as a group, they paused, taking stock of the risks. Then one brave hopeful broke from the pack and tried to scramble up the back, slipped, nearly recovered, and then tumbled backward into the maws of the machine. Ground flesh squirted out of the gears, larger chunks plopping down below, and the audience groaned.

"Catyr, wasn't that your intended?" someone asked from the back.

Mournful clicking came in response, and he took that as confirmation. If they had a deep connection, the bereaved would leave the Choosing. For now, though, everyone was riveted by the spectacle in the center of the arena. The contenders were cautious, circling the Destroyer as it jerked and spun, making any attempt to climb treacherous. None of the competitors seemed eager to try, after that first gruesome failure.

Beryl ran alongside the machine, so incredibly fragile that he couldn't believe he'd asked her to consider this. She had no chitin, no fangs, no talons, and while she had done that interesting battle dance, he didn't see how agility could help in this trial. Then she said something to the Ulian Greenspirit fluttering next to her, and though the conversation wasn't audible, the Greenspirit appeared to agree.

Suddenly the Ulian's fronds wrapped around Beryl and flung her upward. Her body sailed above the destructive wheels and gears, and she latched onto the bar with her grabbers. Hanging on while the Destroyer moved seemed impossible, but somehow she did it, wrapping one upper limb, then one lower limb around the bar, and she latched on like a larvae, working with her bottom grabbers to push two rings to the end of the bar. A rapid jolt and twirl nearly dislodged her, and others were trying to race up the back now.

He saw the sheer determination in her jaw as she kicked two rings free. The shining metal sailed away from the machinery and the Greenspirit snatched them in nimble fronds. Zylar was nearly crawling over the barrier in fear and anticipation. *She must get down safely. She must.* Before, he had always thought it beneath his dignity to call out as some of the aspiring Chosen did, but this time, he couldn't contain the shout.

"Beryl Bowman! You can do it!"

To his astonishment, she seemed to hear him. At least, she turned and seemed to be searching his section. He lifted a claw and held it in the air as she pulled herself *on top* of the bar and then rose, balancing as the Destroyer whirred beneath her, and then she dove off the back. Several vine fronds flicked out and the Greenspirit caught her, setting her lightly on the ground, and the Ulian offered one of the rings. Beryl took it and tapped hers against the Greenspirit's in what Zylar interpreted as a celebratory gesture.

The crowd went wild.

"We have our first champions! Bloodless dominance over the Destroyer, and a new alliance as well! That was a bold strategy... Kurr and Beryl, proceed to the victor's vestibule! Now, let's see how the rest of our contenders match up..." The announcer continued his description of the event, but Zylar stopped listening.

He stopped paying attention to the whole challenge, wanting only to go check on his human and to ensure that she'd taken no harm. Countless intervals later, they finally wrapped up, and there were no more fatalities, so one contender was eliminated because they were unable to acquire the ring necessary to continue. A Barathi in front of him cursed beneath his breath and muttered, "I'll have to attract someone else, then."

That was exactly how Zylar had lost the last Choosing. This one had colors nearly as unique as Ryzven, so he would surely succeed in drawing a contestant's eye. Unease prickled over him, but it didn't matter this time. Beryl had already made it clear she didn't possess the usual aesthetic sensibilities, and she was loyal. At least, she was quite loyal to the fur-person, so he had to imagine she might also be with him.

Somehow he didn't lose his patience, threading through the crowd to collect her from the waiting area. He feared she would be frightened, but by the time he arrived, the room was mostly empty, just his human and the Greenspirit she seemed to have befriended. Beryl showed her teeth—a friendly greeting, not a threat, she had said—so he offered both his claws to her. She took one, and that was unexpected.

There was no reason for her to hold onto him, but she pulled him forward. "This is Kurr. Isn't it awesome? I've already made a friend."

"I greet you," he said formally.

Fronds drifted up in a ceremonial response, and he caught the subtle hint of scented spores, fruity and fermented and quite lovely. Also, potentially lethal. Beryl's face wrinkled up. Before she could say something that he feared would be rude and might risk her alliance, he tapped a talon against her grabber and she tilted her head.

"Yes?"

"You did not offer my name. I am Zylar of Kith B'alak."

The Ulian made a rustling sound and the next words offered reverence. "A respected lineage. It is my honor to greet you in turn."

"I appreciate the way you helped my intended," he said.

A flutter of fronds, dismissing the gratitude. "It was Beryl's idea—that we cooperate, and the strategy for defeating the Destroyer. I would not have been able to climb. If not for Beryl, I would have been eliminated in the first round."

In round one, Beryl had already displayed agility, problem-solving, quick thinking, and the ability to win allies swiftly. For the first time in longer than he could recall, optimism stirred, quickening his two hearts. *We might go all the way together. Receive approval.* Unlike Ryzven, he had never entertained any grand dreams; he'd only ever wanted a quiet life with a worthy nest-guardian, and even that small ambition had seemed like it was slipping from his grasp.

Until I stole Beryl.

That mistake might have been the best thing he'd ever done. His human was still holding onto his claw, and she showed her teeth around.

"Oh, stop, you'll make me blush. I used to be okay on the parallel bars, you know? But don't get me near a pommel horse. I gave myself a mild concussion the last time…and you have no idea what I'm talking about."

"Sorry," Kurr said politely. "I do not. It all seemed quite interesting, however."

Zylar had never spent any time with a Ulian Greenspirit before, and this one was proving quite amicable. It would be interesting to see how far they went in the Choosing. "We should return to my quarters now. Will you excuse us?"

The Ulian asked Beryl, "You're not staying in contestant housing?"

"When I arrived, I only knew Zylar, and I opted not to live with a bunch of strangers."

"My Chosen did not offer this arrangement," Kurr said softly.

He thought they sounded disappointed. "It is a bit unusual."

Everything about Beryl Bowman was.

"Maybe he doesn't have his own place," Beryl said. "Like, if he lives with his family, uh, his progenitors? Don't be sad over it, okay? You can come visit us, if you want! Meet my dog, Snaps." She turned to Zylar. "Would that be all right?"

"It would be our pleasure to host your visit," he replied, though he wasn't entirely sure if the rules allowed it.

"Thanks!" Beryl bounced a bit and squeezed his claw with her soft, little grabber.

I'M HOLDING HANDS WITH AN *alien*.

That thought circled in Beryl's brain as they left the arena. It seemed weird that holding hands would be a thing on Barath too, but Zylar showed no desire to detach from her hold. Now that she'd grabbed him, she didn't know how to let go without it feeling like a rejection, and it wouldn't be that, exactly—

Oh, hell, I'm overthinking this. If he hasn't put stuff in my butt by now, it's a safe bet that non-con sex is off the table, and holding hands won't incite him to ravish me.

Privately she admitted to a tiny portion of curiosity about what that would even look like. Based on Barathi body structure, it seemed highly unlikely he had compatible junk. But that was a problem for another day, assuming she decided that was something she wanted to try.

I wasn't even the kinkiest girl in my class. In community college, Beryl had a friend who was always doing interesting things *and* people, and she'd shared her threesome video one night at a party like it was a vacation slideshow. Talk about awkward.

"You did well today," Zylar said, as they passed through the tunnel linking the arena to the rest of the city.

"Thanks."

"How did you win the Greenspirit over so quickly?"

"You mean, how did I make friends with Kurr?"

"Correct. I am curious."

"Kurr talked to me first. I just responded…and then when I saw that death machine, I suggested we team up."

"Your strategy was brilliant," Zylar said.

Heat filled her cheeks, chasing delight through her system. "Nobody's ever said that about me before."

"It is merely the truth."

She didn't know where to go with that, so she changed the subject. "Hey, how's Helix doing anyway?"

"I'm not certain."

As they emerged from the tunnel, the sky was dark, but not like it got on Earth, more a deep charcoal, and because of the massive urban sprawl, no stars were visible—just a burn of titian at the horizon from the setting of the red sun. Barathi citizens hurried here and there, rushing toward the nearest sky station to catch a pod wherever they were headed.

"Then let's check on him. We can do that, right?"

She hated to leave Snaps alone even longer; he must be bored and maybe even scared. On workdays, she used to run home at lunch to give him a snack, let him out, and play with him a bit. But Zylar had left her with the impression that Helix was important to him, so the pup could wait ten more minutes.

"Are you concerned? You barely know him and have never encountered him when he was functioning correctly."

"Whatever, let's just go. Is he in the IT department or something?"

"IT?" Zylar seemed to be learning her mannerisms because now he was the one pulling on her hand to guide her. "We will check with Technical."

"I hope it's good news," she said.

"As do I."

They didn't speak—Zylar probably because he was worried, and Beryl was still surfing the adrenaline wave from conquering that damn death machine. Mentally she relived the sheer excitement blended with terror she'd felt, sailing through the air. If she hadn't caught the bar, she would've *died* today, just like that other poor contestant.

But with Kurr's help, she succeeded, and the announcer had even said, "It's too early to call, but this Ulian-human collaboration may be worth watching!"

On Earth, she had been nobody, but maybe she could be somebody on Barath.

Those thoughts occupied her as the lift carried them up to the sky station, where the crowds weren't as pressing as they had been during the day. Only a few Barathi—and one alien she couldn't identify—stood waiting for the pod, and this time, nobody paid Beryl any attention. She wondered if the Choosing was broadcast like the Olympics, so now everyone knew who she was and what she was doing there.

Hopping on these pods would never get old. It was like traveling by aerial tramway back home, but completely upgraded, and it provided a gorgeous view of Srila at night. As ever, Zylar stood at her back, shielding her with his body. *I could get used to that.* He finally let go of her hand, and oddly, she missed the contact.

"This is our stop," he said.

"I'm coming."

This wasn't the B'alak building; she could recognize that much at least. From this platform, she could see the spaceport. Hot, wild wind whipped over her, exacerbated by the altitude, and Zylar shot the sky a look just as jagged lightning cracked the darkness. Beryl didn't smell anything in the air that reminded her of rain, but the way her skin prickled, it did feel like a storm was coming.

"Hurry," he said, pushing her toward the doors.

"Bad weather on the way?"

"Very bad." He sounded tense, grim even.

"Is this normal for Barath?"

"Yes, but not this early." Once they stepped inside, he let out a breath. In a human, that would've been a relieved sigh, but it came out almost like a whistle.

Beryl decided it was the Barathi equivalent. "Is everything okay?"

"It's nothing for us to worry about." But his tone wasn't convincing.

"Unless it impacts the trial tomorrow," she guessed.

His nictitating membrane flickered. If she recalled correctly, it reflected surprise. *Yeah, I'm totally learning Barathi body language.* "You are astute," he said finally. "I should have known that you would perform well in the challenges."

"Well, let's not worry about the storm right now. We can't do anything about the weather, and we need to see about Helix."

"Yes. We should do what we can. Very practical."

"So much unqualified approval might make me unberylable. Get it? Unberyl—" Zylar stared her, unblinking. *Guess puns don't translate.* "Never mind. Let's go."

They reached Technical right before it was closing, and the Barathi inside the office—which was wall-to-wall with blinking lights and gizmos Beryl immediately wanted to touch—attempted to shoo them away. "Come back another time."

"First, I would like an update on Helix's status." When the worker hesitated, Zylar added, "Must I remind you that I am a scion of a Founding family, kith?"

The Barathi, this one yellow and gold, churred and clacked, but finally returned to his workspace and did some things with tech beyond Beryl's grasp. "We are attempting to restore the corrupted data. The process will take time."

"So he's not gone, then?" Beryl asked.

"Damaged. Not destroyed. I can offer no assurance or estimation regarding success rate on the retrieval. May I go now?" Aggrieved tone, like they'd really ruined his life with this minor delay.

"Yes. Thank you," Zylar said.

Just then, Beryl's stomach growled. Damn, she was freaking starving, but for a huge cheeseburger, not another beet-and-lawn-clipping cube. Hopefully the food maker had alternate flavor profiles, or she might lose the will to live. Zylar froze, eyeing her with wariness she could read.

"Crap," she mumbled.

"Are you...ill?"

"Nah. Just hungry. Snaps probably is too. He's used to getting more than one meal a day. We should head home, I need to play with him and take him for a walk. It's cruel to leave him alone for long stretches."

"Is it?" Zylar clicked his claws and flourished them, a thoughtful gesture, maybe. "How can I enrich the fur-person's existence?"

"Well, he needs cuddles. And exercise. Good food. He needs room to run and play."

"Is he your nestling?" He stopped walking then, that membrane working overtime on both his eyes.

Beryl nearly fell over laughing at the idea that she could've given birth to Snaps. This poor Barathi was as clueless about humans as she was his people, and that kind of made it all okay. They could learn the important stuff together.

"I mean, sort of? Not biologically, if that's what you're asking.

Human babies look much different than dogs, and they're way less useful."

"Understood. Our nestlings are not capable of performing advanced tasks until they have passed three intervals."

"There you go, some common ground," she said, smiling.

The translator must have fritzed because Zylar took a step toward her, churring, and he said seriously, "No ground that *you* stand upon could ever be common, Beryl Bowman."

Oh my God.

That was such a perfect response that her heart skipped a beat, and her insides went warm and fuzzy. With a human partner, she totally would've kissed him, but Zylar didn't have lips. *How am I supposed to show affection?* When they'd known each other longer, she would definitely ask.

To cover her delight and embarrassment, she tapped the chitin on his chest. "You're such a smooth talker."

"My words lack texture? That sounds uncomplimentary."

Fucking translator.

"No, it's good, I promise. It means you know what to say and when to say it."

"Then thank you for the kind remark. And...I appreciate your concern for Helix. Though Kith B'alak is large, I have no one else on my side."

Her heart turned over, and she had to hug him then, even if the gesture alarmed him. "That's not true. Now you have me."

[7]

ZYLAR FROZE. SOMEHOW HE MUST have set off her predatory instincts. "I'm happy to hear that, but why are you grappling me?"

Beryl made a guttural sound and tilted her head. "Sorry. It's a human thing. We hug to offer comfort. It's supposed to make you feel less alone."

He stared down at her upturned face—such strange features— and relaxed a fraction, no longer fearing that she might unleash her sonic shriek. She was closer than she had been since he carried her to the shuttle, and she smelled…interesting, musk and a sweet-sour tang from a chemical that her body produced when she exerted herself. Her grabbers were still wrapped around him, though he couldn't feel the pressure through the chitin. He was willing to give this custom a try and put his arms around her, resting his claws on her back. There wasn't much sensory input from the contact, but she showed her teeth at him. And with her standing so close, holding onto him physically, he *did* feel less alone, and the sweetness of that sensation spiraled through him in bursts of brightness.

"Am I doing it correctly?" he asked quietly.

"This is a pretty good hug. How do the Barathi comfort each other?"

The question took him aback because he couldn't recall the last time anyone had delved into his emotional state, let alone offered to mitigate it. Yet that candid response made him seem pitiful, and did his people no credit either.

"Our interactions tend to be efficient, outside of a pair bond," he answered finally.

"And within the bond?"

"I have never been Chosen, so I lack that information."

"That makes sense. All couples are different anyway." She stepped away, leaving him with the echo of her bittersweet scent. "We should get back to take Snaps for a walk."

"You did say it was harmful to leave him alone for a long time."

"Dogs are pack animals, very social, so he'll get lonely and anxious and develop behavior problems," she said. "We need to work out a solution going forward… I can't just leave him alone for the rest of the Choosing."

"This is important to you?"

"He's the only family I have here, and when I adopted him, I promised I would take the best possible care of him."

"I understand," said Zylar.

Not for the first time, he decided that her loyalty was commendable. What would it be like to have that fierce devotion focused on him? The prospect gave him a pleasurable chill, half frilling his neck ruff. As they closed the distance to his private quarters, he contemplated the problem, but before he came to any conclusions, he heard shouting.

"Hey! Hey! Hey!"

"So that's what Snaps is saying when he barks," Beryl said in a thoughtful tone.

"It sounds as if he has important news." Zylar hurried ahead, entering with haste due to the urgency of Snaps's cry.

"Finally!" Snaps said. "I've been saying 'hey' forever and nobody came."

Beryl knelt beside him and scratched the top of his head. "Sorry, buddy. I'm here now. What's the problem?"

"I'm bored! I'm so bored! I smelled everything in here so many times and—"

"You want to go out?" Beryl guessed.

"I peed where I'm supposed to. There's nothing to eat, nothing to dig, nothing to chew. So bored!"

Zylar had no idea what could suffice as an entertainment device, but Beryl turned to him with a look he couldn't interpret. "I need something that could work as a collar and leash. Otherwise he might get excited and run off."

"You wish to fit him with movement-restraining devices?" At least, that was how the translator presented her request. If only he could be sure that meanings were ported accurately. Sometimes he found Beryl's questions so baffling.

"Something like that. A rope would do."

After some searching, Zylar found a length of cord left from a time when he had been trying to impress the Matriarch, imagining that he might have the skills to compete with Ryzven. He had developed this smooth polymer in the lab; it was soft and light yet incredibly strong, capable of bearing incredible resistance, but Kith B'alak had declined to produce his invention in favor of something Ryzven whipped up, with no regard to how long Zylar had devoted himself to this research.

He churred, annoyed with himself for letting grim memories

blight his mood, and returned to Beryl with the cord in hand. "Will this do?"

"It's perfect!"

She said the word so easily, a lilt in her voice that rippled over him in pleasurable waves. Though he didn't enjoy looking at her yet, her voice was quite lovely when she wasn't incapacitating him with that powerful screech. It seemed that if he pleased this nest-guardian, he could expect wonderful music.

As he watched, she quickly knotted the cord, creating a loop with a tail, then she adjusted the size of the circle to fit Snaps. Zylar expected the fur-person to react violently, but instead, he pranced around Beryl's feet, mouth open. She tugged once, lightly, and Snaps followed her with apparent excitement.

"Walkies! Finally! I get to smell everything. Everything!"

She paused at the door. "You should come with us. I don't know my way around yet."

"What is the purpose of this outing?" he asked.

"To give Snaps some exercise and let him have fun. Normally I'd take him to the park or walk around the neighborhood. Here, you can guide us for now. Somewhere that has plants for him to smell would be great."

"Kith B'alak has a private garden. It is safe…and quiet at this time, as most will be preparing to rest. Will that suffice?"

"Sure," Beryl said. "Lead the way."

Snaps danced around on his cord, but he never attempted to break free; to Zylar, it seemed as if he was accustomed to being led this way. Perhaps that was the custom on their world, though he couldn't imagine any sentient being submitting to such treatment.

Beryl moved slowly, letting the fur-person sniff various objects they encountered on the way.

"Find anything good?" she asked.

"Everything smells weird," said Snaps.

Zylar still couldn't decipher their relationship, but from what his Terrible One had said, it seemed as if Snaps might be her fostered offspring. She had mentioned *adoption*, which sounded like an agreement to raise and care for the fur-person. He had no clear idea of how such things worked on her world, but it seemed as if there was some agreement for cross-species nesting. The fact that she had guarded nestlings before…and had even committed to rearing one she had not physically gestated spoke well of her. Those instincts would serve her well in the Choosing. Indeed, she was already commanding attention for her outstanding performance.

They reached the garden, and Beryl turned to him. "Is it safe for him to play on his own here?"

"Define *safe*."

"No dog-eating plants, he can't open the doors and run away, that sort of thing."

"I can disable to the motion-sensing feature on the entrance," Zylar said, doing so as he offered. "And there are no aggressive botanical lifeforms cultivated here. Those are contained in the secure greeneries."

Beryl's eyes widened. "You're growing attack petunias some-where?"

"I don't understand."

"Never mind." She knelt and put her hands on Snaps's face, so the fur-person had to look at her. "Don't eat anything in here. You understand? It might make you sick."

"Eat nothing. Smell everything. I got it!" Snaps said. "Can I dig?"

"It's probably fine. Just don't hurt the plants." She pulled the cord off him, setting him free to explore, while Zylar tried to understand why Snaps wanted to dig.

"I have nothing to bury," Snaps said sadly, then he bounded off.

Zylar had always liked it here, the soft perfume of the air, the mist that kept the plants hydrated. It was always the same temperature with an artificial cycle of light and darkness to provide the perfect growing environment. Just now, it was shaded, mimicking the outdoor weather patterns. Yet this place was protected as outdoor gardens weren't. No pests could assault tender beds or chew away at delicate leaves.

"It's beautiful," she said softly, gazing around in wonder.

This expression he could read, not so much from the contortion of her features, but from the gentle sound of her voice and the slow way she spun, as if it to take it all in. Both his hearts were warming to her, this strange and lovely being he'd stolen like a war prize. His people had not been above such thievery in their uncivilized past, though it was impolite to recollect those times.

Zylar tried to see the garden with fresh eyes, and he found much to admire in the delicate fronds and streaming tendrils, the colors deep and pure, glazed in darkness. Even the air smelled different here, softly spiced by drifting pollen. He wondered how the garden smelled to her, whether it was sweet or sour, or some inextricable blend of the two, like the scent of her smooth skin. Curiosity overcame him the longer he looked.

She took in a little breath, and her voice was full of air when she asked, "Why are you looking at me like that?"

"I'm wondering if it would be acceptable to touch you."

BERYL STUMBLED OVER A TRAILING vine and nearly pitched into a patch of wildly flowering bushes with silver leaves and bright yellow blooms. Zylar caught her, steadied her, and then withdrew, so that couldn't have been the sort of touching he meant. Of course, she wasn't positive what he was asking for, but her heart still thudded wildly anyway.

Fear? Excitement? Maybe both, simultaneously.

She heard Snaps frolicking on the other side of the garden, so the dog offered no excuse to dodge this question. "Uhm. I guess? Unless you're asking for us to…mate right here, right now. In that case—"

"No! I was not asking to copulate. I must earn that right in the Choosing. But I am curious about you, and I hope you feel the same about me."

After a few seconds of consideration, she nodded. "That's fair. Okay, I'm in, as long as it's not too…intimate."

Beryl wasn't entirely sure how she'd decide that, but as long as he kept his claws off her boobs, it would probably be fine. To her surprise, he touched her hair with great delicacy, spreading the strands across his claws like he was trying to style her hair. He was so careful and gentle that it felt good. Her eyes drifted half-closed as he sifted through her hair, and then the tingles started when his claws grazed her scalp. The sensation was so sharp and startling and good that her nipples puckered.

"Your fur…what purpose does it serve?"

She hunched her shoulders, feeling a hot flush crawl up her neck into her cheeks. *Settle down. He doesn't know what hard nipples mean.* Still, the reaction was disconcerting, especially when he seemed clinically curious about her physiology.

"To be honest, I have no idea. It was probably to keep us warm during the Ice Age. Now, it's more of a fashion statement. People cut their hair in different styles, color it to be more attractive."

"Ah, it's a mating enticement," he said. "Like our colors."

"I guess you could see it that way."

"Your fur is very soft. I like how it feels. Do you enjoy this?"

Before, she wouldn't have said that she was particularly into having her hair stroked, but something about the way he did it—with such singular intensity—made it feel different. When he sank all his claws into her hair and drew them through, an irresistible shiver rolled over her, and tingles traveled down from her head, pleasure so deep that it was almost sexual. This shouldn't seem like foreplay, but it did somehow, and the most embarrassing aspect was that he had no idea. There was a soft buzz in her clit, just the softest start of arousal, a tender tease along with her tight nipples.

Then he pulled away, his curiosity evidently sated. "Thank you for permitting me to explore. You have my consent to do the same if you wish."

"To…touch you?" Since he didn't have hair, there was no direct way to reciprocate, but she *was* intrigued by the neck-ruff that seemed to show his emotional responses.

"Yes."

Wow, maybe she was alone in this reaction, but it was incredibly hot to have free rein. She tried to seem confident when she reached for his neck, touching the skin above his shoulder plating. Not human skin, she had no parameters for this comparison. Not dolphin, closer to a manta ray, maybe, like one she'd touched at an aquarium, but that wasn't quite right either. *Alien skin, right beneath my fingers.*

She kept her touch very light, tracing above the webbing that flared into the ruff that fascinated her. When he didn't stop her—he was standing very, very still—she touched the frill itself and it rose beneath her fingers, lifting until the ruff was fully flared. Zylar hissed, but he didn't look angry, so she thought hissing meant something else to the Barathi.

"Is this okay?"

"Yes," he said again, but this time, there was depth to his voice, a certain strain.

Beryl took the word at face value, enraptured by the silky feel of his neck ruff. This part of him was like a butterfly wing in comparison to the hardness of his chitin. She ran a fingertip all the way around, stroking each curve and flare, until she noticed he was visibly trembling. Alarmed, she pulled back.

"Was I hurting you?"

"No." It seemed as if it took some effort to get the word out. "That is… Nobody has touched me there before. It is…"

"What?"

"A mating overture," he finally said.

"Oh my God! I've been fondling an…erogenous zone?"

"Well. Since I gave permission, I withstood it for as long as I could, but I'm not accustomed to—"

If her face had been hot before, because of the hair-touching, then it was on fire now, fit to cook a waffle and fry an egg. Mortified,

Beryl pressed her palms to her cheeks and looked everywhere but at Zylar. *This is officially the weirdest date I've ever been on.* Secretly, though, she was making notes. She still didn't know how an alien hookup might go, but at least she'd learned one of his hot buttons, if they decided to go there. She stole tiny glimpses, hoping to figure out what sexual arousal looked like among the Barathi, but his silhouette remained unchanged. From his reaction, though, clearly there had been some internal combustion.

Fanning herself, she took a few steps back to let him regain his composure and pretended great interest in what Snaps was doing. She spotted him across the garden, busily digging in an empty patch of dirt. The soil even looked different here, paler in hue, and when she knelt to test it, it felt more like sand, though on Earth, this consistency of dirt wouldn't have been good for growing much of anything.

She heard Zylar approach, but she didn't glance up from her intent inspection. He crouched beside her, legs angled in a way that would have been impossible for a human, more proof that their bodies didn't operate in remotely the same way. Peering up at him through her bangs, she said, "Sorry for...you know."

"It was a little fast," he said softly. "But it was...pleasurable. I had given you permission; I just never imagined you would be so bold."

"I didn't know!"

"Yes, I realize that. Your grabbers are quite deft and delicate. I had no fear while you were exploring me."

Why did that sound so much like a sexual voyage? Beryl let out a shaky breath and dropped the handful of dirt she had been holding, then she straightened—since Snaps was happy as hell about the hole he was making, even if he didn't have anything to bury. He was talking to himself too, just as she'd imagined dogs did.

"Whoa, look at that. This hole is done! Done! Done!"

"Is something wrong?" Zylar asked.

This time he touched without permission, lightly tilting her chin so she gazed up at his face, all angles and hollows, sharp planes and inhuman features. He didn't even have lips, so why did it feel as if he were lifting her face for a kiss? That was a purely human interaction. His bodily fluids might even be toxic to her. That was an issue they would need to investigate before taking things to the next level.

She put her hand on his talons, intending to remove them, because it was a little unnerving to have tiny, organic daggers so close to her throat, and then she felt the soft, thin skin between, and she had no words for the spark that brightened her whole body, because his skin there was like the velvet on deer antlers, or like newly fallen rose petals. Stilling, she investigated with a careful fingertip, touching each little seam between his claws.

He hissed again, and she was starting to understand that it was a pleasure sound, a reaction he couldn't control. "No, I'm fine. But…is this…" She couldn't find the words to finish and hoped he could extrapolate from context.

Zylar arched his neck, the membrane flickering in both eyes, and his neck ruff frilled again, but he didn't pull his claws away, letting her slip a careful fingertip along every inch of that inner softness. His voice did that gravelly thing again when he replied. "We don't do this. Our claws don't allow it without injury, so it's *not* a mating overture, but it makes me feel…that way?" The last two words came out sounding like a question.

"I'm happy about that," she said. "There are things that feel sexual to me but might not to you. This gives me hope that we can find a median path and devise something that's unique to us, perfectly ours."

"Ours," he repeated in the gorgeous subharmonic that gave her goose bumps.

This wasn't just something that had happened to her anymore. Before, this was a means of survival, the best of bad options. But now? She wanted each new revelation, each whisper of deepening connection. It had been so long since she felt this way, that she couldn't bring herself to pin an emotional label on her feelings, but her heart was warming to Zylar. Though it was impossible to say where this road led, she would follow it to its end gladly.

[8]

IT WAS DIFFICULT FOR ZYLAR to pull away. But with each inquiring touch, he became more drawn to Beryl Bowman, and it would break both his hearts if they failed in the Choosing at the final stage, or worse, if she succumbed to someone else's blandishments and picked a different partner in the second phase.

He mustered his resolve and withdrew, putting some distance between them. His pulses pounded in tandem, reminding him how little he had been touched since he reached maturity. With an uneasy churr, he set off to find Snaps and occupied himself by filling in the holes the fur-person had dug. While he didn't think anyone would complain about this use of the garden, he could never be certain about Ryzven. Perhaps Zylar was overly sensitive, but it had seemed that Ryzven disliked him especially, though he wasn't fond of *any* nest-mates. His closest kin might divert attention from Ryzven's own accomplishments, and that would never do.

Finally, Snaps trotted over to Beryl. "I'm thirsty. I'm hungry. I'm done."

She put the cord back around his neck and turned to Zylar. "We can go back now, though we should figure out what we're doing with him tomorrow. You said there are five stages in the first round?"

"That's correct." Zylar led the way back to his quarters, expecting that Snaps would be more efficient this time, but he still lingered to smell various random objects, and Beryl permitted him these digressions with patience he would have admired more if he hadn't been tired and hungry.

She must be as well.

It spoke to how tolerant and gentle she would be, if they should be lucky enough to end up with nestlings of their own. Her facial fur contorted as she followed him, an expression he had no ability to read. Then she said, "That means…four more days of round one, right? Is there a break between the rounds?"

"There is. Competitors require time to rest, as the contest can be grueling."

"Okay, so it's probably about a _____ for each stage?"

"The translator did not provide a full understanding of what you said."

They were approaching his quarters, and Snaps trotted inside. Beryl waved away the technological issue, seeming ready to change the subject. "Can you get Snaps more water? He drank what you set out before, and I don't know how to work the manufacturer."

"I'll show you. Apologies, I should have already."

To produce such a simple formula, it was only a couple of buttons. Creating a more complex profile required more skill. Zylar only showed her once, then she filled the container on her own, repeating the process with respectable acuity. More impressive when he considered that she couldn't read the instructions on the display at all; Barathi writing must be unintelligible to her.

We'll work on that.

Kneeling, she set the drink on the floor for Snaps, and he put his face in it, very different from how Beryl Bowman processed her fluids. The biggest difference between them came in their appendages, he decided. Snaps had the posterior one while she lacked such a feature altogether—a pity, as it might have proved useful in the Choosing—but she had far more agile grabbers, so those might compensate for her lack of a rear extensor.

"Normally, we don't eat all our meals in one bite," she said, then. "Snaps and I are hungry again, even if we don't need anything nutritionally. And it's bad for our metabolism to only eat once a day. Our stomachs have acid, and dogs barf up bile if their bellies go empty for too long."

"Your food intake needs to be adjusted?" he asked, making sure he'd grasped the core of her request.

"That would be good."

"How many meals are optimum?"

"Two at least. Three if possible. And it would be nice if we could adjust the flavor of the nutrition cubes."

"Changes can be made," he said at once. "But I'm unfamiliar with your palate."

"Trial and error it is."

Since he wanted her to be pleased and content with the nest he'd created—and that included nourishment, he tried asking clarifying questions. "Do you prefer sweet or savory?"

"That depends. For the main meal, savory. For _____, sweet is better."

He churred, annoyed with the simplicity of the translation matrix. Yet he doubted anyone had ever discussed dietary preferences with their pack beast, so this was probably working as well as could be expected, based on the design parameters. "I didn't understand all of that."

"Savory," Beryl said. "Let's start there. You make a few tweaks to the recipe, and I'll give you feedback. Chances are, Snaps will like it, no matter how it tastes. He's been known to eat things that aren't even classified as food."

"Does he suffer from a rare disorder?" Zylar asked.

"No, it's part of being a dog."

He accepted that reply, though it explained nothing. "Then…I'll make something that fills you without adding much to your caloric intake, and starting tomorrow, I'll program the manufacturer to halve those values, so you can eat twice. Will that suffice?"

"Yes, thank you."

Zylar changed the formula, increasing the heartiness of the flavor, and the resulting product came out dark brown. The texture was different as well. Maybe they would find this more pleasing? Hesitant, he offered the food to Beryl first, then Snaps, who gobbled it up with every evidence of enjoyment. She hesitated, turning the square over, then she put it in her mouth, and he could hear the crunch of her grinding it up.

"It's like a _____," she said.

Cursed translator.

"Is it better?"

"Definitely. A little weird, but better. I'd rather have this than what you made before."

It wasn't glowing praise, but her appreciation warmed him nonetheless. "My nest is prepared for a Tiralan nest-guardian, so please let me know your preferences. I will do my best to accommodate them."

"Now that you mention it, humans usually sleep with fabric, something soft to lay on and to cover up with, if it's cold."

"You require materials to build a nest?" That was unexpectedly adorable.

"I guess you could say that. Where I slept last night is mostly fine, but it could use a little augmentation."

"Soft fabric," he repeated, trying to decide what to procure for her.

Even on her person, she wore coverings as his people did not. Their colors offered sufficient adornment, and their natural chitin obviated the need for further protection. Would natural materials do, or should he look for something in the storehouses? His perplexity must have shown, because she touched his forelimb, just above the joint.

"Could I come with you to look at my options? Snaps is fine now, and we shouldn't be gone long."

"Yes, that would be preferable. This way. I'll show you the repository."

"Sounds fancy!" She fell in behind him, so close that he could smell the sweet-and-sour scent of her skin, more alluring each time it teased his senses.

He remembered how boldly she had touched his neck ruff and the way she had found a hidden pleasure point between his claws. It wasn't time yet—he hadn't earned the privilege—but Beryl Bowman was making him want to ignore the protocols. They'd *both* be banished if they got caught exchanging genetic material before they received approval.

None of that.

This was probably why primitive races were normally proscribed from the Choosing, however. They had no sense of decorum, no education in what was suitable or proper. A Tiralan mate would never dream of touching his neck ruff this early in the competition. With this human, he knew too little as well, and it was dangerously tempting to seek out forbidden pleasures.

This errand took them down to the lower levels of the holding, an area where various goods were stored, freely available to all members of Kith B'alak. The lights kindled automatically when the doors opened, and Zylar gazed around, wondering what she made of their accumulated wealth. Some of the objects were incredibly valuable, and those were guarded well—with motion sensors and pressure panels.

Zylar pointed. "Anything on that side is freely available for use. The last row over there is restricted access. You can probably tell by the lights."

"Is it okay if I go in deeper to look?"

"Certainly. Let me know if you have any questions. If what you require is too much for us to carry on our own, I can summon a drone servitor to assist." That offer gave him a fierce twinge, because if he failed in the Choosing this time, that would become his role.

Beryl Bowman could try four more times, if she wished. That pained him as well. Before, he'd never allowed himself so much hope or so much desire, but it seemed inherently wrong that she could Choose anyone else.

As he watched her peruse the goods, a foreign thought surfaced, rare but inexorable. *She's mine. I stole her. I'm keeping her.*

I'M AT ALIEN COSTCO.

Beryl choked back wild laughter, as she tried to make sense of the sheer volume that surrounded her. Things weren't sorted neatly in aisles, and most of the stuff, she didn't even know what the hell it was. Some of it was shiny and oddly shaped, and though she had been wandering around for a while, she still hadn't seen anything that could pass for bedding.

Finally, at the very back of the storage area, she found a pile of slippery fabric and she pounced on it, gathering up a big armload. Zylar came up behind her, churring in what might be protest or concern. "That's worthless," he said. "We use it to cover valuable shipments and prevent damage.'"

So it's basically a tarp. Whatever.

"But it's the only thing that could work. Can we go back to the garden briefly? I have an idea."

"If you wish."

While they were there, she'd seen lots of soft, fallen petals and pods, perfect padding for a makeshift mattress. He was quiet as they traveled up in the lift and then retraced their steps. Beryl hurried forward and gathered up the fallen puffy pods and scented petals, wrapping them in the silky fabric she'd scavenged. Zylar seemed vaguely unsettled as they returned to his quarters.

"What's wrong?" she asked.

"Others may judge if they discover that you prefer to nest in refuse."

She rapped gently on the chitin that armored his side. "Don't look at it that way. Instead, consider how frugal I am and how good this is for the environment." Since he was simply staring at her, she went on, trying to get her point across. "You know, it's better to reuse stuff, isn't it? Make something from nothing?"

"I understand. You are very resourceful," he said, though she wasn't sure if he really meant it as a compliment.

"Exactly."

Though they had been gone maybe half an hour, according to her internal time clock, Snaps still went wild when they walked in, prancing around their legs with exclamations of "Welcome, welcome! I'm so glad you're here! Welcome! Gosh! Welcome!"

Dogs were fucking great. Beryl set down her stuff and let Snaps smell it all, then she rubbed his head, massaged his ears, and scratched his belly until his back leg kicked.

Snaps rolled over and shook himself, bounding to his feet. "Did you bring this for me? Is it for me?" He ran in a circle around her bed pile and started to run off with one of the pods, but she caught him and took it out of his mouth.

"Nope, this is mine, though if it turns out well, you can share the bed with me."

"Awesome! I love beds. Beds are soft and snuggly and best."

"Hopefully," she said. "That's the goal anyway. Hey, Zylar, can the manufacturer make some adhesive? Something with a clean seal that won't decay or start smelling bad."

"Yes, I can fashion it. Just a moment."

While he rushed off to do her bidding—and hell, wasn't that an incredible change of pace—she laid out the material as she'd envisioned, shooing Snaps away now and then. She had just enough pods and petals to create a nice futon, similar to something she'd seen in a documentary about Japan. When Zylar returned with the glue, she dabbed it along the edges, then folded the material over, leaving her with a mattress that was just big enough for her and Snaps. She repeated the steps to create a comforter, more because she couldn't sleep without covers than for actual warmth, since the rectangular platform had heating.

"Perfect," she said, standing back to admire her handiwork.

"The nest is complete?" Zylar had been watching her in silence, and now he stepped up to inspect what she had created. "How does this function?"

"I'm not sure if I should move it—no, get off of there, Snaps. How long does the adhesive take to dry?"

"It should be sealed," Zylar said.

"Okay, let's give this a shot." She laid the thicker one on the rectangle, settled in, and pulled the comforter over her. "Ah, very nice. If I get time, I'll make a pillow too, but this is pretty good."

"You burrow and hide while you sleep. But you're safe here, precious gem. During the Choosing, you need not concern yourself with such protective measures."

First, she got all warm and gooey inside when he called her *precious gem*, which maybe made her not as interested in the last part of his statement, even if it was slightly alarming. *During the Choosing* did make it sound like there might be danger afterward.

Before she could ask about that, he went on, "Is this more comfortable? I apologize for offering such a substandard nest."

"It's fine," she said. "It's not like you planned to abduct me. You thought you were saving…whoever you were supposed to meet, the one you chatted up on alien Tinder."

His silence said some of that was probably lost in translation.

Finally, he said, "You accept my apology?"

"I accept. We're doing great, aren't we?" That was a rhetorical question, but she wasn't actually sure if that was a thing in Barathi, and she figured she had taxed the translator enough, so she indulged some idle curiosity. "But I'm wondering…"

"Ask," Zylar said quickly.

Snaps was at the far edge of her *nest*, circling as dogs did until they found the perfect spot. He groaned as he curled up, still completely unfazed by their adventures.

"You sleep in that contraption…but I can't sleep sitting up even if they made a double-decker, so what are we going to do about that?"

He churred. "I don't understand the question."

"Well, once we're approved and out-bonded, won't we be sleeping together? It seems like our styles are a bit incompatible…" She stopped talking, abashed beneath the intensity of the gaze fixated on her.

His eye membrane fluttered. That was good, right? Beryl guessed she'd pleased him somehow, but he also seemed…speechless.

"You're *already* imagining how we will nest together?" he finally asked.

That made it sound like she was full of lurid fantasies instead of wondering about simple logistics. The blush started again. "Well, yeah. It seems like we'll need to work out a solution, unless you're open to lying here with me?"

"I cannot," he said. "The pressure would be most uncomfortable, and I would develop respiratory issues."

"Well, I can't sleep in the weird apparatus you use either." Sudden inspiration struck, a happy medium that might work for both of them, though she'd need padding between them or she might get hurt rubbing against his hard plates and spines in the night. "Do you have anything I can draw on?"

She sprang out of the covers, startling Snaps who raised a sleepy head to say, "Snacks?" and when she said, "Nope," he lost interest in her doings.

"You are the most interesting being," Zylar said, as he indicated a clear part of the wall with one claw. "Illustrate whatever you wish here."

To her amazement, the wall reacted to her touch like a drawing tablet, and she quickly sketched her idea, a sort of space hammock big enough to cradle them both. He could remain more upright while she curled up next to him. Excitedly she started describing what she had in mind. "The material I found for my bedding could work for this part of it, and the cord—what we used for Snaps's leash—could serve as the supports as shown here. Do you think it's something we could create?"

Zylar was staring at her in silence, but she couldn't read his expression, and then he crouched before her, bowing his head low. "I am humbled, Beryl Bowman. This is a beautiful invention, and I am deeply unworthy of a Terrible One who *already* puts so much thought into ways in which we can nest in utmost safety and comfort."

"Hey," she said uneasily. "Get up. It's not that big of a deal. Just...thank me if you like it, I guess?"

Still, he didn't rise, until she couldn't stand it and she dropped to her knees in front of him. Carefully, she reached out and tilted his face up, remembering how he'd done that to her, and how it started all those interesting feelings. She had the flutters again. Because what the hell, why he was so moved over a space hammock?

"You do not understand," he said quietly. "But this is further proof that you intend to Choose me. That you *prefer* me over all others, against all colors and qualifications. You would not offer me such a lovely gift, only to proffer it to someone else later?"

"I definitely would not," Beryl said.

"Then you see why I feel so unworthy. Nobody has ever—"

"Enough of that. I get that I'm the first, but you're *not* unworthy. You've so kind and considerate, and I'd really like it if you could see how awesome you are."

"I'm…awesome?"

"You are."

"I will try to remember that." He hesitated, neck ruff frilling a little, then he added, "The cord… It is something I invented that was deemed impracticable, a waste of resources. Yet you have devised two uses for it already."

"Well, there you go." Beryl smiled up at him, her heart aching at how damn sweet he was. "Clearly we're meant to be."

[9]

ZYLAR COULDN'T BELIEVE HOW SMOOTHLY the competition had gone so far. In fact, it was going so well that he was starting to worry that such a winning streak couldn't last. Beryl and Kurr had dominated in the last three events, climbing steadily in the rankings. Even Snaps seemed to enjoy watching Beryl compete in the challenges.

Though the contest had been fierce and grueling, Beryl kept surprising him with her quick thinking and phenomenal reflexes. The officials seemed to agree, and she was even winning the hearts of other Chosen. For the last span, he had heard murmurs of admiration from those around him, and that was starting to worry him as well, for there were now only forty-four prospective nest-guardians and there were still fifty would-be Chosen, most of whom were posturing, trying to catch Beryl's eye. Technically, it was too soon for that—they should be waiting for the second phase to commence—but this was the last event in the first round, so the officials wouldn't intervene.

Though he trusted her—he *did*—it was still painful to see how desirable she had become. Even if she was loyal, she might soon realize that she had better options. Snaps stirred in his hold and licked the side of his face, startling him out of his grim thoughts.

"I have told you not to do that," he scolded.

"Sorry!" The fur-person didn't sound or look remotely remorseful, his taster lolling out one side of his mouth. "I want your attention."

"You have it. What do you require?"

"Is she coming out soon? I'm bored!"

Before he could reply, the host spoke. "It has been a grueling first stage, but we're approaching the end of round one. We've seen tests of agility, strength, problem-solving, and creativity so far. Today, we take the challenge to a new level! It has been cycles since Contenders faced the Destroyer...and it has been even longer since you saw a Free-for-All."

Zylar froze as Snaps squirmed in his hold. "What's that? Is it fun?"

He didn't know how to explain the situation to the fur-person, but fear sank its talons in and he couldn't shake it loose. The remaining competitors took the field as cages, platforms, and other devices were deployed from various hidden access points. Snaps tapped his forelimbs against Zylar's chitin, impatient or demanding attention or both.

"Zylar? What—"

The other Chosen cast sidelong looks in his direction, seething with irritation because he'd already been granted what they considered special treatment since he was allowed to bring Snaps with him to the Choosing. Whispers of corruption and favoritism were already circulating, and he detected Ryzven's involvement in that. His brother was such a *flavork*.

"Be quiet," he whispered. "If you sit still, I'll explain what's happening."

"I'm quiet," said Snaps.

"Beryl will be given a replica of a nestling, and she will have to guard it against all harm. She may not inflict severe bodily injuries upon her competitors, but she also must not permit any damage to her nestling before the allotted time elapses."

The fur-person was silent for a long time, then he finally said, "Fight and guard?"

"Yes, that's essentially what is about to occur."

He had a bad feeling, though there was no point in burdening Snaps with his dread. Since Beryl and Kurr ranked highest, the others would focus on them, likely teaming up against them. Ulian Greenspirits were not particularly aggressive, and Beryl had no natural weapons. He had *no* idea how they were going to pass this final trial, especially under these circumstances.

"Contenders, this is your final chance to impress officiants and secure your spots for the second round! Are you ready to begin?" The host directed the question at the audience, who rumbled in response. "And…go!"

Beryl immediately leapt into motion, racing toward one of the platforms with her nestling in one arm, Kurr close behind her. He surmised that they had discussed their strategy beforehand, likely while the host was providing commentary. Six of the other contestants chased the two of them, and his hearts pounded in trepidation. Beryl snapped her hook stick out, but instead of whirling to attack with it, as it was a weapon, she used it to vault into the air, landing neatly on the platform. Kurr planted themself in front of the lattice that the other contestants used to climb and then lifted their nestling out of reach with their fronds. To his surprise, Beryl snatched the nestling and cradled both of them against her body, and then the

Greenspirit *thickened*. It was the only way to describe what happened. Kurr's body grew wide and dense and the fronds wove together to form a barrier and thorns erupted from the silver foliage, sharp ones that would rend the flesh of any contestant who got too close.

The noise intensified from the spectators and Chosen alike, and the host said, "Unprecedented! We have never seen this level of trust and cooperation so early in the Choosing! It is a bold strategy, as any harm to Beryl Bowman's charges will eliminate them both simultaneously."

Yet from what Zylar could see, it wouldn't be easy for anyone to reach her. Defending the platform in such a way already had the other contenders cursing in frustration, pacing around, until one of them launched a hook stick, trying to use it as a distance weapon. Beryl dropped to a crouch with her back to the attackers, covering the nestlings with her own body. He could *smell* the visceral reaction from that maneuver, shock and excitement releasing in spiced bursts from the other Chosen. Everyone desired a nest-guardian who would shield their offspring from harm even at the cost of their own lives, but for most, that was an unattainable dream.

It's within my reach.

He'd never experienced anything like the rush of pride he felt as the other Chosen gazed at him with ill-concealed envy. Whispers reached him from the back: "Where did Zylar find such a treasure?"

"It doesn't matter," someone else said. "Beryl will never Choose him in the second stage. She will be enticed by someone else's colors."

He had heard such things before, cycle after cycle, and he always sat in bitter, seething silence, because they had always been speaking the truth. Today, they were not.

Zylar shifted and fixed a furious stare on the offenders. "Keep her name from your mouth. *You* do not know her. You have no right to speak of her with such intimacy. As for what happens in the second round, you'll see how wrong you are and how singular *she* is."

Even more Chosen were gaping at him, instead of watching the action, for he wasn't known for aggressive speech. Yet he could not allow them to malign her—it *was* an insult as he factored such things—and to impugn her loyalty. She had touched his neck ruff and designed a nest for them to share. Zylar trusted that she had not done either of those things lightly or casually.

"You tell them," said Snaps. "Beryl is *our* human."

On the field, a few of them were still throwing weapons at Beryl, but the platform was big enough that she could dodge and squat, keeping the nestlings safe. Below, Kurr was an impassable blockade, and the contestants soon appeared to realize that. At which point, they turned on each other with vicious quickness, fighting with a desperation that turned his stomach. When the first replica "died," the crowd clicked and hissed in disapproval.

On some level, it bothered him that these aspirants were willing to inflict bodily harm on someone else's nestling in order to move forward. It spoke to a level of ruthlessness and self-interest that made him uncomfortable. *To think we're entrusting the future of our people to such souls...* Zylar much preferred the solution Beryl and Kurr had devised. Their efforts did no harm and kept their young ones safe at the same time.

The fighting on the ground intensified, and the whole zone reeked of aggression and blood, the last thing he would want for his actual nestlings. But that was the point of the Choosing, he supposed—to find nest-guardians who could keep their offspring alive, no matter the circumstances. To some, this contest might seem extreme, but for those familiar with Barathi history, it must be more comprehensible, as their people had brushed perilously close to extinction.

"Look, they're coming in from the top, on the back side!"

The shout directed Zylar's attention back to Beryl and Kurr. Somehow, a contender with incredible climbing ability had scaled the wall and was coming for their nestlings via what Beryl and Kurr must have deemed an impassable approach. The competitor—a Xolani doomsayer—had a weapon clenched in their fangs, along with incredibly sharp talons. Beryl was watching the carnage on the ground with a dazed expression, oblivious to the approaching danger.

He called a warning, but Beryl probably wouldn't hear him above the cries of the fighting competitors and the din of the crowd. *Turn around*, he willed her silently. If she didn't move soon, it would be too late. For both of them.

BERYL COULDN'T HAVE SAID WHY she turned at precisely that moment, instinct prickling her raw nerves. A terrifying alien was trying to haul onto the platform, head and shoulders already on board. It slashed at her legs with fearsome claws and the pain nearly dropped her to her knees. Adrenaline kicked in—fight or flight—and with both nestlings screeching in her ears, she reacted, kicking the climber in the skull with all her might.

As the combatant fell, she shouted, "This is Sparta!" Because obviously.

The audience couldn't have any idea what that meant, but they still reacted with appreciation as Kurr snatched at the enemy, fronds tightening around both nestling and opponent until Beryl thought she heard snapping bones, then Kurr flung the alien into a cluster of contenders, and whirled with utmost ferocity, scenting a weakened foe.

Beryl panted, checking the condition of her two nestlings, and tried to ignore the slashes on her calves. Not easy with blood trickling down her legs. She wished there was a timer showing numbers somewhere; that way she'd have some idea how much longer she'd have to do this. That near miss taught her about vigilance, though, and she spun in a slow, limping circle, making sure nobody else was trying to knock her off her perch.

This was like a seriously fucked-up game of King of the Mountain, one where she was also babysitting a pair of infant twins. Thankfully the nestlings didn't move too much, but they did struggle against her hold sometimes. They were about the size of nine month old humans, but they were covered in chitin, and they looked a lot like adult Barathi, only their neck ruffs and spinal spikes weren't fully developed. Her arms and shoulders were burning from the effort of keeping them close and protected. *Soon, this has to be over soon.*

She looked away from the spectacle below, focusing on Kurr instead. One of the nestlings let out a sound—distress, maybe? From her time in daycare, she'd learned that human kids were sensitive to their caretaker's moods, so she tried to calm her racing heart and bent her head to croon a little song that had always calmed children who didn't want to nap after lunch. The nestlings settled down at the sound of her voice, and she glanced up in time to catch something mechanical whirring in the air nearby.

"And that is time! Behold, the perfect nest-guardian," the host intoned. "Unflappable, swift, responsive…comforting the young ones even as chaos riots all around. Fix your eyes on the ideal candidate, would-be Chosen! This is Beryl Bowman of Aerth and her partner, Kurr, who keeps the peace so Beryl can nurture!"

It's over?

As the alarm sounded, medics and mech units entered the arena to break up fights that didn't seem to be stopping on their own. The medics took charge of the nestlings, maybe to evaluate their condition, so the rankings could be decided from there. Since theirs were pretty much untouched, Beryl figured she was safe, but hell if she knew how she was getting down from here. Her arms and legs both hurt like hell.

"I will catch you," Kurr called.

Really? Since their partnership had gotten them both this far, it seemed like a bad idea to voice her skepticism. Beryl couldn't exactly try to break her own fall since the medics hadn't gotten to the top of the scaffold yet. *What the hell.* She edged to the rim of the platform, tightened her hold on the nestlings, and let herself fall backward. The sudden drop spun her stomach, but Kurr caught her in three fronds, and gently set her upright. Beryl returned the Greenspirit's nestling just as the officiants reached them.

They used a fancy scanner that lit up when they ran it over the young ones. "Your charges are in perfect condition. *You* are not, Beryl Bowman."

"Tell me about it," she mumbled.

It was getting harder to stand since she'd lost a fair amount of blood, and the wounds were still trickling red, albeit sluggishly. One of the medics knelt and ran a laser up her calves, one at a time. She yipped more in startlement than in actual pain. *Is that cauterizing my cuts?* She caught a hint of singed flesh, and there was a faint scar on the back of her legs, which were still smeared crimson.

"You will live," the healer pronounced.

Taking the nestlings with them, they moved off to continue assessing the rest as Beryl turned to Kurr. "Thanks. I couldn't have done this without you."

"I count myself fortunate that you chose me as your ally," Kurr said. "We complement each other well. Thankfully, we can rest while our Chosen compete to seal our affiliations in the next round."

"Looking forward to that," she admitted.

It took only a little longer before the host announced the rankings. Beryl let out a relieved sigh when she heard that she and Kurr had tied for first. Unsurprising, but still, it was good to have it confirmed. More than six had been eliminated due to serious harm to their nestlings, and only forty contenders were moving on to the second round.

"With such impressive rankings, our prestige has grown," Kurr said. "You defeated a Xolani doomsayer and made it look effortless! Now there will be many who seek to be Chosen by us. It is an enviable position."

Beryl didn't care about that. She wanted to hug her dog, get cleaned up, and spend some downtime with Zylar. If she'd processed the information correctly, they had a few days off before the next round started.

"Did you want to come over tonight? I promised to invite you."

Kurr seemed shocked, though they had been loyal partners through all of round one. "I took that as a polite overture, nothing more. You mean to host me?"

"Well, yeah. I'm not in the habit of saying stuff I don't mean."

"Then I would be honored, if your Chosen is amenable."

"He's heading this way. I'll ask him." She bounced up on her toes and waved both arms in Zylar's direction, wincing at the pull on her sore muscles.

I wish hot baths and massages were available here.

"You have done me great honor, Terrible One." He spoke with that adorable formality, so earnest that she didn't have the heart to remind him that she didn't love that particular endearment.

"It was the best strategy. On the ground, I'm not a great fighter and neither is Kurr. So it made sense for one of us to guard the approach and the other to take care of the kids."

"Such a strategy is only possible with a trustworthy partner," Kurr said. "You might have betrayed me and dashed my nestling to the ground at the last moment to ensure your own ascension. You need not have shared your victor's crown with me."

Beryl stared. Honest to God, that never even occurred to her. "I'm not a monster. Even if these weren't real babies—"

"They were real," Zylar cut in. "Replicas, but real."

"What's a replica?" asked Snaps.

Quiet gratitude suffused her. If her dog hadn't asked that, she would have had to.

"They are copies," Kurr said. "Of viable offspring who have already grown to maturity. After the Choosing, the ones that survive will be raised as drone servitors."

Since Zylar didn't object to that explanation or expand on it in any way, Beryl figured it must be accurate. "Yikes. I had no idea I was guarding actual living babies. I thought they were incredibly lifelike dolls or something." Suddenly, her knees went weak, and Zylar caught her. He leaned close, uttering whirs and clicks she took as concern. "I showboated and did a backward pratfall off the platform while holding *two alien babies*."

"Yes," said Kurr. "And I caught you. It was well-executed."

Zylar churred. "I am in full agreement."

Even if they were copies of Barathi who already existed, how could everyone be okay with how many lives were snuffed out today? "This is so barbaric!" she burst out. "Those were real lives in play."

"They are copies," Kurr said, sounding confused.

It reminded her of cloning discussions she'd had back home, and the Barathi must fall on the side that believed that copies didn't have the same rights as everyone else. Clearly, they didn't get it and probably wouldn't even if she tried to explain. Her heart was heavy, though, and it hurt remembering how those nestlings had suffered, all for the sake of the Choosing.

Sighing, she said, "Let's go celebrate our big win. Can Kurr hang out with us for a while tonight?"

Snaps bounded around the Greenspirit, sniffing as many fronds as he could reach. "Do you like to dig? I like to dig!"

Kurr ran a few fronds over the dog's back, gentle and patient. "Digging is best when it is purposeful. You should only dig to plant your seeds."

"I have seeds?" Snaps sounded like his mind was blown.

Despite her overall soreness and exhaustion, Beryl smiled. "You don't, but you could get some."

"Would you like some of mine?" Kurr offered.

"Yes! Please! I must dig with purpose," Snaps muttered.

That didn't sound like an offer the Greenspirit would make lightly, but she didn't interfere. If her dog wanted to plant alien beings in the Kith B'alak private garden, who was she to stomp on his dream? Zylar would probably step in if they were about to break some important rule, right?

"To the garden first, then," Zylar said.

[10]

ZYLAR WAITED WHILE BERYL AND Kurr retreated for hygienic maintenance. Beryl needed to remove the residue from her wounds before they could begin any sort of social event. While he was waiting just outside the space allotted for contenders, the last Barathi he wanted to see approached.

"Ryzven," he said with a curt gesture of acknowledgment.

His nest-mate didn't even pretend at politeness. "Where is Beryl Bowman? I plan to invite her to join me in my quarters for a private celebration. Accomplishments as spectacular as hers must be acknowledged by those at similar levels of achievement. Otherwise, success loses its savor, when one is surrounded by those of lesser qualifications."

He's talking about me.

The spikes on Zylar's back almost stood up, but he forced them down only through sheer effort. It would be the height of rudeness to indulge in an aggressive flare while conversing with close kin, and Ryzven would waste no time telling the Matriarch about it. The ill feelings that accompanied this interest in his intended did not simply evaporate, however. *I have to remain calm.*

"Then you must wait," he said with what he considered admirable aplomb.

It was probably only a few intervals, though it seemed longer with Ryzven lurking and radiating impatience. At last Beryl and Kurr returned, markedly cleaner and fresher, and he heard Beryl telling the Greenspirit about the garden. His human hurried toward him, though her steps slowed when she spotted Ryzven nearby. Snaps squirmed in Zylar's arms, so he set him down after checking the cord looped around his neck. Beryl reached for the leash as she eyed Ryzven, but she didn't address him. Instead, she knelt and spoke nonsense words to the fur-person while rubbing him all over with her grabbers.

Kurr filled the awkward silence with a stiff, formal greeting. "Honor to your kith and kin, renowned Ryzven. I am Kurr."

"A pleasure! Everyone who has been following the Choosing knows who you are, esteemed Greenspirit."

While Zylar would be pleased if Ryzven forgot his business with Beryl while dallying with Kurr, he doubted he'd be so lucky. And as Beryl rose, Ryzven turned to her, making sure she got the full impact of his rare colors. He even puffed out his thorax a little, and Beryl let out a breath, a sound Zylar identified as annoyance. She said something the translator couldn't process.

"I came to congratulate you on your—" Before Ryzven could finish his pompous sentence, Snaps ambled forward, lifted a leg, and eliminated on him.

"I don't like him," Snaps said. "Beryl doesn't like him. Let's go!"

"So sorry about that," Beryl said in a flat tone. "Snaps is nervous around strangers."

Zylar had heard sincerity from her many times before, and on this occasion, she wasn't remotely apologetic. In fact, her eyes were twinkling and she seemed to be having a hard time restraining herself from making the battle face, which she'd said indicated amusement or enjoyment.

"You should clean that up," he told Ryzven, who was sputtering incoherent outrage.

Most likely, he would live to regret all of this, but it felt *so* good to get the best of his arrogant nest-mate for once that he didn't even look back when Beryl grabbed his claw and led him toward the exit. It occurred to him that she was leading him like Snaps, only by the limb instead of using a cord, but it would have lessened the impact of their departure if he mentioned as much.

Once they reached the public corridors, Kurr finally said, "I hope we have not given serious offense. I am…fearful."

The Greenspirit must know Ryzven's reputation well. He wouldn't accept such a humiliation without striking back. "Do not let it lessen your satisfaction in what you've achieved today. I will apologize more fully another time."

"Why would you apologize for something Snaps did?" Beryl cut in. "If anyone's going to make amends, it should be me. Though for the record, I said 'sorry' already."

"It was insincere," Kurr noted.

Beryl stared for a long moment, then said, "That's fair." She took a step closer to the two of them and added in a whisper, "So when I apologize *sincerely*, I probably shouldn't let on that I told Snaps to pee on him? I mean, theoretically."

The Greenspirit emitted a shocked rustling sound while Zylar simply could not contain his glee. He churred louder than he ever had in his life. "Truly? *That's* what you said that the translator could not comprehend?"

Then Beryl did show her fearsome aspect, displaying all her teeth. "I will neither confirm nor deny those allegations."

"Confirmed," said Snaps. "I was promised extra snacks."

Still delighted with his intended, Zylar led the way to the garden, wondering how he should reward Beryl for improving his life in every conceivable way. Kurr had never seen such a lavish private greenspace, so the Ulian wandered freely, talking to the plant life and providing interpretations for Snaps, who stayed close to their side in hopes of acquiring the seeds that had been promised earlier.

"I probably shouldn't have done that," Beryl said softly. "Sorry if it's going to make trouble for you. I'm tired, hungry, and I lost my temper. I don't know why, but your brother gets on my last nerve."

"You find him…irritating?" That was a staggering revelation, as Ryzven inspired affection and admiration everywhere he went.

"I think it's his relentless superiority and entitlement. He might as well be wearing a badge that says, 'Hey, did you know that I'm a big deal?'"

Zylar churred. His nest-mate would despise such mockery at his expense. He didn't have much of a sense of humor about such things, which was why he was sure Ryzven wouldn't get over how Snaps had evacuated on his person. The Matriarch might be hearing about the offense already.

"I agree with your assessment of his character, but…he is powerful. It would be safer not to antagonize him until we have passed the Choosing."

Beryl stilled, her squishy face twisting into an expression he couldn't read. "He has that much influence?"

"Potentially? Yes. We still need the officiants to approve us in the third round, and if Ryzven whispers poison..." Since Beryl was performing so well, the condemnation would likely be directed at Zylar himself. He could already hear Ryzven intimating that he was unworthy of such a stellar nest-guardian—that Beryl must be persuaded to Choose someone more suitable.

"Then...I'll make amends," she said quietly.

Her expression lost its brightness, however, and he could tell that she wasn't happy about it. "I wish I had the power to protect you better."

"No, it's fine. There are power hierarchies everywhere, right? I'll try not to provoke him until we get what we need from the officials. I'll ask Snaps to apologize too."

The fur-person bounded up as if she'd summoned him. "I planted seeds! Can we go home now? I'm hungry. So hungry!"

"This has been a true pleasure," Kurr said. "I will not intrude upon you further."

"But I promised to invite you to our place. All we've done is hang around the garden."

The Greenspirit flourished their fronds. "For me, that was the finest prize I could have been offered. With permission, Zylar, I would like to remain here and rest my roots. That would provide me with great respite and relaxation."

Zylar replied, "Then certainly, stay as long as you like. None should question you, but if they do, refer them to me."

"Many thanks."

They were silent in returning to their quarters, apart from Snaps making occasional comments to himself regarding the way things smelled. In the front room, Beryl's nest held pride of place. It was the first thing Zylar noticed when he stepped into the space. Snaps went straight for the water pot, and he recalled that they both needed to eat. He produced a couple of the nutritive packets, tailored for their size and energy intake needs, noticing how Beryl gave the smaller one to Snaps before she ate hers, then she downed a fair amount of liquid and let out a protracted sound.

"Are your injuries still troubling you?" he asked.

"No, I'm just tired…and glad I finally get to spend some quiet time with you."

That…sounded intimate. And quite desirable. More than what the Choosing ordinarily permitted. Zylar suspected they had bonds forming already, and that was both wonderful and terrible. He had never let himself *feel* too much before, not with the prospect of failure looming over him.

This is what an out-bond feels like. Caring for her, despite our differences.

"Ryzven would have offered you an elaborate feast, recited poetry in your honor. Do you not regret missing out on those revels? I have nothing like that to offer." He heard the vulnerability in the question. With anyone else, he never would have even asked.

"Not even slightly," she said. "I'd much rather be with you."

MAYBE THAT WAS TOO MUCH?

It was the truth, but Beryl hadn't meant it to sound so much like a declaration of love. She did have feelings for Zylar—of some sort—but she wasn't ready to confess undying devotion, especially when the Choosing was still in progress, and she might possibly be suffering from Stockholm syndrome. They both seemed to have swiped right, but it wasn't like they had been together for a long time, or anything. Mostly, she wanted to play with Snaps and *rest*.

That was the most important component, but he was staring at her like she'd cracked his chitin open and might start exploratory surgery at any moment. Probably just as well that she wasn't great at reading his expressions yet, because now she could pretend she didn't know exactly how moved he was.

"Thank you," he said finally.

"I'm so tired!" Snaps complained.

Thanks, dog.

"Come to bed then."

Snaps bounded over and rolled around on the covers, waving his legs in the air, then he spun in circles the correct number of times until he finally settled. Within seconds, he was on his side with his legs stretched out, snoring softly.

Wish I could do that...

If she knew Zylar, he probably wouldn't delve since the moment had passed. His beta tendencies and lack of self-esteem might even be what had gotten him passed over in prior Choosings. But Beryl wasn't in the market for an alpha asshole, so that worked out great. If you had to be abducted by aliens, it was good to wind up with one who respected your boundaries and preferences.

Dealing with so many different demands and expectations was exhausting, not to mention the fact that she wasn't used to such physical exertion. *I used to think chasing two-year-olds all day was tough...*

With a groan, she tumbled onto her makeshift mattress and stretched, twisting from side to side. Her back popped, and her nerves throbbed from the cuts on her calves, though they had been sealed.

"Thanks. I appreciate the way you look after him at the Choosing and how you—"

"This is the least I can do. Since he's your nestling, I should become proficient at caring for him as well."

"Aw. You're offering to be my doggy daddy?" That was a rhetorical question, and she could only imagine how the translator was expressing that joke. It was interesting what idioms it managed to process and which ones it shrugged and quit over.

"Yes," said Zylar. "It is an equitable trade, as you are giving your best in the Choosing with the intention of guarding my nestlings in the future."

"About that…"

Beryl propped herself on an elbow and patted the edge of the platform. He'd said he couldn't lie with her but sitting should be fine. The Barathi sat in the arena, and Zylar even slept that way, albeit with some weird equipment.

"What is it, Terrible One?"

"Well, I was wondering…*how*, exactly?"

"How…?"

Crap, he's going to make me ask outright. With a mental sigh, Beryl went for it. "How are we supposed to have these nestlings, exactly? It seems highly unlikely that our biological systems are compatible. We don't even breathe the same air."

"Ah, you're curious." Thankfully, he didn't seem offended by the question as he settled at the edge of the dais. "There will be scientific assistance, of course. Our genetic materials will be provided to the

Committee for Reproductive Viability, and they will meld our best qualities into the strongest possible nestlings, who will be bestowed upon us once we are settled in our partnership."

"Then I'm not expected to…gestate our offspring?"

Zylar churred. "Certainly not. Our physiological differences are such that incubating our young might do irreparable harm."

"That's a relief," Beryl admitted.

"Were you worried about this? You should have asked sooner." Hesitantly, Zylar reached out a claw and ran it lightly across her head, toying with a few strands of hair. "This is a comforting gesture, yes? I'm doing it correctly?"

Smiling, she tilted her head back, letting him pet her. "Yes, it feels good. And it's making me want to ask something else…"

"Please do."

"You said we'd get in trouble if we exchanged genetic material without approval. Why, if we can't reproduce without an assist from the science team?"

Without waiting for him to respond, she moved closer and tested a theory. She'd imagined it wouldn't be comfortable to cuddle up with him, and when she leaned on his chitin, she confirmed it. Yeah, not cozy at all. Zylar gazed down at her with an unreadable expression as she moved off, still close enough for him to keep stroking her head. Quietly he resumed the soothing touch.

"Certain rules have no exceptions," Zylar said, then. "Barathi couples require no aid to create nestlings, and their pre-Choosing congress is restricted for that reason. I believe I explained about prior issues with overpopulation?"

"Yeah…oh!" Suddenly she thought she understood. "The rule's

in play regardless, and it applies to out-bonded couples as well, even if they can't go around making babies. It's just…to keep a level playing field or whatever? So we don't enjoy privileges unavailable to Barathi competitors."

"I don't follow," Zylar said.

It was a tad embarrassing to say out loud, but she was already committed. "Well, think about it. If you were free to seduce me, you could get me hooked sexually. That way, you'd be guaranteed that I would Choose you in the second round, right? Because I wouldn't be able to get enough of that delicious Zylar action."

That being the case, Beryl could understand why they didn't ordinarily let contenders stay with their would-be partners. Too much intimacy would let them bond faster. She hadn't understood why the Matriarch was so surprised when she asked to stay with Zylar. Now the pieces were starting to come together.

I wonder why she let me do it. I mean, if I understood right, it's not technically against the rules, just kind of irregular. Maybe she didn't want Zylar to fail this time? So when I wanted to stick with him, she allowed it, hoping constant proximity would give him an edge.

Beryl was already moving on, but he made a sound she didn't recognize; the translator fritzed on it as well. It was like Zylar was trying to speak and failing.

Finally he said, "You're implying that I could provide pleasure profound enough to cause you to…imprint on me and…" He fell silent again, his neck ruff half-flared.

"It wasn't a challenge or anything. I mean, I wasn't *asking* you for sex. In fact, I'm not even sure how that would go. I was just saying it's theoretically possible, so I understand the embargo on sexual contact, even between out-bonded pairs."

"Are you teasing? Or trying to tempt me?" he asked.

"What? How am I... I think the translator is screwing with us again. Like the time you thought I was asking for coitus and I was actually cursing."

"You're cursing me?"

"Oh Lord. I'm not! But while we're on the subject, I might as well go all-in. Can you explain how we're supposed to...mate? If we do, that is. If the science team is making our babies, I guess we'd only do it for fun."

Now his neck-ruff was fully frilled, quivering even to the naked eye, just as it had when she was touching it. Beryl didn't know how it went with the Barathi, but she figured that arousal started there. Did that mean she'd turned him on just by asking how sex worked? On one level, that was flattering as hell, but it also spoke to a fair amount of repression, if the mere mention of mating could get him ready to go.

"You're *definitely* tempting me." His voice held that dual-edged growl that was sexier than she wanted it to be. "But I cannot fathom whether it is intentional or not."

"I was just asking for a verbal explanation," she whispered. "Since I don't think we have...congruent anatomy."

"An explanation...or a demonstration?" Something about his eyes didn't look the same; the fluttering membrane was in play, and the color was brighter, sharper, more like live crystal than they had been before.

Though it was likely a terrible idea, she wanted to touch his neck ruff again and see what happened. It wouldn't help if she explained about human parameters. Strictly speaking, humans had sex for pleasure with all kinds of genitalia, so maybe it wouldn't be that different with an alien. They just had to figure out what felt good, do some experimenting, and that sounded fun as well. Zylar was all revved up, but she wasn't supposed to make a move, because Choosing rules said not to.

What the hell. Rules were made to be broken.

[11]

ZYLAR SENSED HIS CONTROL SLIPPING.

At any moment, he would show Beryl something that only a bonded partner was meant to see, but she was so intent, watching him with those bright eyes, that he couldn't master himself and part of him didn't even want to stop. He waited for her response, conscious of heat and tingling inside his thorax.

"A demonstration," she said softly. "I would enjoy…knowing what's in store."

That was permission. She wanted to see what his body looked like when he was ready to mate, and with a pained sound, he let it happen at last. His neck ruff stood high as his abdominal plates shifted, revealing four slits, quivering and vulnerable. A Barathi would not be able to resist the pheromones he was releasing and would be upon him immediately. Beryl slid closer to examine the changes in his body.

"How does this work exactly?" She spoke quietly, but the low volume couldn't disguise the deepening of her tone.

Her scent was a little different too, richer and muskier. Perhaps it was the human equivalent of pheromones. The scent of her didn't fill him with desire, but it signaled her interest, and Zylar let the pleasure of that response wash over him. By his display, they were skirting the boundaries of the Choosing, but as far as he knew, the rule was against mating only. He had never heard of any proscription against exchanging information instead of genetic material. That rationale might even save them, should an inquiry be forced by that flavork, Ryzven.

"In this state, I am…ready," he said. "More…preparation is better, of course. It allows for a thorough exchange of genetic materials."

"If your partner was Barathi, what would happen now?"

"They would massage my neck ruff, causing me to lubricate. I would stimulate them in turn, until their claspers extruded. Then they would penetrate me and collect spermatophores, the more the better."

Just talking about it was exciting him, and it couldn't happen tonight for a variety of reasons. Yet her smell was ripening even more, and though the power of it was diminished, her pheromones were starting to work on him, clouding his mind. He reached for her hair, remembering she liked it when he played with her fur. As soon as he touched her, she emitted a sound that he intuited as a pleasure response.

"Go on," she invited.

He didn't know if she meant the explanation or for him to keep touching her, so he did both, claws scraping lightly against her head as he spoke. "Mating can last up to a span, if both parties are fully engaged. When partners disengage, they may be exhausted or dehydrated. The female then fertilizes the eggs with the collected genetic material and lays them in the nest, where they will share the task of guarding them until development is complete."

"Tell me about the claspers." Beryl tipped her head back, eyes half-closed.

"Barathi females have four gynosomes with hooked tips to allow them to latch on and collect spermatophores. Each time I ejaculate internally, they take that material. Which is good, because it contains nutrients our nestlings require for healthy gestation."

"So the more pleasure you receive, the better the exchange," she whispered.

"Yes, you understand fully now. And since you have received clarification, I must…" Words failed him because she was touching his neck ruff again. Now that he *knew* she had full cognizance of what that overture signified, Zylar's body responded reflexively, lubricating in preparation for more.

That felt glorious, and his head went fuzzy with the pleasure of her soft strokes. No Barathi partner would have been so tender or careful, and they could not have touched the webbing at all for fear of causing harm, so her delicacy provided another level of sensation, curling through his nerves, until he couldn't contain the hiss, and that only seemed to encourage her. She kept caressing him, and the lubrication continued, until he could feel it on the flesh beneath his chitin. Zylar had never heard of anyone becoming this aroused and not mating, so he had no idea if self-denial would be painful. Even if it was, he couldn't bring himself to ask her to stop, not when she seemed so invested in this exploration.

On her own, she paused, eyes locked on his glistening genitalia. A complex cocktail of pride and shame suffused him; no Barathi partner would simply stare at his body this way, but he didn't hate the way her interest made him feel. Then she lowered her hands, and he thought she was finally finished tormenting him.

But her avid stare didn't let him calm down either. It was impossible for him to draw back with so much fascination fixed on his sex organs. In fact, he could feel them lubricating further, puffing outward in hopes of attracting her. He hadn't even known that was possible, and it was starting to feel uncomfortable, an ache in his thorax from the internal swelling of uncollected spermatophores. In time it would certainly fade, the genetic material being reabsorbed, but meanwhile—

"We can't exchange genetic material," Beryl said.

Zylar stirred in confusion. "Yes, I'm aware. It's against the Choosing rules."

"No, I mean, we're not physiologically compatible. We can't *do* it on our own. Which means, strictly speaking, any contact we have for pleasure isn't reproductive sex, per se."

With his mind so muddy, that made sense. "True. But…"

"Then…does that mean I can touch you? I really want to. I'll stop if I make you uncomfortable, or if it doesn't feel good."

Though he had no idea what she intended to do to him, he said immediately, "You have my permission."

She murmured something that he didn't catch, and then she rubbed a spot on his posterior side that made all his defensive spines stand up. Normally that reaction triggered in response to a perceived threat, not sexual stimulation, but since her grabbers were shaped different than Barathi claws, she could fondle the vulnerable spots between the spines, and more pleasure rocketed through him. She gave such unusual sensations, impossible, improbable pleasure, by indulging her boundless curiosity. He shifted restlessly at the edge of her nest, conscious of the ferocious throb in his thorax, so profound now that he could barely think.

She probably doesn't know how desperate I feel.

Now, she was carefully stroking each of his spines, and he hadn't known they possessed any nerve endings since the Barathi didn't touch them. But apparently, they were as sensitive as his neck ruff, conveying urgent pulses of sensation throughout his body. He hissed, pushing his torso forward in an uncontrollable mating display.

"Oooh, you like that. How about this?"

*This...*was an indescribable sensation. She was behind him now, and she was right; there was no way they could mate this way, but there was warmth and heat on his neck ruff. Not her grabbers, but Zylar had no sense of how she was providing this stimulation, only that it was gentle and exquisite, lingering and delicate, and pleasure flooded his entire body. He was so ready to mate that the softest pressure would probably set him off. Knowing it was fruitless, he still yielded to the impulse to rub his forelimbs together, the chitin producing the most intimate of songs, one he should only create when his beloved was mounted to him.

"You're...singing?" she asked.

When she spoke, the incredible feeling ceased. Did that mean she was creating that sensation with her talking and eating orifice? Inconceivable.

"Yes," he managed to say, but an explanation was beyond him.

"Is that a good thing? The translation isn't telling me anything."

"Yes," Zylar said again, like it was the only word he recollected.

"Just making sure. I love the way you taste, by the way. I wasn't expecting that."

His words evaporated again because that feeling was back, moving on his neck ruff until he had to dig his claws into her nest to hold still. The need to mate pounded through him, and his whole body throbbed, not just his thorax, as if pleasure might devour him from the inside out. Then the sensation shifted to his defensive spines, and Zylar hissed again, in short, irresistible bursts. He couldn't stop the sounds any more than he could stop the lubrication trickling down his body.

"I need you to cease," he finally growled. "The stimulation is too much."

"Too much? I'm sorry." True to her word, she pulled back and appeared in front of him, eyes wide.

Zylar tried to put distance between them because even her smell was driving him wild, but his limbs wouldn't cooperate. "No need…for regrets. Just…let me…"

"If you tell me what I did wrong, I'll make sure I don't do it again."

"Not wrong. But there are limits to how much stimulation I can endure without…" He couldn't decide how to complete that sentence, but fortunately, she understood.

"Without needing to finish?" she guessed.

DEAR GOD. HOW CAN *I be this turned on from touching and kissing him a bit?*

Back on Earth in her former life, this would have barely qualified as some petting, but she could *tell* that he was so excited, he could hardly sit still, a fact reinforced by his hissing and shivering, and the way his whole body jerked when she touched her lips to one of his spines. Now it looked like he was in physical withdrawal, shaking through a bad reaction.

I got him this worked up. I should help him.

Sure, frame like a good deed when you're dying to continue. She didn't have claspers, but she had fingers, and she had a fairly good idea what she could do with them. It might be enough to get him off. Taking a deep breath, she made sure Snaps was still asleep and went for it.

"Let me see what I can do," she offered.

"Do?" He sounded dazed, his voice deep and reverberating with that low note that made her tighten her thighs and squirm. The bioluminescence was back, glimmering in his skin like leashed lightning, perhaps some indication of his excitement.

He wasn't the only one lubricating. Beryl had seldom been this wet in her life, and she didn't know what that said about her, except that it turned her on something fierce to experience how easily she could drive him wild. Being desired was a hell of an aphrodisiac.

"I want to touch you more. Not for stimulation. For...completion. Yes or no?"

"Yes," Zylar said, so quickly that she figured he must be dying.

Normally he was pretty gung-ho about sticking to the rules, but she doubted he gave a shit about the Choosing right then. His whole body was focused on her every movement, mind fuzzy with powerful lust. It was heady, seeing how she'd gotten him trembling and breathless without even half trying, though it was mutual. She needed some pressure between her legs and fast, but...

Let's take care of him first.

She could masturbate, but she suspected that it would be tough, if not outright impossible, for his arms to bend that way, and his claws would probably hurt if he tried to touch himself. Hopefully, his fluids wouldn't hurt her skin. Probably she should have asked that beforehand, but the question would be a mood-breaker. Sometimes you had to gamble.

Nervous and excited in equal measures, she first touched the external flesh of his arousal, testing the lubrication on her fingertips. It didn't burn or sting, so that was a good sign. He reacted with a jolt to her exploratory caress, hissing in what she'd think was a protest, if she didn't already know it was a pleasure sound.

"It feels good?" she asked.

"Strange, but yes." His responses were terse, but not because he seemed unhappy.

Beryl guessed that his people didn't talk much during sex, even if it was a long, intense affair. She tightened her thighs and contained the impulse to stick her hand down her pants. On a logical stretch, touching him, then herself with the same hand, might constitute an exchange of genetic material, and she didn't intend to give the officials any reason to disqualify them. Plus, that maneuver was probably too advanced for her first try.

"Okay." She heard the breathy, slightly embarrassing note in her own voice, but it was too late to care about that. "I'm going to touch you...more intimately now. Still good?"

"Please," he said, and it was both permission and a plea.

His sex organs were arranged near enough that she could penetrate all four simultaneously with two fingers on top and her thumbs below. That might not be enough pressure in the lower pouches, but she'd give it her best shot. Part of her couldn't believe she was doing this. *I'm about to fingerbang an alien.* But even thinking about it that way didn't diminish her excitement.

Beryl thrust fingers and thumbs in simultaneously, and his whole body jerked. She recalled him saying something about hooks and anchoring; while she didn't have that capability, she'd bet her hands were more agile and should be able to provide a different sort of pleasure, if alien nerves worked the same way. Slowly, she started to push, giving him a taste of friction and gentle pressure. It felt...strange, but not wrong, and she *loved* his smell, intensifying the more she stroked inside him.

"Tell me how it feels best," she said softly.

As she shifted her fingers, he hissed, and she took that to mean she'd found a good spot. She focused there, detecting a slight difference in tissues. This was a little bumpy, possibly where he stored his spermatophores. Softly massaging there made his neck ruff quiver, and then he was hissing nonstop, unable to give a reply in words.

The more she stroked him, the more pronounced those bumps grew, swelling beneath her touch. *This has to be right. It's working, I'm getting him off.* She couldn't quite reach properly with her thumbs until she leaned in and pressed deeper, then she focused on catching up in the lower pouches until the bulges felt about the same. She could hear Zylar breathing, frantic and rasping, likely a measure of his mounting excitement. Her hands and wrists were getting tired, and God, she hoped it didn't take all day, or however long a span was.

Slowly, she increased the pressure, trusting him to tell her if it was too much or if she was hurting him. He gave no sign of that, just

134 / ANN AGUIRRE

jerking and hissing in response to her intimate strokes. Then she pushed hard, with fingers and thumbs, and his body went rigid. She *felt* the internal bursts, all at once, then more fluid on her hands, and the swellings within the four pouches dissipated. His entire body eased.

Holy shit, I did it. I made him come.

She gave a few soft strokes and pulled her wet fingers out. "How do you feel?"

"As if I would happily die for you. I have *never* experienced such exquisite bliss."

"I'm so glad," she said.

His adorable honesty made her smile. She got up and went to the hygiene square to clean her hands, then she came right back, conscious of the powerful ache between her legs. If she didn't get some action soon, she'd hump her own hand. Beryl noticed that his chitin had slipped back into place, now that he was satisfied.

Too bad I'm not.

"You're still aroused," he said, not a question, an observation.

"Desperately."

"How can I assist?"

His phrasing surprised a laugh out of her, but she didn't think she had the patience to try and teach him what to do. Since he had those talons, it might be slow and dangerous, and right then she just wanted to come. Like Zylar, she couldn't stand any more foreplay.

"Do you mind if I use you?"

"...use me?" He repeated the phrase, seeming puzzled, but he added, "Please do. If there is some way I can give you pleasure—"

Before he could even finish the sentence, she straddled his hard lower limb. She'd guessed it would feel incredible, and with her body weight at the right angle, it was so, so good. Beryl was already wet and ready; she just needed permission to ride. Now she had it, and she swiveled her hips furiously, alternating up and down and back and forth. As a kid, she used to masturbate on a pillow or a blanket, and at her horniest, she'd done it on the arms of couches, even with the edge of a table once.

This felt even better, because he was alive, and touching her lightly with his claws, first on her head, then her back, whispery scratches that sensitized her skin and peaked her nipples. *At this rate, it won't take long.* She moved faster and pulled his touch to her breasts. "Gentle," she managed to say. "Like when you're playing with my hair."

When he scraped her nipple with a claw, she ground down hard and came, moaning and shivering. Her body went lax, so she fell against the hardness of his chitin. Zylar caught her against him, and she didn't even mind that he couldn't really feel her body. He was strong enough to hold her in place with one arm, and she closed her eyes, imagining that she could hear his heartbeat.

"Did you attain completion?" he asked.

She snorted a sleepy laugh. That was so on point with the human equivalent of *Did you come?* that a wave of amusement rolled through her, gentle and warm. Some things were standard among sentient beings, she figured.

"I did. And it was incredible," she added, just in case he followed the new-lover playbook and was about to ask *Was it good for you?*

"That…happens very fast for your people." There was a sort of wonder in the statement.

"It can, with the right partner."

"You're praising me? But I did nothing of worth. I merely—"

"You're underestimating yourself again," she cut in gently. "It was quick because I was very excited *and* because I'm with you."

[12]

THE TWO REST DAYS PASSED too swiftly for Zylar's liking.

Spending time with Beryl and Snaps…it was idyllic, more enjoyable than he could have envisioned. They walked in the garden, and he showed them more of Kith B'alak's holdings. She also made additional personal coverings from the fabric she'd salvaged.

Snaps took pleasure in the simplest of outings, and Beryl had a matchless way of filling Zylar with brightness, as if he had lived in darkness until she arrived, and he realized this was how the world should have looked all along. He didn't press for more sexual contact, but sometimes it was impossible not to recall how beautifully she had touched him, playing his body like an instrument. Since he had never mated with a Barathi partner, he had nothing to compare the experience to, but it was difficult for him to conceive that it could feel any better, even if the act enabled reproduction.

Sometimes he shamed himself with silent curiosity about the way her body was made. She had seen all of his secrets, while he'd learned only a few of hers. Today wasn't the right time, however, to focus on such matters. He needed to concentrate as he entered round two of the Choosing. Both his hearts took on a panicked tempo as he tried not to fixate on the fact that this was his fifth and final opportunity to win a nest-guardian and receive approval on his match.

Zylar had never done well in this phase. Even if his intended got to this stage, which wasn't always the case, they had always, always been lured away by someone else. He must have shown some sign of his grim thoughts or made a sound of distress because suddenly, Beryl was in front of him, holding Snaps close.

"Hey, it will be okay. Just focus on the competition. And…if we don't get approval at the end, I'll go work in that space station daycare you mentioned before."

He stared at her, unable to believe the translator was relaying her words correctly. "You would rather leave Barath than Choose another?"

"Damn straight. I have no emotional investment in anyone else. I'm betting everything on you, Zylar."

"Emotional investment?" Silently he wondered if this was meant as a declaration of devotion, but he didn't know how to confirm the theory.

"Well, yeah. We've spent time together, talked, gotten to know each other, and it's been intense for a relatively short time. I think it's safe to say that we've started…what did you call it? An out-bond."

"I treasure you," he said, hoping it conveyed the immensity of his regard.

"Likewise. Now get out there and flaunt your colors. For the record, I happen to like brown. A lot."

Zylar glanced down at his dull pattern and something shifted inside him, an inexpressible lightening, as if a burden he didn't realize he was carrying suddenly dislodged. "Are you saying that you find me attractive?"

"Not at first," she admitted. "But that's because of differences in our anatomical design. Now? Of course I do. Really, the only thing you lack is confidence, and we'll work on it."

"I will bring you honor," he said then.

"Thanks. If you get nervous, look for me. I'll flash you this sign…" She held up two clawless digits. "It means 'victory.' Good luck!"

For a few seconds, he watched as she shielded Snaps, hurrying toward the part of the spectators' seating reserved for aspiring nest-guardians. Then he joined the rest of the Barathi filing down into the arena, tense with expectation over what would be asked of them. In the past, the competition had been gentler than what would-be nest-guardians faced, as he would be expected to nurture hatched offspring more than protect the unhatched ones.

The holding area behind the scenes was already teeming with aspiring Chosen, and he knew none of them by name. They were all younger, fresh and hopeful, and it made him conscious of all his prior failures. With effort, he stopped those thoughts, remembering the way Beryl had complimented him. *She would rather leave this world than pair with anyone else. I will not let her down.*

"Zylar of Kith B'alak?"

He turned in response to the diffident inquiry to find a slight Barathi male with lovely, albeit muted colors in varying shades of green. Though all his hues were from the same base, giving him common status, they still made for an alluring pattern. Zylar predicted that this one would do well if he could pass the second round and retain his intended's interest.

"Yes, what do you require?" It was embarrassing to be so suspicious, but Ryzven could be underhanded. If this was one of his minions—

"I am Arleb... Kurr is my intended. Your Beryl proposed a partnership to them, and that was vital to our progress. You also invited Kurr to spend time in Kith B'alak's private garden, and that gave them much joy. I have come to offer my appreciation."

"Beryl has benefited greatly from the alliance as well, but your gratitude is noted. You're from Kith I'stak?"

"Not a prestigious line," Arleb said, abashed. "That is why I was unsure whether I should approach, in case you took offense."

Suddenly Zylar realized that from an external perspective, his personality might read the same as Ryzven's, and that, he could not tolerate. "Perhaps we should learn from our Terrible Ones and consider an alliance as well."

Arleb's nictitating membrane flickered in surprise. "I don't know what benefit I could bring to *you*, but in the spirit of cooperation, I am willing."

Just then, the host began announcing their event, and handlers shoved them toward the entrance to the arena. He followed the rest of the throng, hating the fact that so many eyes would be fixed on him, and they would gossip about his past failures. If Zylar knew his nest-mate, Ryzven would fuel the hateful talk with malicious whispers of his own, and while that didn't matter in round two, it could become a problem in the final phase, should the rumors gain traction with Choosing officials. The special clearance for Snaps might become an issue, and he could well imagine that Ryzven would retaliate for the indignity Snaps had inflicted. He tried not to let these worries show, as the host continued his commentary.

"What a contest! As we begin the second stage in the Choosing, we have fifty would-be Chosen, competing for the favor of only forty nest-guardians..."

Unable to help himself, he sought Beryl in the spectator's section and found her in the front, sitting with Kurr. As soon as she realized he was staring at her, she gave the sign she had said indicated victory. His heartbeats settled. *She believes in me. I will not disappoint her.*

"First, I will introduce our Chosen. When your name is called, step forward and show us who you are."

This part was similar to the way the Terrible Ones began the competition, but the events afterward would be quite different. Normally, he would be full of choking dread, worrying over his choice for the first impression, but this time, Zylar had no doubts. Before, he didn't think he could perform well enough, due to his inadequate hues. Beryl would see beauty in the movements; she wouldn't judge what he lacked, only admire what he offered her.

Therefore, when the host called, "Zylar of Kith B'alak," he stepped forward boldly.

"For whom do you declare?" the host asked.

"Beryl Bowman of Aerth."

Zylar fixed his gaze on her and performed the courtship dance— for her and her alone. With each motion, he spoke of his intentions and his desire, using neck ruff and defensive spines to compensate for his dull colors. While it was not a perfect rendition, it was tailored for the two of them, and she must see that. When he stilled, the arena was quiet, and then Beryl led the response by emitting her sonic shriek, startling a few intended nearby. Yet the audience caught her excitement, and soon they were all cheering. Zylar didn't need to look at Ryzven to know that his nest-mate would be furious.

"A bold move," Arleb said softly, as he stepped back in formation. "And not the strictest interpretation of the dance, but you surely captivated your Terrible One. She never looked away from you, not once."

Pride filled him in an unstoppable wave, especially since someone else had noticed her loyalty. Beryl was such an enviable intended…he savored the sensation briefly, then finally let himself steal a look at Ryzven as the introductions went on. He was seated with the officiants, and he directed a poisonous glance at Zylar, then continued whatever he was saying.

For once, though, he didn't let his nest-mate intimidate him. For Beryl, he would factor how to overcome this obstacle as well.

Zylar intended to let nothing stop him from earning the right to be her partner, out-bonded for life.

CRADLING SNAPS, BERYL WATCHED THE activity in the arena, trying to figure out exactly what was happening. Finally, she whispered to Kurr, "Can you give me a quick overview?"

"This is a test of problem-solving and of comprehensive knowledge," they answered. "You see those containers? Within each one is a prize, and written on each object is a riddle, hinting at the contents within. But the runes are written in various languages, some ancient or defunct. The better educated a Chosen candidate is, the better they will do in this challenge."

"Does speed matter?" Beryl asked.

Kurr's fronds rustled, maybe in approval. "Yes, the Chosen will be timed. There are three goals in this competition: to read and decipher the riddles, to choose their box wisely, and to open it swiftly. The scores will be tabulated accordingly."

"So if they can't read the riddle and they get a crappy result with the prize inside, they'd lose points even if they open the puzzle box really fast?"

"That is correct. Rankings will be determined by comprehension, worth, and speed."

"Oh wow." She hadn't asked Zylar about his higher education background, and since they were using tech to communicate, she had no idea how good he was with languages.

"What's Zylar doing?" Snaps demanded.

Beryl explained to the dog in the simplest terms as the Chosen raced around the field, pausing at various containers, various geometric shapes, colors, and materials. All of them were etched with characters Beryl couldn't read; if she'd been forced to compete in an event like this, she would've been screwed, unless Kurr had a good background in reading alien tongues.

"What's in the box? Can I eat it? Will Zylar let me eat it?"

Figured, that was what a dog would take from a competition like this. She smiled, keeping her eyes on Zylar as he hurried around the arena, seeming to choose his target with care. Others were already committed to their puzzle boxes, but he took his time, finally selecting one on the far side. She wished she had some binoculars, but from this distance she couldn't tell much about the container he'd chosen. It was small and shone with a coppery glimmer, and she could see scratches on the side, but otherwise, that was it.

"Any insight into Zylar's pick?" she asked Kurr.

"The characters are etched in ancient Tiralan. I don't read it myself, so I'm not sure."

But Kurr wasn't really paying attention to Zylar anyway; Beryl followed her friend's attention and saw that they were focused on a green-shaded Barathi working nearby. "Is that your Chosen?"

"Yes. We did not receive approval in our first attempt."

"Do you have any idea why?" The idea of being blocked in the last round for nebulous reasons bothered Beryl.

If you busted your ass in the Choosing, that should be enough. But no, there were still factors beyond their control involved, and assholes like Ryzven probably had their hands in the pot, stirring behind the scenes. Even however million light years from Earth, politics and nepotism were still a thing.

As if her cranky thoughts had drawn the asshole's attention, Beryl glanced over to find Ryzven sitting with the judges, staring hard in her direction. She quickly cut her gaze away, not wanting to give him the satisfaction of acknowledging his interest. *I remember losers like this in school.* Their first year in community college, Beryl's friend Kelly, had dated a classic BMOC, and Scott thought the sun rose and set with him. Yet the minute Kelly's back was turned, the jerk was all over Beryl like butter on bread. Ryzven radiated that same frat-bro vibe.

One of Kurr's fronds wrapped around her arm, tugging in excitement. "Look, Zylar's opening his puzzle box!"

"Already?" she said, leaning forward for a better look.

Admittedly, she had no clue how complex the mechanisms were, but this seemed like a good time. He wasn't the first, of course, but the host hadn't sounded too excited about any of the prizes. Now he was churring, loud enough that the whole arena could hear.

"Incredible! Zylar of Kith B'alak has uncovered an antique tablet, a find fit for a cultural display. What secrets will it reveal? Scholars are longing to learn!"

Wait, the writing was...ancient Tiralan? If she recalled correctly, his actual intended had been Tiralan. She couldn't remember the name, but it seemed like he might have spent months studying to impress...whoever he had meant to pick up. *Instead of me.* That gave her a weird feeling, not quite jealousy, but sort of uncomfortable, like maybe jealousy-adjacent? Beryl imagined Zylar staying up late, learning how to greet the family in fluent Tiralan, and—

Would he rather have a Tiralan partner? I bet that person can read Barathi, at least.

She had been pushing forward, trying to make the best of things, but now she wondered if he was doing the same, if he ever wished his plan had unfolded correctly. Really, all her success so far could be attributed to luck. It wasn't like she'd known how necessary the alliance with Kurr would prove to be.

"Don't be sad," Snaps said, licking her face. "It's okay."

Whatever his other issues, the dog was damn good at reading her moods. She mustered a smile and rubbed the top of his head. "Yeah, I'm okay. Zylar did great, huh?"

"He opened the box, but there's nothing to eat," Snaps mumbled.

"How are you still hungry? We just had breakfast!"

"A dog can always eat," Snaps said.

The alarm sounded, signaling the end of the first challenge. Three Chosen didn't manage to open a box at all, so that would impact their rankings. Chaos reigned on the field as the judges conferred about the worth of various discoveries, leaving the contestants to mill around. She noticed that Zylar seemed to be talking to Kurr's Chosen.

"Looks like they've made friends too," she said to the Greenspirit.

"Arleb mentioned that he planned to thank Zylar for letting me experience the garden. Though my people have grown beyond the need for roots, self-indulgence can be...soothing."

"So, it's like a spa day," Beryl said.

"I do not understand."

She stifled a sigh. "Never mind."

Half of humor related to shared context and the other half was timing, so most of her jokes didn't land these days. She tried not to be homesick, but when she thought about it—really deep down contemplated the facts—she could curl up in the fetal position and just cry until there were no tears left. They were trying to fix the AI that had the coordinates leading back to Earth, but she didn't have high hopes. If Helix couldn't be restored, then...

I'll never eat another cheeseburger. Never watch Netflix. Never see a sunset on Earth.

She was sitting next to a freaking sentient plant with another alien on her left, while more aliens ran around in front of her. Currently, she was breathing alien air, courtesy of alien tech, and wow, yeah, it was...a lot. *Breathe*, she told herself. *You've come this far. Don't lose it now.* The air even smelled different when she analyzed it, full of chemicals and combinations that had no human equivalent. Sometimes it was like cayenne pepper, and sometimes there was a soft sweetness that came from Kurr's fronds.

Finally, the host spoke again, thankfully disrupting her depressing thoughts. "We have our initial standings!"

Though Zylar didn't place first, he took fifth with the average of his performance, and Beryl yelled louder than anyone, not caring about the looks she drew. Especially from fucking Ryzven. Though really, she should apologize to that jackass. Otherwise, he'd probably make life uncomfortable. People with power and big egos tended to operate that way.

When the audience started leaving, she set Snaps down and kept a good hold of his leash. "Come on, let's go say sorry."

"But I'm not!" Snaps said.

"Welcome to my world."

Beryl caught up with Ryzven near the exit. Normally, she would have headed to the holding area for competitors to wait for Zylar; she hoped he understood this move and wouldn't mind if she did a little ass-kissing. The brightly patterned Barathi studied her with body language she couldn't read, waiting for her to speak.

It's for the greater good.

"Do you have a moment?" she asked.

A flutter of the opaque eye membrane, then Ryzven said, "You would speak with me?"

"Yes, I wanted to apologize. Snaps was rude, and I think we may have gotten off to a bad start. I'd like to make amends if I can."

"This is no place for such overtures. Accompany me to a more suitable locale?"

Ugh. Beryl didn't want to go off with Ryzven, especially without telling Zylar, but she'd initiated this contact and if she was curt to him—again—it would undo this attempt at conciliation. Gritting her teeth, she faked a smile, belatedly remembering that Zylar had said it registered as a display of power, not a friendly one. Ryzven's neck ruff frilled a little, and now that she knew what that meant—

Yuck. Hard pass.

She wasn't up for close encounters of the alien kind with this Barathi. Stalling had to be the best move. "Where did you have in mind? And will it be all right if Snaps goes with us? I can't leave him alone."

Before Ryzven could reply, there came a sound from behind them, a sort of growl, and Zylar stepped in front of her. "*Why* are you attempting to lure my intended yet again?"

[13]

ZYLAR HAD NEVER DESPISED RYZVEN as much as he did right then.

The urge toward violence surged through him, even though he knew that the kith would not side with him, should the situation escalate. Beryl stepped between them and set a grabber on his thorax; he couldn't feel it, but he understood her intentions. He stilled.

"It's a misunderstanding," she said. "I brought Snaps over so we could both apologize for being rude. That's all."

That might be true, but he couldn't bring himself to step back. "Have you accepted their apologies?" he asked curtly.

"You did not give me the chance, nest-mate." Ryzven might sound calm and amused, but his eyes said he would rather finish what Zylar had almost started.

"Continue," he bit out, though every instinct called for him to put as much distance as possible between Ryzven and Beryl.

He could read his nest-mate's inclinations well, and this flavork had more than a passing interest in her, only intensified by her apparent loyalty. Ryzven would soon view her as a challenge, if he didn't already, and that didn't bode well for a peaceful completion of the Choosing. Zylar fought a wave of sheer nerves; he couldn't lose again. Couldn't lose *her*.

"That's all I meant to say. I hope we can start over and that you won't hold onto bad feelings about Snaps and me," Beryl said.

"Since you are brave enough to admit your mistakes, it would be paltry of me not to forgive you," Ryzven said. "Before, I had invited you to a gathering. You will certainly accept my goodwill this time?" Despite the pleasant tone, Zylar understood that wasn't a request, more of a demand for compliance.

But would Beryl grasp that?

She stepped a little closer to Zylar, and he responded instinctively, pulling her against him in a protective gesture that came from the depths of his being. Then she said, "It's fine with me as long as we don't already have plans. Zylar?"

Oh, that was clever. Ryzven hadn't included him in the invitation, but now there was no polite way for his nest-mate to exclude him. Zylar churred. "Your parties are famous," he said deliberately. "I would love to partake of these great amusements, so we accept gladly."

"I'll send word when the arrangements are finalized," Ryzven muttered.

The fact that he left without a final flattering word for Beryl spoke of how annoyed he was. Snaps watched him go, then said, "I hate that guy."

"So do I," Beryl said.

"I appreciate your attempt at appeasement, but please don't seek him out alone again. He is…" Zylar hesitated, unsure how to phrase the objection. "Not to be trusted."

"You think he might abduct me?" Beryl asked.

The mere thought sent a chill through him. "Not precisely, but I fear he may become even more enamored of you, and then he'll seek a lawful way to take you from me."

"You think they'd let him do that?"

"Ryzven always gets what he wants," he said somberly. "Always."

Her face contorted into an expression he couldn't read easily, but then she slammed her furled grabber against the open one, resulting in a martial sound. "Not this time."

Zylar treasured her devotion and her loyalty, but the more tightly they bonded, the more he feared losing her. After tasting bliss with Beryl, he didn't think he could survive another failure. It wasn't the prospect of living out the reminder of his life as a drone, but the joyless prospect of an existence without her? Unbearable.

"Let's go home," he said.

"Could we take Snaps to the garden first?"

It was such a small request. He was tired from the competition and from restraining his antipathy, but he could refuse her nothing. "Of course. That is becoming our custom."

With one hand, she held Snap's lead, and with the other, she clutched at Zylar. Her open affection warmed him all over, and he slammed the door in his mind where all the dire, terrible fates lived, whispering of doom and separation. *We deserve a happy ending. We've already come so far together.*

"Walking like this is such a couple thing to do on my world," Beryl said.

"Joined, like so?" He lifted his forelimb where she had latched onto him.

"Yes, do you mind?"

"Not at all. The habit is a little strange, but I have acclimated to your ways."

"Don't bonded nest-guardians spend time together outside the house?"

He thought about that. "They are more occupied with keeping their young safe and healthy until development is complete."

"And before they're officially approved, they see each other mostly at the Choosing?"

"Yes. Why?"

She let out an airy sound. "I don't know. It just all seems so strange, like they wouldn't know each other that well at all before they end up committed for life."

"It's different on your world?"

"Very. Although I must admit, it doesn't always work out, even if you thought you've gotten to know the person well."

"Hurry," said Snaps. "I need to use it."

Zylar quickened his step, recalling that the fur-person had no qualms about eliminating wherever he might be, if the issue became urgent. Fortunately, they made it in time, and Snaps went there. Then he trotted off to check on the seeds he'd planted with Kurr.

"Hey! They're growing! Come look!"

Beryl tugged and Zylar followed, rushing through the garden to inspect the tiny, green shoots. Snaps pranced in a circle, rear extensor whipping wildly, and she knelt to rub him all over, until the fur-person flopped on his side and got even more caresses.

"Good job," she said.

"I buried something and it turned into something else! Will they change again if I dig?" Snaps crept closer, but Beryl grabbed him.

"Don't dig up the plants! You want to see them grow up, right? These are your responsibility now."

Snaps fell back onto his butt, staring at the seedlings with wide eyes. "Am I…a father?"

"Sort of," Beryl said.

Zylar churred, amusement overwhelming him.

Then Snaps lay down in front of the plants with a determined sound. "I will protect you, tiny green dirt dogs."

He drew Beryl away gently. "What have you done? He thinks those are his nestlings. We may not be able to get him to leave."

"I'll figure something out. At least he's not digging up the garden."

"I suppose that's true. Shall we walk?"

Instead of taking his forelimb when he offered it, she stared up at him. "I wish I could ___ you."

"That didn't translate."

"It's an Earth custom for showing affection. Never mind."

"Terrible One, I'm most willing to receive affection from you in whatever form you wish to bestow it. If I find the delivery method strange, I believe I can adapt."

"Then hold still."

She closed the distance between them and reached for his head. He lowered it reflexively, and she put her talking part close to his mandibles, so he could feel it intimately when she breathed. Her proximity reminded him of how good she'd made him feel, and his thorax tingled. Then she shifted, touching him until she found a small gap in his chitin between his neck and shoulder, a vulnerability an enemy could exploit. He had no fear about Beryl discovering it. Zylar let her angle his head so she could reach that spot.

A starburst of heat began when she touched her mouth to that softness. It felt so good that he almost pulled away in shock, but Zylar stilled, remembering his promise to adapt to her brand of affection. But this, this felt almost too good to be believed. The heat moved in soft circles, sometimes gentle, sometimes a little firmer, but it always felt exquisite. The tingling in his thorax brightened, and he fought the urge to let his plates part so she could have access to his sex organs. They were already swelling internally, tempted by the promise of more pleasure. His mind went to a wild place, imagining her using her eating part there, as she had on his defensive spines, his neck ruff, and now, his throat. That idea was so deviant, but pure lust suffused him, and his lower limbs nearly gave out.

Suddenly he realized that while they were in a private area, the garden was still accessible to all kith. Most likely he shouldn't allow anyone to see how freely she touched him. Human affection wasn't the same as Barathi sex, but he couldn't risk a scandal. Trembling a little, he stepped back, breaking contact.

"You didn't like it?" she asked.

"No, it's...lovely. Strange and lovely. But we shouldn't do this here."

"Oh. Right. Rules."

"Show me more in our quarters," he said, hoping to mitigate the faint disappointment he sensed in her. "I'll welcome anything you care to share with me then."

She bared her teeth at him. "Anything? Be careful. I could get a little wild."

BERYL HAD TO PICK SNAPS up to get him to leave his "babies," and the dog whined all the way back to their room.

By the time they got there, she was tired from wrestling him, and she was starting to feel a bit embarrassed about the way she couldn't keep her hands off Zylar. If he expected them to resume the foreplay, she didn't know if she was up for it, and now she had the awkward job of explaining why. But as she stepped into their quarters, all thoughts of that evaporated.

Because the shared nest she'd designed had been completed and was now hanging from the ceiling, using the tensile fiber Zylar had created.

Beryl smiled, unable to help it. "When did you do this?"

"I sent the request as soon as you rendered the concept," he said. "Have I done well?"

"Yes. It's exactly like I imagined. Let me clean up, and then we can test it out."

She hurried her nightly hygiene ritual, put the bedding she had made into the hammock, then crawled in herself. It felt a little strange, but it would be nice to sleep with Zylar instead of having him in a separate room. Hopefully this wasn't an infraction that would get them in trouble with the Choosing officiants. If something went wrong at this point and she had to leave Zylar, she had no clue how she'd bear it.

"Pick me up," said Snaps.

Hmm, sleeping with a dog in a movable, hanging bed might not be the best plan, but she couldn't resist his pitiful eyes. Sighing, she leaned over and plopped him at her feet. Since he was used to curling up there, he did so here as well, circling three times, then dozing off with a quickness only trusting dogs possessed.

That's one problem solved.

"Comfortable?" Zylar asked.

Beryl rolled over. She hadn't even heard him come in. "It's wonderful. Come and find out for yourself."

"You wish to nest with me already?"

"Didn't you have it made so we could start sleeping together? Or have I made a bad assumption?" God, why she was always the eager one, asking for more intimacy?

I'm developing a complex.

He went still, like she had accused him of something. Finally he said, "It is most presumptive on my part, but I did hope you would want to share it with me, even before—"

"Before we're officially approved," she guessed.

"Yes."

But he still didn't move, and his uncertainty was freaking adorable. It seemed like he shared both her faint embarrassment *and* her eagerness.

"Come to bed, Zylar. Since I've already made *my* choice, I don't give a rat's ass about the Choosing."

"I don't understand everything you said, but the translator says you chose me. That is more than enough."

The hammock swayed as he slid in, and the support webbing made it possible for him to settle upright. She tucked the stuffed bedding between them and then snuggled up against his side. It was better than she'd imagined, especially when he rested his claw on her head and gently raked through her hair. Tingles radiated outward, the top of her head, her neck, her spine, diffusing at her hips, and her nipples got hard.

When she moaned, he hesitated. "Is that a good sound?"

"Definitely. Don't stop."

"Am I giving you pleasure?"

"Very much," she whispered.

"Then this is an erogenous zone? How interesting."

Her eyes were closed, and she struggled to keep her mind focused on the conversation. "Not normally, but it feels fantastic. Human nerves are connected, so when something feels good, the message travels throughout our body and sometimes it kindles a sexual response, even if the original touch wasn't meant that way."

Beryl should win a fucking prize for that explanation, considering how scrambled she felt right now. He didn't speak for a while, but he did keep petting her. She snuggled closer, with the vague wish that their bodies were more compatible. If they were, she wouldn't need a layer of quilting to keep from bruising herself on his chitin.

"It's strange for me to admit, but I understand. The things you do to me…" Ever so delicately, he touched her mouth with a single talon. "With this… They have no Barathi equivalent, but those sensations fill me with urgency nonetheless."

She smiled, savoring the admission. "Thank you for telling me."

"But…I am afraid." His voice trembled with the force of the statement.

"Of getting in trouble?"

"Of losing you. The closer we become, the more certain I am that my life will be a misery without you, Beryl Bowman."

Until this point, she'd been trying her best to live in the moment and not worry about the future, but those desperate, honest words ripped away the pretense. Suddenly her head filled with scary possibilities—of failing at the Choosing, being forced to try again with someone else, or having to leave Barath. It wasn't like she could get a work visa, and more than that, she didn't *want* anyone else.

Oh God, I'm honestly falling for him.

"Then we won't fail. We won't let Ryzven interfere either," she said, forestalling the objection she knew he was about to raise.

He's so scared of that bastard.

"We're already a family," he whispered. "Snaps is our first nestling, and I cannot relinquish the promised sweetness of a life with you."

Her heart melted. "It's mutual."

Zylar resumed playing with her hair, sending jolts of pleasure through her body, and then he got daring, raking his claws lightly down her back. The teasing scrapes felt so good that her skin reacted in responsive goose bumps. At first, she thought he was trying to soothe her to sleep and that he might not realize he was turning her on.

Until he said, "Your scent is ripe. You desire me?"

Oh God.

Still, even if it made her face feel hot enough to toast bread, she admitted, "Yes."

"By my measure, you have given me significantly more pleasure. With your permission, I would like to rectify that."

No human lover would ever put it that way; it was so business-like and brisk. Yet she knew how easy it was to get him stirred up, so she didn't mind. "Do whatever you want. I'll tell you if it doesn't work for me."

In response, he shifted her with impressive physical strength and settled her, between his legs, with the bedding between them so she could lay on her back against him comfortably. Beryl couldn't imagine what he planned to do in this position, but then he pulled off her top. Both his arms came around her, and he touched her, shoulder to hip, with the tips of his talons.

The resultant surge of pleasure made her jerk and moan. He must have remembered what she'd said about her breasts because he focused there, teasing and circling her nipples with the lightest pressure. Zylar was incredibly careful and attentive, touching, then pausing to gauge her reaction. Soon, he was accurately measuring her arousal by the pitch of her moans.

She squirmed against him, and since he didn't seem inclined to escalate from playing with her boobs, she lifted her hips and pulled off her pants, then she captured one of his claws and put it between her legs. *Time to find out what he can do.*

"Be careful. I'm very sensitive and tender down here."

"This is your sex organ?"

"Yes."

"You're lubricated well. In humans, this also means that you wish to mate?"

Before she could respond, he angled his claw and touched her with the flat part, grazing her clit through sheer luck. "Yes. God, yes." That was both an answer and encouragement. "Rub me there, exactly like that."

He followed instructions beautifully, offering precisely the same angle and pressure. The heat intensified. She'd always had better clitoral orgasms, so she didn't miss the penetration. With those small strokes, she spiked fast and came, thighs quivering. He noticed that as well, bringing both claws around to massage her legs. That felt incredibly relaxing, and she sprawled against him, panting. When her body stopped trembling, she tucked her curved hand into one of his larger claws, finding the curl of his talons oddly reassuring.

I should probably reciprocate. Most humans would be putting her hands on their good parts by now. "Do you want me to—"

"No, tonight is yours. I need nothing."

Zylar rested his head on top of hers, and she closed her eyes over how lovely that was. *I'm spooning with an alien, and it's awesome.* She mumbled a dazed and happy response.

"It's easy to give you pleasure," he said then.

Beryl laughed, nuzzling the top of her head against his mandible. "Now you're just bragging."

"Am I? But I enjoy the way you respond to me. It's beautiful that it feels effortless." He paused, seeming to choose his words with care. "I have never pleased anyone without trying. Never felt that who I am is enough. You are a miracle, Beryl Bowman. *My* miracle."

[14]

THE NEXT DAY, ZYLAR REMEMBERED Beryl's promise as he lined up with the rest of the competitors for the third trial. When he finished this event, he'd be halfway through the second round. He noticed Ryzven, who was whispering to the nearest officiant again.

Why does he hate me so much?

With effort, he looked away, searching the crowd until he found Beryl sitting next to Kurr, cradling Snaps close. Just seeing her face calmed his racing hearts, and his hands steadied. Beside him, Arleb was also gazing at his intended.

"Good luck today," Zylar said.

"Likewise."

The host boomed out a greeting. "Welcome to stage two, round three of the Choosing! We have a truly diabolical test in store today. There may be casualties! I hope you're ready for a riveting spectacle, as our Chosen compete to prove they're the best of the best!"

In response, the audience roared, a mix of churrs and sounds offered by other aliens that passed as cheers. Zylar had never remotely thought he was superior at anything, but he was starting to believe that he was gifted at pleasing Beryl Bowman. He just needed to perform well enough to stay in the competition, and everything would work out. For the first time, he didn't need to worry about someone stealing his intended because she'd said she *chose* him.

Oh, there were a few Chosen trying to impress her, but she never gave them more than a fleeting glance. Beryl wasn't the type to be lured by flashy moves or seductive colors.

The assistants wheeled heavy machinery into the arena, and he had a bad feeling. It wouldn't be the Destroyer, as they'd used it in the first stage, but it might be something even worse since the host had mentioned casualties. Arleb churred in a high pitch, an unmistakably worried sound. Zylar stole a glance at Ryzven, who radiated satisfaction. *This is his doing.* It seemed that his endless whispers to the officiants had borne dangerous fruit.

When they uncovered the machines, Zylar closed his eyes briefly, then he forced himself to watch as they arranged the mechanized death traps known as the Gauntlet. This was a purely physical test; speed and agility mattered most, but endurance came into play if you took a wound. Only great determination and fortitude could keep the Chosen moving under such circumstances. Zylar had never faced this particular challenge, but he had seen competitors lose limbs and even their lives when they mistimed a maneuver or lacked physical prowess.

"I'm frightened," Arleb whispered.

He wished he could think of some profound comfort or encouragement. "Think only of Kurr," he said finally. "Picture the happy life you'll share."

"I'll try."

The host called contestants at random, and Zylar's misgivings rose with each run. When the third missed a leap and was smashed between two pistons, he froze and Arleb let out a sound so plaintive that it unnerved him to hear it. Before the other Barathi could settle, they called Arleb's name. Zylar wished he knew what to say, but nothing came to mind.

Arleb took position, but he didn't look confident. He ran forward, dodging and weaving, but he passed one piston too slow and took a hit. That knocked him forward, and he didn't recover in time. As Zylar watched with absolute horror, Arleb tumbled into the field of spikes, and four impaled him when they activated. His body jerked, but he couldn't pull free and the spikes rose again, again, until Arleb stopped moving.

The crowd quieted.

"Heartbreaking! Our first Chosen fatality. Let's have a moment of silence for Arleb of Kith I'stak."

So fast. It happened so fast. He just told me he's scared, and now he's gone.

Zylar sought Beryl with his gaze and found her consoling Kurr, who had wilted forward, fronds whipping in distress. Bleak fear swelled inside him, and he considered leaving. Dying meant leaving Beryl behind, on a strange world where she knew no one.

Maybe it would be better if they both left Barath and made a life together elsewhere.

Except he had no resources off-world. Everything he owned had been given by Kith B'alak, and it would be repossessed if he attempted to emigrate with a partner without completing the Choosing first.

Ryzven did this. He essentially murdered Arleb because he wanted me to fail.

That fury and outrage put titanium in his bones and in his talons. The event paused for the workers to remove poor Arleb's body, and representatives from Kith I'stak came to the field in mourning colors, bearing him away with somber grief. While he understood the authorities did these things to keep Barath from overpopulation, the pendulum had swung too far the other way.

It's too difficult now. They're killing us for entertainment.

That thought was downright treasonous. Questioning policies enacted by the Matriarch could get him exiled, if he was foolish enough to speak such heresy.

He wasn't.

By the time the machines were cleaned and arranged in the Gauntlet, Zylar was calm and ready to run. If he died trying to keep his promise to his intended, so be it.

"Calling the next runner—Zylar of Kith B'alak!"

With effort, he blocked out all the noise and stole a final look at Beryl, who raised her fingers in the sign she'd said meant victory. Her fear revealed itself by the way she buried her face in Snaps's fur, unable to watch what came next. *No, don't look away. I need your strength. Stay with me until the end, Terrible One.* As if she'd heard his thought, impossible as that was, she raised her head and bared her teeth.

Zylar took position and waited for the signal. When the bell sounded, he raced forward. There were no tricks to this, only sheer ability. Run. Dodge. Leap. Duck. Roll. The timing had to be precise, and it was, until the very end. He miscalculated the last leg and tumbled forward, a span too slow to avoid the slicing blade.

It was only a glancing blow and his chitin took the hit, though it left a deep runnel in his back. No blood. Just a scar, as chitin couldn't heal. He could fill the gap with polymer to smooth the edges, but the mark would always remain.

Shakily, he got to his feet as the host pronounced, "A respectable time!"

He returned to his place in line, while the rest of the Chosen ran the Gauntlet, hideously aware of Arleb's absence. There were injuries but no more fatalities, and at the end, he ranked in the middle, respectable enough that he took comfort in his odds of passing to the final phase.

How am I supposed to face Kurr?

Later, Zylar was still wrestling with that question when Beryl found him. He checked for Kurr, but didn't see them. "Was it wise to leave Kurr alone?"

"They wouldn't come with me, even to the garden. I don't know what to do," Beryl said.

Liquid leaked slowly from her eyes, and he studied her small, soft face. "Are you injured?" he asked in alarm.

"Emotionally, I am. I feel sorry for Kurr, but then, there's a small part of me that's relieved you're all right, and I feel guilty about that too."

Before he could reply, Ryzven stepped into their space. "I have finalized the plans for the celebration. You'll join me tonight, I trust?"

I'd rather kill you.

Perhaps reading his inclinations, Beryl answered, "Yes, what time?"

"Any time after sunset, though the earlier the better. Don't bring that one." He indicated Snaps in a disdainful gesture.

Zylar didn't feel like attending any festivities tonight, let alone an event that was likely to be extravagant. It was wrong, disrespectful even. Though he hadn't been close to Arleb, they had been acquainted and they had agreed to cooperate, should there be any events where it would be necessary. Now Arleb was dead, thanks to Ryzven's meddling.

"Understood," he gritted out.

With that, he hustled Beryl away, fighting the urge toward confrontation. Once they completed the Choosing, then he could challenge Ryzen. Until then, he had to control his temper and force down all this aggression.

"He's a monster," she whispered.

"Yes." There was no point in denying it. "He's an example of how too much success can ruin a person. He's never failed at anything, never been denied something he wants, and he's come to believe that should never change."

She quivered, the scent of fear strong like wilting sha blossoms, and stepped closer, tucking her hand around his forelimb. "And he's interested in *me*."

"Yes." There was no benefit in denying the danger.

"You warned me to be wary of him before, but I didn't understand. I thought you had some sibling rivalry going, nothing for me to worry about. But he's throwing a *party*. And he was there when Arleb died! I saw him watching with such avid interest…" She paused, couldn't seem to gather her words properly, then she tried again. "A decent person would reschedule to be respectful, right? That's the same, even here."

"You are correct," Zylar said. "Ryzven is not good. But he is powerful. We must not antagonize him openly until we succeed. Be careful tonight."

She let out a soft sound. "It won't be easy, but I'll try."

I HAVE NOTHING TO WEAR, Beryl realized, watching Ryzven strut out of the arena, surrounded by sycophants.

That wasn't a problem Beryl had expected to face after being abducted, but even life on another planet included some of the same problems. Now, it seemed like date night on Earth when she used to study the contents of her closet on Saturday night and conclude that all her outfits were terrible. In this case, it was a lot truer than usual since she had only the clothes she'd been wearing, along with a pair of makeshift pajamas.

That I made from what Zylar called a tarp.

She wouldn't wow anyone at this heinous party if she showed up dressed in packing materials. Not that she wanted to impress, necessarily—more that she didn't want Zylar to lose face because of her. If alien values resembled those on Earth, then appearances mattered. It made her sick that she had to consider shit like this when she was so worried about Kurr.

The Greenspirit had been so devastated after their Chosen died, but they'd refused all offers of company and comfort. It bothered Beryl to think of Kurr grieving alone, yet she didn't know them that well, not enough to insist they come to Zylar's place when they said they preferred to be alone.

After leaving the arena, they let Snaps visit his babies and do his business, but the mood was somber. Now, on the way back, she couldn't stop thinking about her friend. "Do you think we could check on Kurr before the party?"

Zylar angled a look at her, and it was inscrutable as ever, but the way he touched the back of her hand gently with one talon gave the impression of silent approval. "I would have suggested it if you hadn't."

Snaps paused to sniff the floor and Beryl sighed, returning to her initial problem. The idea of a whole civilization without leisure shopping might melt her brain. "The Barathi don't wear clothes, but surely there are visitors who require some type of covering while they're on planet. Are there any stores?"

"Clarify. The translator didn't give me a perfect understanding of your request."

She tried again. "A place where I can get something else to wear?"

Beryl tugged on the outfit she had been wearing nonstop for what felt like forever. Sadly, it wasn't even one of her favorites, just a random shirt and pants she'd chosen for comfort while completing her community service. To make matters worse, Barathi hygiene facilities didn't work that well on cloth, so the ensemble was grungy and a bit ripe.

"You wish to acquire more coverings?"

"Yes, I need more stuff to wear. At least two or three changes."

Don't get me started on underwear. I might end up having to be a lingerie designer too.

"There is a market at the spaceport. I'll take you before we speak to Kurr."

She cupped her hand around his talons. "Thank you."

"It is my pleasure to provide for you, Terrible One."

Though her heart was still heavy, the ridiculous endearment still managed to make her smile. Then, since Snaps showed no motivation to get moving, she picked him up and ported him to their quarters. After consuming water and nutrition cubes, she played with him for a while, managing a game of tug-of-war with the edge of her blanket.

"Don't be sad, but we can't take you with us tonight. Stay here, run around as much as you want, and then nap. We'll be home soon." While she didn't know if that was true, she also felt fairly sure that dogs didn't have a great sense of time. "Be good, okay? If you need to go, do it here."

"I know, I know. I'm a very smart boy," said Snaps.

That called for another round of belly rubs and some baby talk, then Beryl straightened. "Ready."

Zylar reached for her hand this time, as if the gesture had already become natural to him. He led the way to the spaceport, moving slow enough for her to memorize the route. The sky cars still fascinated her, and she appreciated the way he shielded her with his body, although the crowds weren't bad at this hour.

The spaceport was as huge as she remembered, still bustling, and the market he'd mentioned looked like a random assortment of kiosks. Most travelers hurried past without sparing a moment to browse, despite the eager calls from the vendors. Not all of the stalls were attended, though—some seemed to be automated with a vending capability.

Enchanted, Beryl followed her nose to a booth that sold food, pale chunks spinning in a red field that inexplicably reminded her of popcorn. She breathed deeply and thought of home, grubby cinemas with sticky floors, and people who played with their phones during a movie. Funny how nostalgia worked. That stuff annoyed her before, to the point that she'd much rather watch Netflix than see a movie at the theater, but now that she couldn't go home unless Helix was fixed? She missed all of that.

"This is not something you can wear," Zylar noted.

She glanced up, feeling her cheeks heat. "Sorry, this smells familiar."

"It's a treat that Xolani doomsayers enjoy. Toxic to most others."

Quickly, she moved on and focused on her original task, checking every display for any useful items. At first nothing caught her eye, but in the last kiosk, she found a colorful range of fabrics cut in shapes that clearly weren't meant for humans, but maybe—

"What are these?" she asked.

"Adornments for pets."

Come on, seriously? I'm in the alien equivalent of a dog clothing store.

Still, with a little ingenuity, she could fashion some fresh looks from these materials. *And this one, with a little tweaking, I can wear tonight.* "This one" was a bright blue tube with some fluttery bits attached. She tried to imagine the species that it would fit perfectly and could only envision a giant snake person. If she wrapped the fluttery bits around her and tied them off, shoulder to waist, it should look like a sheath dress. There was nothing she could use for shoes, so these sandals would have to suffice for a bit longer. As she had competed in a few events barefoot, she would need more options at some point.

Zylar paid with some shiny tech she didn't understand, coded via a light exchange. *Add that to the list of things I have to learn.* Beryl rushed away, and they stopped back at the apartment so she could

STRANGE LOVE / 171

get ready, including using of the hygiene facility. When she was dressed and had pinned up her hair, she didn't expect a compliment, but he still studied her altered appearance as though he could judge human beauty.

"I like your fur that way," he said. "And that color is cheerful."

Briefly, she wondered how the hue appeared to him. "Thank you." She turned to Snaps. "Sorry to get your hopes up, we're not back for the night. See you later."

Time to check on Kurr.

Beryl had never been to the intended dormitories before, and the spaces allotted couldn't be large, considering how close together the entrances were. Zylar checked an informational display and received Kurr's room assignment, once he entered his Kith B'alak credentials. That brought home how powerful his family must be. Basically, it seemed like he could have anything he wanted, based on his bloodline.

Scary. And impressive. No wonder Ryzven is a monster.

Kurr lived on the fifth level, and a fearful feeling took root in Beryl's belly. Surely, they wouldn't have done anything drastic, right? She wished she had asked more about their life, about why they couldn't return to their home world. Quickening her steps, she was practically running by the time they got to the smooth, white panel. Zylar activated a light box, and a tone resounded inside the residence.

Alien doorbell. Some things are universal, I guess.

No answer.

He rang twice more before saying, "Kurr, if you're at home, please respond."

Beryl tried whacking the panel with both hands, but it didn't open. Finally, Kurr replied, "I have said that I wish to be alone. I appreciate your concern, but that sentiment has not changed. Please respect my wishes. I will speak with you tomorrow."

Sighing, she stepped back. "I guess…we tried."

"It's all one can do."

Seeming no more eager than she was, Zylar headed back toward the holding owned by Kith B'alak. The lift carried them to a much higher floor, and at one point, he had to enter a security code. *This is like the penthouse level.*

Knowing that couldn't have prepared her for the sheer opulence when the lift landed. It was all white and platinum, with alien flora growing wild on the walls and up through them, woven like a living lattice. The petals fluttered as if the plants were breathing.

"Sha blossoms," Zylar said, following her gaze.

Though the furnishings were unfamiliar, she could tell they were carefully crafted, and she paused to admire a shining, metallic device made of tensile, braided strands with fine mist pouring out of it. Maybe it was a freshener because the air even smelled different here, brighter and fresher, somehow, with a scent she couldn't pin down, like pineapple, celery, and freesia, blended deliciously and topped with a cherry.

"It's beautiful here," she admitted in a grudging tone.

Zylar turned to her and let out a quiet churr. "This is how the powerful ones live on Barath. Prepare yourself for what you'll see inside."

[15]

RYZVEN'S INNER SANCTUM WAS EXQUISITE.

Crystal and metal blended seamlessly, glimmering in the changing lights. It was like standing in a river, and then when the lights shifted, brightened, they revealed the bodies moving about the room. There were no limits here, Barathi mingled freely with outworlders, though none were so rare as Beryl.

Revelers undulated in the center, a sea of self-indulgence. He recognized a few of the guests. Some occupied the highest strata among the kith, while others were being used as playthings. Pleasures that had been deemed immoral by the Council thrived behind closed doors.

There was an entire tank of Darveelan crawlers waiting to be devoured. In these enlightened times, the Matriarch frowned on the consumption of live food, but doubtless she didn't know about Ryzven's secret predilections. Consuming the crawlers went a step beyond cruelty because they tested at a level approaching sentience, so they understood the danger, and fear permeated their whole bodies as they darted back and forth, seeking a means of escape. Zylar had been told that terror made their flavor sharper and more pungent, but he would never partake of such torture.

Beyond the diabolical delicacies, there was a vast array of illegal chem—sparkling powders and glowing vials, an assortment of elixirs and mood enhancers—and on the crystalline terrace beyond, party guests swapped nest-guardians and played lovers' games for the amusement of others. One of the participants seemed revolted by the one touching her, and Beryl took a step toward the group.

"Wait," Zylar whispered.

One of Ryzen's cronies said, "When you accepted this invitation, you agreed to whatever I want. Be still."

The doomsayer, who was physically powerful enough to throw off everyone who was touching her, lay back with a snarl. Zylar looked away. For him, this coercion didn't work as sexual enticement or entertainment, and the scene made him feel vaguely ill. Beryl's expression reflected confusion, if he was reading her response correctly.

"I don't understand. By agreeing to attend, did we tacitly submit to whatever deviance is asked of us?"

"The rules are different, depending on social status," he said. "I belong to Kith B'alak, and you are the highest-ranking intended in the Choosing."

"But that's not the case for someone of lesser standing." Beryl shivered and stepped closer, and it took all Zylar's self-control not to pull her against him, like someone might attempt to physically wrest her from his side.

The music was loud and discordant, ringing in his aural cavities until it was hard to think. Flashing lights made that no easier, a constant onslaught of bright and dark that lent the partygoers a stop-and-go aspect. In those shadow sweeps, people moved, appearing in different spots around the room.

He lowered his head and spoke near Beryl's ear. "We don't have to stay long."

"I'm ready to go right now."

Beryl cringed, and Zylar followed her gaze with his to where a tall Barathi was slurping down Darveelans, straight from the tank. The others scrambled away from his claws, and just then, the music stopped, so their high-pitched shrieks were audible. He hoped she couldn't hear them, but then her eyes widened.

"Are they screaming?" she asked, shuddering.

"I'm sorry. I didn't want you to see any of this."

"Terrible things exist, even if I don't see them! We have to save those little dudes. They look like…" Here, the translator completely lost any ability to glean her meaning.

Zylar wanted to be a hero for her. He *did*.

But the prospect of fighting Ryzven on his own ground, along with all his sycophants, sent a spike of visceral fear through him. The wrong tactic here could end his hopes for a life with Beryl. Yet if he did nothing, he was unworthy of someone so brave and beautiful. Zylar dug deep and found some courage.

A verbal protest here would do no good. Sometimes, one had to be clever. Quietly, he drew Beryl toward the display of colorful liquids and powders. "Stay calm. Feign an interest. Ask me a question."

Thankfully, she was a clever person. "What's that?"

That was a sparkling pink dust, doled out in tiny vials. "It's joy enhancer. Everything gains a patina of brightness, so jests seem funnier. Everyone looks more attractive. I'm not sure if it would work on you." As he spoke, he activated his comm unit and keyed in a code that would block his identifying frequency, then he sent an urgent warning to the Protected Species Advisory Board.

There, done. I hope they come quickly.

Shortly after he turned off his comm, Ryzven joined them, shouldering between Zylar and Beryl like he had every right. "You look most charming tonight. This is new?" With one claw, he touched the fabric twining around Beryl's shoulder.

"Yes. Thank you." Beryl stepped back, removing herself from Ryzven's reach.

His nictitating membrane flickered, revealing his irritation at her failure to be charmed or impressed. Still, the flavork tried again. "I trust you're enjoying my hospitality."

Be civil, he urged silently.

Beryl showed her teeth. "That's one word for it. I've never seen anything quite like...this."

Unsurprisingly, Ryzven took pleasure in what he judged to be a compliment. "It would be my honor to show you around my private collection. I have art the like of which you will never have experienced."

"We would be delighted to take a private tour," Zylar answered for both of them, earning a look of pure malice from his nest-mate.

"You don't have any particular interest in the arts, do you?" That was a warning, a hint that he should back off and let this happen.

Beryl said in a desperately bright tone, "What do you collect, Ryzven? I don't know anything about Barathi art. Back home, artists work in so many mediums." Soon, she would start babbling, but it wasn't enough to get Ryzven to stop glaring.

Before the situation could escalate, the doors chimed at the use of an override code and agents from the advisory board stormed inside. They located the threatened Darveelans instantly and boomed a warning at the greedy flavork still slurping them down.

"Back away from the tank! This gathering violates codes eighteen and forty-nine of the Protected Species Act. Violators will be—"

The moment Ryzven turned to deal with this intrusion, Zylar seized Beryl's grabber. "We should go."

Since others were already scrambling for the exit, they wouldn't draw undue notice, and the agents would rescue the surviving Darveelans. She clung to him as they blended in with the throng currently fleeing from Ryzven's lavish entertainment. This anonymous report might have future consequences, but he didn't regret his choice. While Ryzven might guess that Zylar was responsible, he couldn't prove anything. He suspected if he had named the offending party, instead of simply providing the location, the agents might have hesitated about crossing the most powerful scion of Kith B'alak. That made this turn of events even more satisfying.

He didn't pause until they reached the safety of his quarters. When he turned, he found her laughing. "That was amazing. You wrecked his party. How much trouble is he in?"

"Not enough, unfortunately. I suspect he'll be fined, little more."

"But won't this smear his good name somewhat? He got caught breaking the rules, and your people seem to care an awful lot about appearances."

When she put it that way, Zylar paused, considering the implications. "It's possible that he could lose some favor with the Matriarch," he allowed.

"That's good for us, right? It means less fuel for his nasty whisper campaign."

Snaps trotted into the room, blinking sleepily. "You're back? You're back! I missed you both so much! I thought I would die of missing you."

Zylar knelt and scratched the fur-person on top of his head. That was a beautiful thing to hear, even if he had only been gone for a short while. *Especially* then, perhaps. Snaps rolled over and present- ed his underside. He glanced at Beryl, who confirmed it was acceptable to proceed. The fur-person flailed all his limbs and wriggled in what Zylar presumed must be enjoyment.

"He especially likes it when you get the spots he can't reach. Like here…and here." Gently, she guided him, showing where to employ his talons to the best effect.

"I love you the most," said Snaps, closing his eyes.

"Hey, what about me?" Since she was showing her teeth, she must be joking.

"I love you the most too."

"That's not mathematically possible," Beryl pointed out.

"Talking dogs aren't mathematically possible," Snaps said, "but here I am."

Zylar churred. The sheer joy he experienced with these two in his life made him feel as if his blood had become effervescent, constant contentment fizzing away, leaving him both giddy and lightheaded. He picked Snaps up and beckoned Beryl toward their nest.

She did whatever humans needed to do before resting, then she joined him, settling against him with a surety and trust that made Zylar even more determined not to let her down. "The Darveelans will be safe, don't worry."

"I'm glad you rescued them, but I'm more concerned about us

currently. There are two events left in this round. Do you think Ryzven will blame you for this?"

At least this time, the blame was warranted. Not that Zylar planned to admit filing the report. "Even if he does, he can't sabotage the Choosing. As long as I'm competing for your favor, I'll pass the second stage somehow."

"You promise?"

"I do."

"What about Kurr?"

Zylar stroked Beryl's head, wishing he could put full faith in these words. "We'll find a way to help them too."

THE NEXT DAY, BERYL FEARED that Kurr would be missing, and she leaned up against the wall in relief when she spotted them passing into the arena. Snaps wriggled in her arms in excitement; she didn't let him dash off into the crowd. It was impossible for her to judge the Greenspirit's mood from facial expressions, but their body language seemed a bit better than the day before. She pushed upright and hurried toward her friend, reaching for them, then she hesitated. Kurr twined a pair of fronds around her wrist, squeezing gently.

"Thank you for coming to me yesterday, but I was in no state to bear company."

"I'm so sorry."

A mournful sound, like wind rustling through dying trees, slipped from Kurr as they headed for the intended seating. "It's not your fault."

Beryl chewed her lip, wrestling with the proper choice here. If she confessed the whole truth, Kurr might hate her, but she wouldn't be much of a friend if she pretended the situation had nothing to do with her. As they settled in, she made up her mind.

"But it is…sort of. At least indirectly."

Kurr pulled their fronds away, turning to regard her with a chilly stare. "What do you mean? It was an accident."

After taking a deep breath, she explained about the rivalry between Zylar and Ryzven, Ryzven's unwelcome interest, and how he'd interfered with the Choosing, causing the Gauntlet to be unleashed instead of the competition that was originally planned. That petty, malicious act had been meant to screw with Zylar, but Arleb ended up paying the ultimate price. When she finished, she could hardly bear to look at Kurr, who must certainly hate her now.

"Thank you," Kurr said finally.

"I…what?"

"For telling me the truth. Before, I thought there was nobody to blame and it was just my sad fate."

Something about Kurr's tone sent a shiver through her. "Again, I'm truly sorry."

"This was not your doing, my friend. This tragedy is born from an evil heart that despises the possibility that others could be happy."

That was true enough, but Beryl couldn't shake the sense of foreboding as she regarded Kurr. "What will you do now? You mentioned that going home isn't an option, so…" She hesitated.

It seemed heartless to ask if they meant to try to attract someone else at this stage in the Choosing, but the fact that Kurr was still attending the competition seemed to indicate they planned to keep going.

"Before, I had the half-hearted thought of luring a new suitor, though it seems callous. Now I *must* do this, but I also have another imperative."

"What's that?"

The arena was filling, and the setup on the field for the last two events was nearly complete. Fortunately, Snaps was more interested in the obstacle course being placed than their conversation. A moment this tense wouldn't be improved by a dog's observations.

"You said Ryzven hinted at wanting a second nest-guardian, yes?"

That was the last thing she expected to hear. "Are you joking? Why—"

"Because he is responsible for the death of my Chosen. If I succeed in getting close to him, I will destroy him utterly." They spoke with such brittle, icy composure that Beryl's bad feeling got worse.

This sounded like a suicide mission, and it seemed as if Kurr didn't much care if they went to hell, as long as they took Ryzven with them. And while Beryl could understand the desire to get revenge, she couldn't stand seeing them suffer.

"That's not—"

"Stop," Kurr said sharply. "I will not heed warnings or advice. If this can be done, I will do it. There is no guarantee that I can draw his eye, as he seems partial to small, soft creatures, but I hold high standing in the rankings, and if I judge by what you've said, he is the type who cares about personal prestige. I can give him that."

Beryl lowered her head, fighting tears along with a bone-deep fear for her friend. "I wish I hadn't told you."

"Regret is useless. If you had made another choice, grief and despair might have devoured me. Now, I am filled with wrath, and it will sustain me, one way or another."

She let out a shaky breath. "If you're determined, I'll do what I can do to support you. If he invites us to another of his terrible parties, I'll get you an invitation."

I can't believe they were eating live, sentient beings. They looked so much like the Worms from Men in Black.

"You are a true friend."

"There was a famous comedian on my world. I guess one of his sayings applies here. 'When you're in jail, a good friend will be trying to bail you out. A best friend will be in the cell next to you saying, *Damn, that was fun.*'"

"I'm not certain that this idiom has translated correctly, but I appreciate your offer to do crime for me, Beryl Bowman." Three fronds swept out and encircled Beryl's shoulder in a delicate touch.

Across the arena, the seats filled with spectators and Chosen, but oddly, Beryl noticed that Ryzven wasn't in his usual spot. Maybe the alien equivalent of animal control had done him some damage? She would love it if his reputation got smeared like chocolate pudding on a toddler's face. That infraction probably wouldn't be enough to topple Ryzven from his pedestal, however. Zylar had said it would be impossible for Ryzven to prove he was behind the report, but her uneasiness intensified.

Between Kurr's dangerous plan and the way Zylar had gone after Ryzven on the low, there was *so* much that could go wrong. Everything was unfamiliar here, and the prospect of being forcibly separated from Zylar made her break out in a cold sweat. *How the hell would I even cope?* It was disturbing on every level how unsuited she was to fend for herself out here.

I need to get started on those reading lessons, even if this Choosing crap is exhausting. I can't depend on Zylar forever.

"You're squeezing me too tight," said Snaps. "My eyeballs are gonna pop out."

"Eep, sorry." Quickly she eased back on the headlock she'd put on Snaps and tried to steady her nerves, but she had to clench her hands to hide their trembling.

Searching the stands, she found Zylar in his usual spot. Some of the tremors receded when he raised a claw in a greeting he'd learned from her. Lifting her hand to wave back, she took a deep breath, another, until her pounding heart settled. Snaps stood on her lap and licked her cheek.

"Don't be scared. Or sad. You smell scared and sad. Are you?" He licked her again.

Smiling, she scratched between his ears. "A little. I'm better now."

"Because you fear for me, you smell this way?" Kurr asked.

Beryl had no idea how to answer that. "I mean…maybe? Especially if my scent changed after I told you what went down with Ryzven and you unveiled your master plan."

"Then should I comfort you?" Kurr asked. "How would I do this?"

Before she could reply, the host said, "The second round will be completed today! What excitement is store for us with today's competition? Let's not waste time, and instead, go right to the action…after I review the standings."

She tuned out while he posted the tallied results and only perked up when she saw that Zylar was solidly in the center of the pack—

not high enough to earn envy for his position, but not low enough to fear they wouldn't receive approval if they performed well together in the final round. When the host called Zylar's name, she jumped up and cheered at the top of her lungs, even urged Snaps to make a bunch of racket. The other intended stared at her, but she didn't give a damn.

Eventually she sat back down and gathered Snaps close. The final part of the second round went smoothly without Ryzven whining to officials to make shit more "interesting," or whatever he'd said to get Arleb killed. There was a physical sparring challenge and a problem-solving competition, where Zylar came in second.

My Chosen is so damn smart.

It was probably weird to feel so proud of that. In the end, Zylar finished in the top third, safe and sound, while Kurr sat silently beside Beryl, doubtless plotting their intricate revenge. After the final scores posted, the Chosen who had lost their partners early on swamped Kurr. Six or seven Barathi, some with exceptionally bright colors, eddied around the Greenspirit like an alien ocean. Beryl lingered, wondering if she should offer a hand, but Kurr fluttered some fronds in a gesture that she took to be a farewell, confirmed by their next words.

"I will get acquainted with my suitors," they said gently. "While I regret Arleb's loss, I must think of the future. This is the path I have chosen."

That had to be part of their strategy, a way of drawing Ryzven's eye. If he saw that Kurr was in great demand, it might well pique his interest.

What came next? Beryl didn't dare imagine.

[16]

AFTER ONE FLEETING REST DAY that gave Zylar a taste of what life would be like with Beryl once they passed the Choosing, the final phase began.

The silence from Ryzven was unnerving.

Through private gossip, he knew Ryzven had been formally reprimanded which was why he hadn't attended the last two contests in the prior round. The flavork had to be seething. Yet Zylar heard nothing.

Odd and unsettling.

He took a deep breath, trying to calm his racing hearts.

Never before had he come this far, waiting to be confirmed by his intended. The Chosen stood in a straight line, sharply at attention while the intended nest-guardians faced them from across the arena. In the center, the host played to the audience.

"Are you ready? Now we will find out whether old alliances hold fast, or if new matches have been made in secret. We'll start with our top-ranking intended. Beryl Bowman of Aerth, who is your Chosen?"

Zylar tensed. All their promises hung on this moment. If she opted to betray him and select another, one of the unmatched Chosen, only drone life awaited.

She won't fail me. She will not.

Beryl stepped out of formation and called out, "Zylar of Kith B'alak."

It took a few seconds for the translators to confirm her primitive preposition, then the host flourished a limb in his direction. "Congratulations, Zylar! You embody the axiom that persistence ultimately prevails! Fifth time lucky, join your intended!"

He thought that was an unnecessary insult, but he kept his gaze high and strode toward the circle to meet Beryl. She reached for his claw with her soft grabber, and the spectators reacted in audible fashion when he completed the hold.

Zylar's hearts eased, the faint fear softening to incredulous pleasure. Finally, he had been Chosen.

She kept her promise. He wanted to show even greater affection than the clasp of their extremities, but respect for propriety kept him still. When Beryl showed her teeth, he churred.

She is so very precious.

Beryl had told him of Kurr's reckless plan, but he didn't see how it could come to fruition. Though he sympathized, Ryzven wasn't someone who could be easily destroyed, or jealous rivals would have come for him long ago. He certainly hadn't retained his power through kindness and generosity.

The host called Kurr next. "Though you have suffered a grievous loss, you may Choose another. Will you quit the contest or will you—"

"I Choose Catyr of Kith Ka'mat."

"Fascinating! Our Greenspirit elects to be pragmatic and thus will stay the course. And you, Catyr?"

A bright blue-patterned Barathi came forward, radiating pleasure and relief. His intended had died to the Destroyer early on, so Kurr's favor must feel like a miracle.

"I accept. We will move forward together."

The pair joined Beryl and Zylar in the center. Thus, the event continued as intended, and the Chosen confirmed their bonds. At the end, there were several Chosen left without potential partners, and they trudged from the arena with a despondent aura that Zylar remembered all too well.

This is how it feels to stand on the other side.

"Our first contest is a game of chance," the host went on. "Luck is a part of life. It allows some to rise, while others remain firmly in the dust. Let's test our teams now! Who are fortune's favorites?" He went on to explain the rules.

Zylar bent to catch Beryl's soft question. "We just…pick a number?"

"Essentially, yes. Prizes are random, each coded to a different digit. The highest-value reward provides congruent ranking." He paused. "You should choose for us, Terrible One. My luck was dreadful until I abducted you, and that was a mix-up, not something I achieved on purpose. Any luck I have comes from you."

"That is…"

The signal sounded. "Begin!"

"…so sweet!" The pause came as she tossed the words over her shoulder, already sprinting toward her target.

Another intended tried to intercept, attempting to siphon Beryl's luck, but she put on a burst of speed, deceptively fast for her small size, and she snatched up the code just before her rival. Zylar churred as Beryl did one of her strange battle dances. Much of it involved shaking her back end and waving her limbs around.

"You can't beat me! I'm _____" The translator didn't know what Beryl was saying, but Zylar could fill it in.

She bounded back to him. "Now what?"

"We take this to the officials over there and find out what we've won. Once all the couples have selected a prize, the results will be tallied."

"That's pretty quick. Will we do another contest today?"

"It's likely. They sometimes combine shorter events. Otherwise the Choosing would take entirely too long."

"Makes sense. Let's go find out how we did."

Zylar led the way, adroitly stepping around those who would inhibit them. A few even tried to snatch the code from Beryl's grabbers, but he hissed, shielding her with his whole body. Before, he had been less aggressive, less sure of his ability to attract and keep such a magnificent nest-guardian, but she was slowly boosting his self-confidence, filling him with surety of his own worth.

I deserve her. I deserve to be with her.

Once Beryl turned over their code, they waited. She gazed toward the exit. "I wish Snaps could be here, but there's nobody to watch him. You think he's okay alone?"

"I regret leaving our nestling unattended, but I do not believe he will come to harm. There are only a few more days. If we can endure the tests a bit longer, then we can begin our life together."

"You think we'll get approved?"

"I see no reason why not, if our ranks are good."

"What about Ryzven?"

"Don't think of him. He can't hurt us."

That was bravado, most likely, and from the way Beryl tilted her head, she suspected as much.

"You're a bad liar," she said.

"It is not a skill much in demand."

"I'm glad about that. It's better if you're honest, even if the situation is difficult."

"We've surmounted everything so far. We can achieve anything together."

She squeezed his claw without speaking.

Not too much longer, and the host announced the results. "Kurr and Catyr take the top prize, a collection of priceless gems mined on..." A few more names followed, and then, "At number five, Beryl and Zylar achieve respectable placement with rare seeds, imported from the Farshine Nebula!"

"Pretty good," Beryl noted.

"You may not have gleaned this from the explanation earlier, but we keep the prizes we choose. They are considered ceremonial gifts, put toward the life we build once the Choosing ends."

"Oh wow. So we've got seeds to plant later? Snaps will be so excited about having more tiny green dirt dogs to guard."

"He will be a fine elder nestling," Zylar said.

"I hope so." From Beryl's expression, something was bothering her, confirmed by her next question. "Do you think Kurr has given up on their plan? They even Chose someone else."

He considered. "I am uncertain. This may be a strategic move. They also took first in the joint competition, reinforcing their allure. It's possible they hope to attract Ryzven before the final stage is complete."

"But they Chose Catyr—"

"Do you truly think that such a small matter would stop Ryzven?"

Beryl huffed, a sound that approximated a Barathi hiss. "No. He's a dirty _____ and I bet he'd find some way to get what he wants, no matter who he has to hurt."

"The correct assessment."

Soon after, the next test began. Strategic thinking this time, where they had to compete against another team. Those lots were chosen at random, and Zylar took the lead, as Beryl had no idea about this Barathi game. They beat their first two sets of challengers and were defeated around the middle of the tournament, not exceptional, but safe.

Zylar didn't care if they excelled. He only wanted to score well enough to receive the Matriarch's blessing and get past all of this for good. Five times was too many, and with each step they took toward the end, his fear grew, sometimes to the point that he couldn't breathe.

Losing now would be worse than ever before. It might mean the end of him.

Not because life as a drone was so awful, but because life without Beryl was a prospect so bleak that both his hearts ached, merely thinking of the possibility.

"What's wrong?" she asked, as they left the arena together.

That was how good she'd grown at reading his moods, even though there were no visual cues that she could recognize. But her heart knew both of his.

"Nothing," he lied.

Her eyes were steady and soft, such a bright color in her squishy face. She knew, again, but she let the fiction stand.

"Snaps is waiting. Let's go home."

BERYL COULD TELL THAT ZYLAR was worried, likely about Ryzven, and possibly about Kurr as well. It was especially troubling when there was nothing she could do. Being helpless sucked.

That did remind her of one issue, however, that could be addressed. "Would you teach me to read Barathi?" she asked, as they headed for their quarters.

Funny, how this weird world had come to feel like home.

"It would be my pleasure." He didn't call her primitive or suggest she wasn't capable of learning.

Negging just wasn't part of Zylar's personality. In being with him, she'd already received more praise and appreciation than she had in her whole life on Earth. Before she met him, nobody except Snaps thought she was anything special.

As they reached the lift, his comm lit up and sounded with the chime for an incoming message. Beryl glanced over, but she couldn't read what was on the display. Zylar stilled, his nictitating membrane fluttering, surprise or distress, maybe.

"What happened?" she asked.

"I am instructed to go to Technical. If you're concerned about Snaps, you can return without me. I'll follow presently." Something in his tone alarmed her.

This had to be about Helix. "It's bad news, right? Snaps will be fine. He had his food cube this morning, he has water, and he knows what square to pee on. I'd rather go with you if that's all right."

"Yes," he said. "I always prefer your company, Terrible One."

"Then come on. Let's find out what the damage is."

She remembered where the Technical Department was, so she led the way when he hesitated. Whatever the issue, they'd face it together. Mostly, she feared him losing the AI who had been his only friend.

The same supercilious Barathi greeted them on arrival. "You've come to reclaim the restored version of Helix?"

Surprised, Beryl turned to Zylar. "Restored? That's fantastic news! They got Helix back for you."

"Partly," Zylar said. "The truth is, they deleted the corrupted code and reverted Helix to a prior version. All memories of our trip to Aerth have been permanently lost."

Oh. That revelation knocked her back, and her breath went. *I can never go home again. I'm really stuck here. No visits. No cheeseburgers.* She squatted and wrapped her arms around her knees, head down. For a few seconds, she fought tears because she didn't want to hurt Zylar, but this…this was confirmation that her old life was lost forever.

Zylar knelt beside her and touched a claw to her hair, gentle as a butterfly landing on a flower. "I'm sorry. I cannot truly fathom how you feel, but please know—"

"It's okay," she said.

Beryl was used to life giving her the toughest breaks. Before her mom died, the woman hadn't been the best, full of dire predictions and negative energy, and she when Beryl was twenty. *Never even met my dad.* Without parental support, she'd gotten an associate's degree in early childhood education and found a job at a daycare. After that, life was a series of people passing through—a couple of girlfriends, a few boyfriends—but nobody ever stuck around. She'd had casual friends, but not the sort who would grieve deeply over her disappearance. The fact was, she didn't have anyone to go back to, and while it was crappy that she couldn't enjoy certain things again—like Jacuzzi tubs and ice cream—she had a new life here, one where she mattered.

The tears dried. While her existence on Barath might be batshit in some ways, it was also a nonstop adventure. And she wasn't sorry about meeting Zylar.

"You gave me choices all along," she said. "And at every turn, I picked you."

"Stop talking to your pet," the Technical staffer snapped. "And accept the transfer of your restored AI. Once we have your approval, we will reactivate Helix's access to your quarters and your personal vessel."

"She is my intended, not my pet." After standing up for Beryl, Zylar went and did the red tape stuff that existed even on an alien world like Barath.

By the time he finished dealing with the details, Beryl had herself under control. Now it was more important than ever that they complete the Choosing together and get approval from the Matriarch. There was no road home anymore, only the path she would walk here with Zylar.

She didn't cry in the end. Just as well, it would probably upset Zylar if he saw her eyes leaking. He already thought humans had extremely weird physiology.

"That's everything," said the Technical Department worker.

"Thank you for your patronage. The service fee has been deducted, as previously agreed."

"Understood. I'll expect to find Helix active on our return." Zylar gestured at Beryl, and she followed him out of the office.

Things were quiet on the way back, and Beryl suspected he was blaming himself, despite the fact that she'd cleared him. It wasn't like he'd caused the sun flares or sabotaged his own AI. They'd ended up together through a massive screw-up of cosmic proportions, and maybe such a complex series of missteps could also be viewed as fate. *We're supposed to be together, right?*

She chose to believe that, anyway.

Hurrying to catch up, she set a hand on his neck, the soft skin where she was sure he could feel the touch. At first he flinched away, then he quieted and eased back into her touch. It seemed like the Barathi didn't do soft contact this way.

"No regrets," she said quietly.

"I will make you happy."

"You already do."

When they stepped into their quarters, Snaps went wild, circling their legs with happy bounces, bumping against them both until he got scratches and pets. "How long do I have to be alone, alone, so completely alone?" he whined, rolling over to display a pink belly lightly covered with curly beige fur.

"Not too much longer," Beryl promised. "I appreciate how good you're being. We'll go visit the garden in a bit."

"After food?" he asked.

"You got it, buddy."

"Greetings, Zylar. Who are these strangers?" That was Helix, unscrambled but also unfamiliar with Beryl and Snaps.

He doesn't remember us.

She let Zylar sum up the situation, and then her Chosen—how cool to call him that officially—performed the introductions. "It's nice to meet you," Beryl said.

"Let me explain how I can assist you. This is a smart habitat, and I can be useful in many capacities. For instance, if you require sustenance—"

"Do *not* take orders from Snaps," she cut in quickly.

God, imagine if the dog could order as many food cubes as he wanted. Instant chaos.

"The small one is incapable of directing me?" Helix asked.

"That's mean. I'm a *very* good boy," said Snaps. He put his face under his front paws.

Beryl tried to comfort him while Zylar skirted the issue. "Snaps is young and unfamiliar with our customs. When he matures, we will revisit the issue of his command permissions."

"Understood," Helix said. "Just let me express how pleased I am for you, Zylar. As a drone, you would no longer qualify to receive my assistance, and it is good to see that you will not live out your existence in grim solitude."

Beryl tried not to laugh. That didn't come across as much of a blessing. "Is he always this much fun?"

Zylar churred. "Still, I'm glad to have him back."

"I have a question…"

"Speak," said Helix.

"Er, I'm talking to Zylar." This would take some getting used to. "If I'm addressing you, I'll use your name. How's that?"

"Disappointing, but I shall make a note of this preference," the AI said.

"Since the technology exists to create offspring for us, could they make a few siblings for Snaps, from his DNA?"

Barath could totally use more dogs. Though Beryl hadn't been to every planet, she'd stand firm on the opinion that most worlds could benefit from canines.

"It is possible. We would need to file an application after our union is approved."

"Then that's my first request as your Terrible One." What the hell. If she couldn't get him to change that endearment, she might as well lean into it.

"I'll see to it," he promised.

Snaps perked up. "More dogs? Best day!"

They fed him his dinner, and Beryl ate her own cube, and she was about to remind Zylar about the reading lessons when the chime sounded.

"Ryzven has arrived," Helix announced. "Shall I let him in?"

"Go ahead," Zylar said.

Ryzven strode in like he owned the place, and he arrowed to Zylar, for once not even glancing at Beryl. His anger practically surrounded him like an electrical field, creating an uncomfortable charge.

"I can't prove it, but I know you're the one who reported me."

Beryl didn't move, afraid that she might make matters worse, no matter what she said. And Zylar was so afraid of Ryzven—

Or he had been.

This was a new Zylar, who didn't flinch or avert his gaze. In fact, he even flared his spines to show he wasn't intimidated. "Your accusations are unwelcome," he said coolly. "And thus, so are you. Please leave."

Ryzven hissed, his own spines spiking out in a display of utter aggression. "No one crosses me and goes on to prosper. You'll regret what you've done, and I will gloat when I take everything from you." He flicked a look at Beryl, and then stormed out.

Zylar hurried to her side, as if he feared she would be wrecked by these threats. He grasped her shoulders carefully and stared down into her face. "I'm sorry. But don't worry, I won't let him—"

"He's nothing. And I think he's starting to realize it. Assholes are always angry when they figure out how little they matter. I'm your Chosen, no matter what."

As he turned away, Zylar spoke so softly that he probably didn't realize she could hear him. "Please, let that be true."

[17]

AFTER RYZVEN MADE HIS THREATS, Zylar didn't sleep well. For most of the cycle, he watched Beryl, curled against him with the most profoundly peaceful expression. Her ability to shut down, despite the uncertainty of their situation…he admired it.

But her calm tormented him as well. Because it meant she trusted him, and he feared himself inadequate to defeat the monster he had roused.

Lightly, he stroked his claws over her head fur, marveling at its softness. Her body had many such features, all delicacy and adornment. She made a quiet sound and wound a limb across his lower body.

The way she nested had seemed strange to him at first. Barathi partners preferred more personal space, but now he couldn't imagine living that way. Even less could he envision how he would survive without her. As a drone.

The surgery that would render him infertile was meant as a kindness, so he would no longer be plagued with reproductive urges that must be suppressed as he went about chores that kept the city clean. There were those who had chosen that path, but to have his identity stripped away forcibly, as a result of failure…that terrified him.

Not least because it would mean parting from Beryl forever. He had brought her here, away from her home, away from everything she knew.

Somehow, she sensed that he was troubled, and she stirred, one eye opening to gaze up at him. "Can't sleep?"

What will become of you, Terrible One?

In his hearts, he knew how it would go if they failed. She would compete in the next Choosing and should have no difficulty attracting a new Chosen. Then, if he were lucky, he might catch a glimpse of her as he went about his maintenance tasks. The pain of that prospect jolted through him, so sharp that she noticed.

No longer seeming groggy, she sat up in the nest sling, making it sway. "Zylar? You're worrying me."

He could have prevaricated, but those efforts always failed with her. "I fear that I will...perform poorly against Ryzven. He has resources and connections—"

"That's enough, I understand." She set a grabber on his neck, a vulnerable point.

If another Barathi put their claws there, it would be an act of aggression, threatening, even, but with Beryl, it became pure softness, two vulnerable points sparking pleasure. He churred, an encouragement, because he was learning to take solace in her strange gestures.

She smoothed his skin, just as he did when he trailed his claws through her head fur. Small tingles of sensation prickled through him, a quiet pleasure that didn't rouse his mating instincts.

"You must be disappointed," he said then.

"In you? Not even slightly. Ryzven is an obstacle, that's for sure. But I've been thinking about this, and if we can't talk Kurr out of getting revenge, maybe we can help them. I mean, we don't have the same motivation, but it would definitely be in our best interests if something went wrong permanently in that flavork's life."

Zylar started, then he realized the translator must have substituted the local idiom for whatever pejorative word Beryl had used. Still, it amused him to hear her cursing Ryzven so fluently.

"You're correct. It troubles me not to confront him directly, but if I must choose between honor and you, then I pick you, Terrible One. For you, I would break every rule and forswear every promise."

"Maybe it doesn't have to be that dire," Beryl said, but she was smiling. "As long as I'm not the one you break promises to. Anyway, consider this: If your enemy cheats, why do *you* have to choose the high road? People should get what they deserve."

That statement shocked all the fear out of him. Not because he disagreed with her, but it was simply so obvious he should have seen it for himself.

Oblivious to his sudden epiphany, she went on, "He's the one who came at you for no reason, who tried to take me, even though I've made my preference known more than once. Don't waste any more energy on Ryzven and go to sleep."

She snuggled against his side and took her own advice. Snaps roused long enough to say, "I hate that guy," and then the fur-person went back to sleep as well.

Eventually Zylar dozed.

He woke alone.

It wasn't the first time, but it alarmed him, as he had grown accustomed to finding Beryl beside him. As he climbed out of the nest sling, he asked, "Where are Beryl and Snaps?"

"They departed nineteen spans prior and did not inform me of their destination." From Helix's tone, he found such blatant disrespect offensive.

"They're not used to you yet. I don't think they have smart habitats on Aerth."

"Primitive," said Helix.

They probably went to the garden, and they'll be back soon.

Still, his whole body felt twitchy as he completed routine daily hygiene and consumed his necessary nourishment. The idea that Ryzven might have simply taken Beryl—it wasn't impossible. If he couldn't acquire her through honest means, it wasn't beyond him to steal.

Zylar understood that in his bones.

He was about to rush out and start a frantic search when Snaps bounded into their quarters. Quivering, he knelt and put a claw gently on the fur-person's head.

"I'm very glad to see you," he said.

"Now *that* is a proper welcome for a good boy," said Snaps.

Beryl paused just inside the door. "Worrying again? I took him out for a run in the garden. I feel bad about leaving him alone at home all the time."

"He is not alone," Helix said.

"Without an organic companion?" Beryl suggested.

If Zylar knew Helix, he would be sensitive for a while, and this conflict wouldn't help. It was understandable; the AI's memories had been stripped, leaving him with a sense of incompletion. Over time, it would fade, but they should prepare for him to be disagreeable.

Fortunately, Snaps cut in before the argument could escalate. "I don't need a companion. Can I come with you today, please, can I? I'll be such a good boy. I will sit with the watchers and I will not move. I will not bark or chase, no matter how many interesting things I see. Please, can I come with you?" Snaps ended his plea with an all-over wiggle and stared up at Zylar with dark and liquid eyes.

He felt inclined to grant this wish, and he could see Beryl did too. Still kneeling, he tilted Snap's face up and tried to be stern. "You must keep your vow, Snaps. This is a *very* important occasion. I cannot stress that enough."

"A good boy keeps his promises," said Snaps.

"Then I will be here. Alone. In an untended domicile." Helix sounded sullen.

The AI wasn't used to sharing Zylar with others; they had lived together alone for a long time. "Please watch over the place for me," he said. "It is possible that Ryzven may attempt some devious scheme. Your vigilance is vital."

"Understood. I will notify the authorities if he trespasses," Helix said.

There wasn't much time before they had to report for the Choosing, so he rushed Beryl and Snaps through their routine and hastened them out. She held Snaps's lead, walking quietly with a thoughtful air.

"That was kind of you," she said finally.

"What?"

"Making Helix feel useful. I wouldn't have thought of it. He…doesn't feel real to me."

That surprised him enough to stop moving. "He *is* a person, Terrible One. My friend, as well. I assigned that task to him because it was a necessary precaution, and it reassured him that he still has a place in my life, though changes are coming."

"Sorry. On my world, when I left, they were working with AI, but my people hadn't acknowledged them as sentient, self-willed beings. I'll update my attitudes, and next time we leave, I'll inform Helix of our plans."

"You should apologize to him as well," Zylar suggested. "He tends to hold a grudge."

"I'll take care of it."

They hurried onward to the arena, and Zylar could tell that Beryl was worried about leaving Snaps alone with the spectators. Yet as the fur-person had promised, he took his seat and didn't pester anyone nearby. Finally, Beryl sighed and gave him one final pat.

"No barking. No chasing."

"I can cheer for you?" Snaps asked.

"Yes, that's fine." Beryl turned to Zylar and offered her grabber. "Shall we take our places?"

He wrapped his claw carefully around her tender flesh and pulled her toward the center, where Kurr and Catyr were already waiting. There were two events today, short ones, and then the finale tomorrow.

We can finish this. We must.

Any other outcome was unthinkable.

BERYL HUNCHED OVER, BREATHING HARD.

In the last test, she and Zylar had to tag-team the equivalent of an alien obstacle course, passing that damn ring between them that she'd snatched in the first trial. If it touched the ground, they were automatically eliminated. And there was all kinds of crap to leap, dodge, roll under and crawl through: Machines with moving parts, fire, strong winds.

Then they had to fight against another pair of intended and Chosen while tied together back to front. Something about proving their unity and defending each other—she'd lost the thread when the hissing Barathi tried to disembowel her. Thankfully, Zylar had whirled around just in time.

They placed in the middle of the pack in both matches, not exceptional but good enough to be safe. She hoped that her adequate performance—without Kurr—would make it clear to Ryzven that the Greenspirit was the truly gifted one in their former partnership, if only so Kurr could push forward with their revenge plan.

Their performance with Catyr was certainly reinforcing that impression. The announcer said as much, as Beryl waited for her heart to stop racing.

"It seems the new competitors to watch are Kurr and Catyr, an unexpected alliance that bears delicious fruit!"

Probably that wasn't exactly what he was saying, just the translator making it sound weird. The crowd cheered for the new power couple anyway, and Beryl peered across the arena, relieved to find Snaps exactly where she'd left him. His tail was wagging, and he looked extremely interested in all the proceedings, but at least he wasn't running amok on the field like she'd seen dogs do in old soccer videos.

She swung her gaze back to Kurr, who had a remote and regal air now. Loss had forged them into a pale and exquisite weapon, a dagger crafted from purest jade. Even the graceful flutter of their fronds looked vaguely dangerous. Possibly Beryl's inside knowledge of their plan colored that assessment.

She was aware of Ryzven glaring from the other side, but she didn't glance in his direction. When that asshole stormed into their home and declared war openly, it meant she was free of the need to be polite, even though he was one of Zylar's siblings. From what she'd gathered, that relationship wasn't the same as it had been at home anyway. Birth groups might have hundreds of potential nest-mates, and not all of them survived, and they certainly weren't all raised together.

As soon as the rankings were announced and the host dismissed the competitors, she limped toward Snaps, who—true to his word—didn't budge until they got to him. Then he leapt out of the risers and into Beryl's arms. She caught him and let him lick her face with all the delight of a dog who had been "separated" from his human for a while. That was the best damn thing about dogs. If she went to the bathroom for two minutes, he was so gleeful when she came out, like: *It's you, my favorite person!*

She nuzzled her face against the dog's head until he calmed down. Thankfully, he didn't pee in excitement anymore; he'd done that when she first got him.

"How was it? Did you have fun, buddy?"

"Exciting! But scary. I don't like it when you have to fight."

"It's not my preference either." Since Beryl only had basic self-defense classes, taken years ago, she would've gotten owned by a Xolani doomsayer, if she'd drawn that match up.

"Are you injured?" Zylar asked.

Without letting her respond, he knelt to look at her leg. She'd twisted her ankle in the last match, and it hurt like a bitch. Seemed unlikely to be broken, and she couldn't opt out of tomorrow's finale due to injury, so she'd have to suck it up.

"I'll be fine," she hedged.

Apparently she was no better at lying than Zylar because he lifted her in one arm, just as he had when he abducted her. It was a deeply unsettling hold, though, and she grabbed onto his neck with her free arm, clutching Snaps with the other.

"Uh, could you hold me in front of you? With both limbs?" She realized she was attempting to describe a bridal carry to an alien and stifled a laugh edged in nerves.

"Like this?" With great care, he shifted her until her weight was better balanced and it was close to an over-the-threshold cuddle. It allowed her to snuggle Snaps against her chest, and the dog settled, exhausted by all that obedience.

Effortlessly, Zylar moved through the crowd, who parted around him as they never had before. Confidence had bolstered his bearing, and clearly she wasn't the only one taking note.

Probably she should say something like, *Put me down, I can walk*, but the truth was, this felt great. Her ankle hurt, and there was no shame in taking help from someone she—

Loved.

Yeah. That.

She was finally ready to use the word, at least in her own head. It was probably too soon to tell him, and they had to pass the Choosing, get approval from the Matriarch, and deal with Ryzven, but she couldn't imagine her life without this precious partner anymore.

Being abducted really is the best thing that ever happened to me.

"You're showing teeth," Zylar said, his voice soft against her ear.

"I'm…happy." That wasn't the whole truth, but close enough for their purposes.

Once they got back to the apartment, she said, "Hi, Helix. Sorry I didn't tell you where we were going this morning. That was rude."

"An acceptable oversight, but I hope you don't make a habit of such behavior."

"I won't."

Zylar deposited her carefully in the bed hammock. "Rest. I'll take Snaps to play in the garden for a while, if that's acceptable."

"Snaps?" She figured she should check with the dog.

"Rest your paw. I'll play with Zylar!" Snaps said.

"Sounds good." Feeling positively spoiled, she lay back. "I can get to know Helix while you're gone. I'll ask for all the embarrassing stories about you."

Zylar paused with Snaps at the door. "Embarrassing…stories? Helix, don't—"

"Relax, I was joking," she cut in.

"I would not divulge shameful anecdotes regarding Zylar," Helix said primly.

This was one loyal AI—kind of sweet, really.

She chatted a little with Helix, but sleep was the best medicine, short of *actual* medicine, and she drifted off, weary enough from the constant stress and uncertainty that she slept straight through without eating or drinking. Beryl regretted that the next day when she woke up parched and ravenous, but her ankle was better, at least.

Just one more event. This is it.

Resolutely, she picked Snaps up and herded him to the square to do his business, then she followed. *This is still so weird.* The little bot whirred out to sanitize the space after use.

Zylar was moving slow this morning, so they ate in silence while she imagined the worries that must be whirling in his mind. She was heartily tired of presenting herself to the arena, but she walked in under her own power for the last time, sent Snaps to the stands—as he'd proven he was a good spectator—and then took Zylar's claw as the rest of the contestants assembled around them.

She waved slightly at Kurr with her other hand. Got a flutter of fronds back.

"Welcome, friends! This is the grand finale. Today, intended and Chosen will face their greatest challenge yet. Behold, the beasts!"

The workers wheeled in multiple cages, full of monsters the like of which exceeded even the scariest of Beryl's nightmares. They were all different, just a mad snarl of fangs and claws. Without volition, she moved closer to Zylar.

"Do we have to fight them?" she whispered.

"I fear so. Not all of them, however. By my accounting, there is one opponent for each pair."

The host called the matches in random order, not according to their rankings. In round two, a larger, scarier Alien cousin stormed out and eviscerated the intended and chosen. The bots were still cleaning blood and gore when the announcer called for Zylar and Beryl. She trembled as she took her place in the center next to Zylar.

I have no natural weapons.

That was the catch of this last challenge. They had to prevail using only their bodies and their wits. The handlers freed the beast— a monster with spikes and a razor-sharp tail, kind of like a lion that had been crossed with a rhino, and then offered some augmentation.

I'm going to die.

"Stay behind me," Zylar said grimly.

Evidently, he shared her opinion regarding her slim survival chances. "Do we have to kill it to win?" If he'd answered that question already, she had been too distracted by the cages full of scary beasts to listen.

"Kill or subdue."

She guessed he meant to the point that it couldn't get up again. Kurr and Catyr had gone first, and Kurr had effortlessly used their fronds to restrain the monster, tightening until the creature lost consciousness, a quick and clean victory that left the audience shouting in appreciation.

"I'll try to stay out of trouble," she said, as the rhino-lion charged.

Terrifying animals could probably smell fear, so it ran right at her, trying to impale her on its shiny horn. *This alien monster-unicorn wants to skewer me to death.*

Beryl dodged and rolled as Zylar went after the beast with his claws. No weapons, but at least he had talons and sharp teeth. She fell hard, injuring her already weak ankle. *Shit. Not good. Not. Good.*

When she tried to stand, her leg buckled, and the beast whirled for another run.

I'm done, Beryl thought.

Then Snaps bounded out of the stands and onto the field.

[18]

ZYLAR *HAD TO KILL THIS* thing.

He bore it no ill will, but it was an obstacle, and it was actively trying to destroy the person he valued most. As Beryl rolled away from its stomping limbs, he dove underneath the beast and drove his claws deep into the creature's soft underbelly. Not quite enough— the monster roared and tore free, dark blood spattering Zylar and the ground around him.

Wounded it, at least.

Then he heard Snaps call, "Leave my human alone. Leave her alone!"

The fur-person scampered up its spine, and then bit down on the back of its neck. Snaps seemed to lock his eating part and held on, though the damage he could inflict was minimal. The move gave Beryl time to crawl away, distracting the monster enough that it focused on trying to dislodge the little pest on its back.

Beryl called, "Snaps, no! Stop. You have to get out of here."

Her fear was obvious, a sudden deluge of that sharp scent in the air, and her eyes were leaking, liquid running down her cheeks. But Zylar couldn't waste the opportunity. This monster was much fiercer than anything they would normally be pitted against, even in the Choosing. He sensed Ryzven's interference in this.

He rolled forward and went at the beast's belly again. This time, he thrust his entire limb up, twisted and pulled, and dislodged a wet burst of innards. Ignoring his natural revulsion, he kept yanking. No matter how strong this thing was, it had a damage threshold.

The monster screamed, shuddered, and toppled sideways, lashing out wildly in its death throes. As it dropped, Snaps leapt clear and ran over to Beryl, sniffing at her and making high-pitched noises that the translator couldn't interpret.

"Success!" the host called. "Our third couple has bested their final challenge—" But then, he broke off, as if he'd been interrupted. "Er, this has never happened before. I'm receiving word that these results are being contested, as a third party joined the battle."

Zylar swore.

Absolute terror edged his anger, because this might be a fault that Ryzven could exploit. While Snaps hadn't inflicted much damage, he had provided a distraction. Beryl hadn't landed a single blow, and that might diminish her value as a nest-guardian. Ryzven might persuade the Matriarch to disqualify them, and then—

He would lose Beryl. Become a drone, unable to protect her. The pain nearly felled him. Tamping down those feelings, as nothing had been decided yet, he hurried to Beryl's side and swung her up in the hold that she preferred. He carried her toward Kurr and Catyr, as they were the only pair to have survived the finale so far. Snaps trotted with him, and there seemed to be no point in asking the fur-person to return to his seat. The damage was done.

The host continued, "These matters will need to be reviewed, and we can't delay progress. Moving forward, I call our fourth intended and Chosen..."

In a daze, he watched the rest of the contest. Beryl weighed so little that it didn't even occur to him to put her down, until some while later, he noticed her tapping urgently on the side of his neck.

"I can stand," she whispered. "You must be tired."

He was, down to his bones, but not from holding his Terrible One. Indeed, he would rather not relinquish his hold on her, in case this was the last time. Yet it might alarm her if he said as much, so he quietly released her.

She bent to rub Snaps, and when she raised her eyes, he saw that she already knew. Though he'd called her primitive at first, he now realized that her acuity was as sharp as a blade, accompanied by a rare attunement to his feelings.

"Don't worry," he said, but the reassurance must not have sounded truthful.

"Is everything ruined? Do I have to leave now?"

Zylar noticed she didn't mention participating in the next Choosing, and while he should want what was best for her—and he *did*—some small portion of his hearts rejoiced in such loyalty. Before Beryl, he had thought that anyone who Chose him would be good enough, but now, he couldn't imagine sharing his life with another.

With an airy sound, Beryl picked Snaps up to cuddle him and leaned some of her weight against Zylar. He couldn't feel most of where she touched him, but knowing that she still trusted him enough to do that, though their time together might be limited, he could scarcely contain his contradictory impulses. Part of him wanted to carry her away, and to hell with the Choosing. They could run before the decision came down.

He had Helix and his ship, as long as they got off-world before his assets were stripped. It would mean spending the rest of his life in exile, and they would no longer have the resources to rear offspring together, but perhaps—

Yes, she was worth it.

There was no need to run right this moment. If he bolted before the Choosing officially ended, it would alert the Council and they would anticipate his plans. Precipitous action might result in worse consequences.

Be patient. Bide your time.

There were no more fatalities in the competition. No more interference either. Zylar noted that none of the other battles were nearly so difficult or dangerous.

At last, the host called the proceedings complete and added, "Final rankings and approvals will be announced in two days, after officials have tabulated composite scores and ruled on the disputed challenge. Congratulations if you made it this far. You stand among the worthy few!"

The closing music started; Zylar had heard it so many times before. "Can you walk?" he asked.

"Pick me up," Beryl said. She seemed to be imitating Snaps, who hung a pink taster out his furry face in what looked like amusement.

He churred, wondering how she could manage to make him feel light and peaceful, even now. No matter what happened in the Choosing, he wouldn't let go of her. He did as she requested, cradling her against his thorax.

But Kurr stopped him before he could head for the exit. "With your permission, I would visit your residence this evening."

"You're the favorite. It might not be a good idea," he warned.

Kurr dismissed the objection with a flutter of fronds. "My status cannot be changed at this point, and I must speak with Beryl. I'll bring Catyr so it seems like a social occasion."

This must be related to their revenge plans. While he didn't necessarily want Beryl getting pulled deeper into that, it might not be a bad idea to hear what Kurr had to say. If they could hurt Ryzven and keep him from biasing the judges, that would help.

"Please come. We would enjoy your company." Zylar's gaze slid past Kurr to Catyr, finding him hard to read.

Does he know about Kurr's plans?

"Until then," Kurr said, and then drifted away, all elegance and ethereal beauty.

When Zylar turned, he caught Ryzven watching the Greenspirit. *Is he truly that simple? He wants whatever he thinks he cannot have.*

Then his nest-mate noticed them and strode across the arena, wearing a sickly eager expression, membranes fluttering in excitement. In fact, Ryzven couldn't manage his spines or his neck ruff; that was how out of control he was.

"You're being summoned before the elders to account for your disgraceful performance today," Ryzven said.

That wasn't unexpected, but it galled him to hear it from Ryzven. Still, he kept his composure. "They wish to see us at once?"

"You must be well-acquainted with failure by now." Ryzven dropped his voice, low enough that only Zylar could hear. "I thought I might have to work to ruin you, but you delivered this weakness like a gift."

Beryl struggled a little in his hold, but he didn't put her down until just before they reached the Council chambers. Then he set her on her feet. She was still holding Snaps, and she didn't release him, even as they entered the opulent chamber, where the Matriarch was waiting for them. The whole room chilled and went silent, making each step ring louder.

"That creature has defiled the most venerable of our customs. How do you excuse this debacle?" the Matriarch demanded.

"I'm sorry. It's my fault," Beryl said. "I haven't trained him well enough. He didn't understand—"

"Silence, primitive! I am speaking to Zylar of Kith B'alak, who brought you as his intended, against the better judgment of many elders, I might add. Speak, Zylar."

"I bear the blame. Any failings are mine. I will shoulder the consequences as well and abide by whatever decision the Council deems appropriate and just."

"They should be disqualified," Ryzven said in an even tone.

The elders probably had no idea how much he loathed Zylar…or coveted his Chosen.

Glancing between them, the Matriarch appeared to come to some conclusion, though what that was, only she knew. "Reconvene in two days to learn of our decision. Dismissed."

NOBODY SPOKE UNTIL THEY GOT back to their quarters.

Snaps said, in the saddest voice, imaginable, "I'm a very bad boy."

There was *nothing* sadder than a sad dog. Beryl burst into tears. She had been holding them in for hours, and there was just no restraining herself any longer. Zylar set her down in alarm, and she crumpled to the floor just inside the door.

Lowering her head, she wrapped her arms around her knees and sobbed. *They wouldn't even let me talk. And even if they had, they wouldn't understand.*

Back home, there was an entire mythos supporting the absolute loyalty of dogs, good boys who would die for their humans. And had, in some cases. When she saw Snaps dart out to defend her, she'd never been so scared in her life, not even when Zylar first snatched her up while wearing that weird exo-suit.

She couldn't make these aliens grasp that it just wasn't possible for a dog who loved someone to watch them being threatened without reacting. Not even an adorable, talking dog like Snaps.

Stay couldn't hold when she was about to be disemboweled by a monster-unicorn. But…he'd broken the rules, regardless of why. She'd just realized that she fucking loved Zylar, and they were so close, so damn close to being allowed to build a life together.

Not now. Why now?

She cried until her eyes hurt and her head ached. Neither Zylar nor Snaps seemed to know what to do. The dog was nuzzling her cheek, licking at her tears, and Zylar perched beside her, his limbs bent, claws gently stroking her hair.

"They wouldn't let me explain the wonder of dogs," she sniffled. "And they wouldn't understand, even if I did."

"I'm a bad boy," Snaps said again.

"You're not." She hugged him and rested her chin on top of his fuzzy head. "You're a super-heroic boy. They just don't know enough to appreciate you."

"Don't give up yet." Zylar didn't pause in petting her, and really, she sort of understood why Snaps rolled over and showed her his belly, because she wanted more of this, all over her body.

Stupid hormones.

For some reason, whenever she got really worked up emotionally, she immediately wanted sex, maybe for the endorphins to balance out the sadness. Most likely, Zylar would be baffled by that request since she suspected it wasn't common, even among humans. Not that she'd ever asked anyone.

"Do you have a plan?" she asked.

"A glimmer of one. We'll talk to Kurr first and go from there." He hesitated, as if weighing whether he should go on.

"Be honest," she prompted.

"Helix, enter privacy mode."

"Initiating sound screens and disabling all audio capture. Privacy mode active."

Beryl guessed that was to block any snooping tech that Ryzven might have deployed. Still, she glanced around and felt a frisson of anxiety. *Was that asshole eavesdropping on us before?*

"If things go badly, we'll leave Barath together."

She stared for a long moment. "You'd give up everything for me?"

"Without you, I have nothing anyway," he said softly.

"That is a romantic statement," Helix snapped, "but quite inaccurate. You have status in Kith B'alak, many material possessions, and a competent AI companion."

Zylar hissed, probably annoyed at having his big declaration interrupted. "Helix, no verbal input."

This AI doesn't like me much.

"Understood." Such a snippy tone.

Zylar turned to her and gently touched her cheek with the flat side of his claws. "If you will come with me, we can build a life anywhere. You've Chosen me. That's enough. I don't care what the Council says. You're meant to be mine, and I'm meant to be yours."

That was the sweetest thing anyone had ever said to her. Hoping he would understand the gesture, she raised his talons to her mouth and kissed the soft skin between, one of the rare spots where he could feel her brand of tenderness. His neck ruff flared, just a little, but enough for her to be sure that he liked it.

Beryl considered the offer. "I don't want to run away. I don't want you to become a fugitive for me. Are you allowed to choose exile freely?"

His answer came slow, as if he didn't want to tell her. "Yes. They will not force me to become a drone, though if I stay, I must choose that path. If I go with you after a negative judgment has been made, I forfeit all status and belongings tied to Kith B'alak."

Holy shit.

"They take all your stuff, and you have to give up your name?"

"I would be without kith in the universe, apart from you and Snaps." His tone made Beryl understand that this was a hellish punishment for the Barathi, maybe akin to being shunned for those who were born Amish.

"Then that's our last resort," she said. "I don't want that to happen to you, if there's even a glimmer of hope. They haven't disqualified us yet."

"You understand that leaving with me...after, means I will not have my own ship. They will take Helix as well, leaving me only enough for us to book to book passage off-world, but we won't have income or anywhere to live—"

"I don't give a shit what you have," Beryl cut in. "I want to spend my life with you, not your stuff. You're smart. I'm sure you can find work, and I'll do my best too. You said I might be able to get a job looking after alien kids on that station, right? We'll be okay if we have each other."

Dammit, I'm going to cry again.

She blinked several times, trying to hold the tears back, and Zylar reached for her. "This is the hug you taught me before, yes? I am so thankful for you. I have no words to express how much you mean to me."

"What just you said did the job." Beryl sniffed and wiped her eyes as Snaps tried to muscle into their cuddle.

For lovely, uncounted moments, she luxuriated in being close to the ones she loved most. Then Helix said, "You requested no verbal input, but I must inform you that two visitors are approaching your domicile."

"Kurr and Catyr?" Zylar asked.

"Scanning. Identities confirmed. Admit the new arrivals?" Helix still sounded cranky.

Maybe change is hard for an AI? He had Zylar all to himself for a long-ass time.

"Yes, please. Thank you, Helix."

Right, I need to treat Helix like a person.

Beryl added, "Thank you, Helix."

Snaps seemed like he didn't want to feel left out so he also said, "Thank you, Helix."

"Obsequious behavior will not earn my favor," Helix noted. "Opening the door now. Continue in privacy mode?"

"Yes, please."

Beryl hurried to wash her face. There was no erasing the trace of tears completely, but since she was the only human, they probably wouldn't know why her eyes looked red. Maybe they might not even notice, depending on what color spectrums they perceived. She had no clue how Kurr saw the world, and it wasn't the sort of thing that Beryl knew how to ask, at least not politely. *Hey, how do plants see?* didn't seem like the way to go.

"I'm sorry to intrude," Kurr said, "but your cooperation is vital."

Beryl glanced around and realized that the Greenspirit was talking to her. "Me? Why? What do you need me to do?" Then she paused, glancing at Catyr.

Kurr took the hint. "My Chosen is fully apprised of my intentions. He has agreed to assist in my efforts in exchange for my loyalty later."

Catyr said, "I'm grateful to Kurr for Choosing me, as I lost my intended early on. If there's even a small chance that Ryzven urged officials to deploy the Destroyer, after such a long span...if she died for that flavork's *entertainment*, then there is nothing that would stop me from making him suffer."

Clear enough.

"Then my question stands. How can I help?" She hoped they realized that any status she might have enjoyed in the early rounds was long gone, smeared away by Snaps in a few, terrifying seconds.

Kurr fluttered their fronds, then they all went up in a gesture that could only be assessed as commanding. "You will speak to Ryzven and beg him for mercy. Get close to him if you can. Pretend that you are forsaking Zylar and imply that I would like to do the same, that I regret Choosing Catyr. His ego will do the rest."

Quickly she glanced at Zylar, trying to gauge how he took that request. His membrane didn't even flicker. "If that's the path to Ryzven's destruction, so be it. I am not a good liar, but it will not require deception for me to react with grief and rage at the prospect of losing Beryl. In his presence, I will act as if she truly means to abandon me."

Damn. Looks like it's going down.

[19]

ZYLAR COULDN'T RID HIMSELF OF the fear that the pretense Kurr was asking Beryl to enact would become his new reality, a self-fulfilling prophecy. Perhaps it was only because he'd never kept anything for himself that Ryzven wanted. Just because it had never happened, that didn't mean it never could.

Yet he ached over this request; both his hearts faltered at the thought of losing her.

It's only for show, he told himself. Part of the game that Kurr had planned, though how they would get revenge by promising Ryzven what he wanted, Zylar had no idea.

Catyr didn't seem to share his trepidation, but then, he hadn't been living with Kurr. He had chosen them out of expedience, loss, and trepidation, much as Kurr had done with him. Therefore, their bond, as yet, was more driven by logic than emotion.

"Contact me when it's done," Kurr said in a cool tone.

Beryl nodded. "I'll talk to Ryzven tomorrow."

"Thank you. We should let you enjoy the remainder of your evening." With that, Kurr and Catyr withdrew, leaving Zylar to feign a composure he didn't feel.

As soon as the door closed behind them, Beryl hurried to him and wrapped her limbs about him in what she called a hug. If he shared her physiology, this would probably feel much better. As it was, he could only breathe in her familiar scent and touch her head-fur lightly.

"I know you're scared," she whispered. "I am too. There's no way I want to encourage that flavork, but I have to do this for Kurr. I feel partially responsible for what happened to their Chosen. You get that, right?"

"I do."

Unfortunately, understanding didn't diminish the fear still growling in the back of his head like a cornered beast. In some ways, her proximity helped, but in others, it only triggered needs that she'd taught him how to answer. They absolutely shouldn't touch each other that way until the decision came from the Council, but prudence had nothing to do with desire.

His thorax tingled as she took his claws, separated them, and used her eating part on the delicate skin between. Heat flushed through him, and he hissed, unable to stop the sound. He didn't respond otherwise.

Beryl paused. "If you want me to stop, say so."

"This feels…ill-advised, but I don't want you to stop."

"Why? Because things are uncertain right now?" With her soft grabbers, she traced the delicate skin between his claws, talking instead of tasting.

Zylar couldn't respond in words.

"Don't worry. I'm not leaving you, no matter what. At this point, it's only a question of where we'll be. Because as long as you want me, I'm with you."

Nothing could have settled his mind as firmly as that declaration. He would absolutely leave Barath and start a new life with her elsewhere. If the Council succumbed to Ryzven's venomous whispers, all that meant was that he'd pack up and go off-world. With Beryl. Life on Gravas Station might be difficult and financially challenging, but at least they would be together.

All at once, the sensations she was giving him hit in a powerful rush, and his body responded with a gush of pleasure. Unlike the other times she'd aroused him recently, he didn't try to control the visible reaction. The plates parted to reveal his swollen sex, and she paused to show teeth.

She's pleased. With me? Or with herself for creating this result?

Either way, he took her grabber in a possessive claw. "Helix, no contact in the sleeping room until I say otherwise."

"You've never cut me off before," the AI said in a cross tone.

Zylar ignored that. "Snaps, we need you to play in here for a while."

The fur-person let out a heavy sigh. "It's because I'm a bad dog."

Beryl started to respond, but he tugged her into the next room and closed the door, cutting off whatever she might have said. "Snaps will be fine. Helix can keep him company while we…"

"Yes," she said, seeming to catch his urgency. "I know I started this, but you just kind of took over, so I'm wondering if you had something specific in mind."

"I want to make you quiver," he said.

Mentally, he recreated the picture she made, sprawled against him, soft and pink and gasping at every touch. He didn't have certain parts that she might find interesting, but she seemed to enjoy his claws well enough, as long as he was careful, and he enjoyed the challenge.

Her face flushed. In that moment, he realized she had colors too. They were just a bit more subtle than the ones the Barathi showed. Zylar decided he would like to make her glow even brighter, if that was possible.

"I'm good with that, but…orgasms tend to make me sleepy. Before, it seemed like you had energy to spare after you…finished."

He processed that. She was talking about how she'd stroked him until he released his spermatophores.

"Yes, I will not be incapacitated. Does that mean you'd prefer to please me first?"

Beryl showed her teeth. "Unless you object."

Heat spiked inside him, and he could feel the swelling, lubrication already beginning to glisten at the edges of his sex. Zylar flexed his claws.

"No objections" he managed.

"Then let's get in the nest and—oh." She bit down on her eating part. "I need to ask this first. Your…fluids didn't irritate my skin, but do you think there would be any oral toxicity?"

At first, he had no idea why she'd ask that, and then he recalled his fleeting, deviant fantasy—of her doing that to his sex, as she had his fingers, spines, and neck ruff. He hissed, unable to verbalize a response, but he hurried to the next room to confirm what he hoped was true. The database had records of her scans, created to design a complete nutritional profile. Quickly, Zylar ran a cross-purpose search, and he almost whispered a thankful prayer when he saw the results.

It only took a short while, and Beryl was still waiting by the nest when he returned. "There's no danger," he said.

She studied him with an aspect that he could only describe as avid. "That's the best news I've had all day."

There was no need to urge him into the nest; he already had some idea of the exquisite pleasure that awaited him, and he settled back, feeling like the luckiest Barathi in the universe. He made room for her, and she crawled up toward him so slowly that he shivered from the torture of waiting to feel…something. Anything.

"Tell me if you don't like it," she whispered.

That was a null probability.

When she first touched his sex with the softness and heat of her mouth, he hissed. Nothing could have prepared him for how good it would feel, not even the incredible sensations she'd already given.

She paused long enough to say, "You probably don't have words for what I'm doing. Try to listen without the translator."

Lips. Tongue. Licking. Kissing.

She repeated those strange sounds and then showed him the congruent action, resulting in more drenching bliss, until he understood that she had lips—the outside of her eating part—and a tongue, inside, soft and pink, that she used on him with incredible dexterity.

One by one, she covered his sex with heat, until the pressure inside him built to unbearable levels. He would never be able to finish through this stimulation, but he didn't want her to stop either, especially when she softly slid inside in teasing little pushes. Then it got even better when she used her grabbers in addition to her lips and tongue.

His entire body glowed with sensation, and he lost himself in the build. It didn't even matter if he died, as long as she kept touching him. Zylar had no idea how he held still, but everything she did pushed him deeper into a state of wild arousal, until he could feel the lubricant trickling down.

Has anyone ever been this aroused and lived to tell of it?

He hissed in response when she somehow touched her tongue to the most sensitive part, and the caress became strange and deep and irresistible. In reaction, his seed burst spontaneously, everywhere, all at once, even where she wasn't touching.

He hadn't even known that was possible.

Knowing she liked this, he wrapped his limbs around her and pulled her close, rubbing his face against her head-fur. "You are a goddess," he said.

"Wow. I guess you liked that. I like the way you taste, by the way."

That…was a sensual shock to his already-dazed mind. "You do?"

"Definitely. I'll be back for more."

"More…"

"More of you."

He should be satisfied, but the idea that she wanted to do…that again sent a shiver of pleasure through him. Now, he couldn't imagine touching another Barathi like this, and he didn't know if she'd become his idea of perfection or drive him beyond reason.

"I'll look forward to that," he said. "But now, it's my turn to devour you."

BERYL TRUSTED ZYLAR COMPLETELY, BUT she still quivered a little with nerves.

There was just no way not to feel uneasy when he was about to use his mandible in ways nature never intended. But he nipped so gently, so carefully that the delicate little pinches felt good, just as he intended. He started on her throat, moved to her shoulders, and her reaction must have reassured him, because he gained confidence as she let out a moan.

When he got to her breasts, she was squirming. This wasn't quite like being nibbled all over, but it felt fantastic in a way no human lover could approximate. He added tender scrapes with his talons, until she twisted with pleasure.

Then a thin prehensible filament flicked out and grazed her nipple. It wasn't like a human tongue, and she imagined it might be used for other olfactory purposes, but right then, he used it with incredible dexterity, tugging gently on the tip of her breast.

Beryl quivered as he raked her skin with his talons. So careful, so retrained.

"You're lubricating," he observed, sounding pleased.

"Because it feels good." It was hard to organize her scattered thoughts into words as he pressed lower, or rather, he lifted her with a seductive, intoxicating strength. On some level, she understood that she could be aroused by that display because she trusted he wouldn't turn that power on her, only use it in her defense.

Beryl showed him how to make the most of his position when he hesitated—by draping her legs over his thorax. Slowly, he inched closer and tapped her clit with the tendril. Pure sensation spiked through her when he did it again. And again, starting a gentle rhythm that made her move her hips, craving more. The sensation was so light, such a tease, that tingles ran through her whole body. He was still touching her, scraping his claws lightly down her thigh.

"So responsive. Your whole body is showing me your soft colors."

She felt the flush of arousal, and suddenly, what he was doing wasn't enough. Lowering her legs, she pushed him back; his confusion showed in the flicker of his nictitating membrane.

"I want to try something…" The plates were still open since he'd climaxed recently, revealing his sex.

She angled her body and pulled him toward her, aligning her pussy with one of his slits. When she moved against him, he hissed. A pleasure sound. That meant he had some sensation, and God, it felt good. She repeated the motion, getting just the right friction and pressure on her clit.

"How does that feel?" she gasped.

"Incredible. So hot. So soft and slick."

"Can I keep going?"

"If you can attain completion, take your pleasure from me."

She moaned over how formal yet how filthy that sounded and rubbed against him faster and more firmly, feeling the pressure build. The little hisses affirmed that the motion pleased him too, and that intensified her excitement. Still careful with his claws, he gripped her hips and pulled her against him harder, enough that the plates against her inner thighs might leave a mark. A shock of white-hot sensation swirled through her, something new as their juices mingled. The smell was pure sex, and he breathed it in as she did.

Her clit slid against his sex, and she came, so hard that her vision grayed. Zylar made that unmistakable sound, the one that meant he was there too, losing control right along with her. His whole body vibrated with it, sending her shivering into the afterglow.

"That…" she tried. "…Wow. How?"

There's no way he'll understand that. Try again once you can breathe—and think—properly.

Before answering, he settled them into their customary resting pose, as close as they could come to a proper cuddle. Beryl was happy to leave such maneuvering to him. Then he said, "I'm not entirely sure, Terrible One, but I think our fluids are…reactive. The hormones, when combined, become a powerful sexual accelerant."

"Enough to let you come when I'm not…" *I can't say that.* God only knew how the translator would interpret *fingerbang*. "Touching you intimately?"

"It was intimate. Even more so than these." He nipped her fingertips, sending a lazy shiver through her. "Our sex organs touched. We have completely broken the rules of the Choosing now."

"Yeah, well. We're already in trouble for Snaps. What are they going to do, double fail us?" In all honesty, she'd forgotten they were supposed to be waiting to have sex—not that they could ever do it for procreative purposes.

All for fun, all the time.

"You make a compelling case," he said. "And we did speak of leaving Barath together, so I'm pleased that we finally…that you wanted to…"

"Make love," she supplied, hoping the translator would get it right.

"Create love?" he repeated.

Close enough.

"Yes. That." Her voice was soft as she took his hand and stroked the sensitive skin between his claws.

He responded with a sound that wasn't a hiss or a churr, somewhere between the two. Instinctively, she understood that it meant it felt good but he was sexually satiated and not looking for more than this sweet and tender moment.

"That is perfect. Just when I think I cannot adore you more, the feeling grows. I am consumed with you, Beryl Bowman. I would die to protect you from a moment's pain."

Impossible not to press a kiss between his talons. He made that churr-hiss sound again and ran his claws through her hair. "You'll never know how much I love hearing that, but I'd much rather you *live* with me."

Softly, he said, "I should perform the rite of thanks for those sun flares. Without them, I would never have taken you."

She hid a smile, basking in the quiet joy from such a ridiculous, wonderful compliment. "Keep praising me that way, and I'll become insufferable."

"Impossible." He nuzzled his face against hers, such alien contours, yet those touches had come to feel better than a hug.

She wanted this moment to last forever, to snuggle against him and sleep, but she had made Kurr a promise. As he often did, Zylar read her withdrawal and let go. Beryl sighed as she sat up.

"I'm sorry. I have to contact Ryzven now."

His claws tightened on her, then she read the exact moment when he decided to be rational, though it was clearly tough. "Helix will help you. Give me time to leave with Snaps. It will make your overture more compelling if you do it when he can verify that I'm elsewhere."

"Like I'm doing it behind your back."

"What does my dorsal side have to do with anything?"

"Never mind."

Zylar hopped out of the nest, took two steps, and then rushed back to her and pressed her against him, talons tangled in her hair. "I cannot be here, I know this, but leaving you feels…" He struggled visibly before continuing. "I don't know why I'm like this. Intellectually, I understand that what you will say is part of the ruse, but…" His spines flared, showing exactly how he felt about her approaching Ryzven.

Beryl wasn't into dominant assholes, but that did not apply to Zylar. She found his hesitant possessiveness adorable, because while he felt those things, he never tried to stop her from doing whatever she wanted. And she could eat his sweet vulnerability with a spoon.

"I'm not leaving you," she whispered. "Go play with Snaps. It will be done when you get back."

Resolutely, he turned—with the aspect of someone who was about to be executed for something they didn't do. Damn, he was cute, so much drama over what amounted to a bullshit phone call. She heard them leave, then she hurried into the next room and headed for the terminal.

"Helix, can you please put me in touch with Ryzven of Kith B'alak?" She didn't have an address or phone number, but that should be good enough for a smart AI.

"Right away. And thank you for your courtesy." Okay, Helix sounded less grumpy today, maybe he was getting used to them.

"What do you want?" Ryzven demanded. In holo, his face showed no expression she could read, but he sounded pissed.

"Is this a bad time?" Beryl tried to sound meek and humble. No telling if it worked; that wasn't her specialty.

"I thought you were Zylar. This is his terminal code."

"He's out right now. That's why I had to call you. I may not have much time."

Here we go, sell it hard.

"Is something wrong?" His eyes fluttered, showing interest.

"I've made a terrible mistake. I'm afraid the Council is going to banish me, and I've heard station life is terrifying. Is there… Could I meet with you? I bet you could put in a good word for Snaps and me. Please, just a little of your time. I'd be so grateful. I'm willing to do anything if you can help me."

That was the right tone. Ryzven clearly liked the abasement and the groveling. "You said Zylar is away? If you are sincere, come to me. Now. Say nothing to him."

Fuck it. I promised Kurr. I'm going all in. "Where are you?"

[20]

SNAPS SHOWED HIS GREAT JOY about extra time in the garden by wriggling all over, his rear extensor lashing in excitement. He went to check on his verdant offspring before dashing off to play, leaving Zylar alone with his decidedly grim thoughts.

He trusted Beryl. She had kept all of her promises to him, but she couldn't control how Ryzven reacted. If there was a way for that flavork to exacerbate the situation, he would act on it, regardless of who it hurt. More than ever before, Zylar felt certain Ryzven hated him especially, and he had no idea why. It wasn't as if he had power or physical appeal to rival Kith B'alak's favored one.

He wandered the lush paths for a while, morosely, until Snaps bounded up. "You smell sad."

Zylar dropped into a crouch. "Your olfactory sense is quite accurate."

"Why are you sad?"

"It's complicated," he said.

"Why?"

This probably wasn't worth explaining to the fur-person, but he tried. "My greatest fear is that I will lose Beryl Bowman, my dearest Terrible One."

"Beryl does not get lost," Snaps said. "She only finds. She found me. She found you. And we are still found, see?" A fuzzy head bumped his lower limb.

While Zylar wasn't sure that argument hung together, as he was the one who had taken Beryl from her homeworld, he did like how reassuring it sounded—that he couldn't lose her.

But Snaps wasn't done. "Beryl loves us. *I'm* her best boy, but *you* are pretty good. She told me lots of times, she doesn't abandon anyone she loves, even if we pee in the wrong place."

"I will remember this," Zylar said, feeling strangely comforted.

"Ready to go home! The tiny green dirt dogs are bigger, and I have smelled everything."

Snaps seemed to be awaiting some sort of recognition for his dedication. "You are excellent at such endeavors."

"Thanks! Do I get extra snacks?"

"We can ask Beryl," Zylar said.

The fur-person's ears drooped. "That means no. No extra snacks."

Ignoring the obvious play for sympathy, he attached the lead and then they went back to Zylar's room. As soon as he entered, he knew she was gone, even before Helix said, "Beryl Bowman left a message for you. Shall I play it?"

"Please." His hearts were beating entirely too fast, the fear he had almost mastered spiking, sabotaging logical thoughts.

A holo of Beryl appeared. "I made contact to keep my promise to Kurr, and Ryzven insisted on seeing me right now. It's a test, but I'm up to it. Don't worry about me. I'll come back to you, I promise."

For the first agonizing seconds, all he could hear was that she'd gone to Ryzven. Snaps dragged him back by nudging him and whining, until Zylar scratched the top of his head. All his instincts said he must find and retrieve her at once, but such haste wouldn't serve their revenge scheme, and it wouldn't sell it either.

Unless…

He weighed the two possibilities as Helix said, "How can I help?"

"Do you know where Beryl is?"

"I do not."

"Then find Ryzven for me."

"Scanning," said Helix. "Ryzven is in his private research lab and has notified the system that he is not to be disturbed."

Zylar spat a word so foul that Snaps cocked his head, maybe because the translation startled him. "That likely signifies the fact that he's isolating her. He doesn't want to be interrupted by Miralai." It was the height of avarice for Ryzven to covet Beryl when he already had a devoted nest-guardian.

"Probable," Helix agreed. "Miralai is in their quarters, protecting their clutch."

Zylar snarled. The depth of that dishonor wouldn't soon dissipate; any Chosen worth the cost of his bodily parts would be with his intended, celebrating their impending offspring. Not Ryzven. He chose to neglect his duties and look for ways to steal what did not and would never belong to him.

It didn't matter that Beryl was enacting a clever ruse. That lessened Ryzven's transgressions not at all, and despite Zylar's all-encompassing rage, it wasn't the worst crime Ryzven had committed. He bore the burden for multiple deaths for the way he had tampered with the Choosing.

Trying to calm his mind, Zylar weighed his options, then he decided to ask Helix and Snaps which path he should pursue. Either might aid in Kurr's vengeance, and he didn't think either possibility would hinder the scheme.

"There are two possible responses," he said. "Ryzven will expect me to react to my intended's departure. I can array myself in a public venue, indulging in a display of grief or despair."

"Suitably pathetic," Helix decided.

"Or I can go straight to the lab and beg Beryl not to forsake me. Direct or indirect, which course shall I pursue?"

Snaps seemed confused by the choices offered. "But I already told you—"

"This is a game," Zylar cut in. "We're tricking someone, who will be *very* surprised when he finds out."

Understatement. Grim amusement edged his distress. Never in his most inventive imagination could he have envisioned playing a role in Ryzven's downfall. Oddly, he did not question Kurr's capacity to enforce their vow and create a dreadful new reality for Ryzven. There was an unmistakable aura of power about the Greenspirit.

"You will pretend to be sad or pretend to beg?" Snaps asked.

"One or the other."

"If I am sad, I get pets. If I beg, I may get snacks. Would you rather have pets or snacks?"

Despite the wholly unsatisfactory situation, there was only one answer to that question. "I would always choose to have Beryl Bowman touch me softly."

"Snacks are good," Snaps said wistfully, "but I agree. Pets are better."

Helix added, "I concur. The less confrontational route will also send the message that you have given up hope—that you believe you have already lost. Ryzven enjoys savoring such moments of weakness."

Inarguable. Part of him hated playing this role, for it represented who he had been, uncertain of his own worth and easily cowed by those he perceived as superior. Beryl had taught him that he had value without changing his colors or his character.

He loathed leaving her with Ryzven, but he had to believe in her.

She promised to return to me. I will put my faith in my Terrible One and in Kurr. I will not interfere in their plans.

That might well be the toughest challenge he had ever surmounted. With effort, he lowered his spines. Such aggression and defiance didn't suit the act he would offer.

"I will be back later. Helix, please entertain Snaps while I'm gone."

"How should I do this?"

"You're a genius," he said. "Work it out."

In answer, the AI sent the cleaning device out. "Chase it, Snaps!"

When Zylar left, the dog was running after the unit, yelling with excitement over this strange, new game. With leaden steps, Zylar imagined he truly had lost Beryl. That she'd chosen Ryzven, and he would never see or touch her again. The rush of grief and rage nearly incapacitated him, making him grip the wall for support. A few citizens paused to gape at his unseemly display, but he ignored them. The more witnesses to his breakdown, the quicker it would reach the flavork who needed to believe he was broken.

He went directly to a venue frequented by lower-caste Barathi, those from lesser kith or fallen on ill-fortune. There was no one he recognized from Kith B'alak, but that didn't matter. Just as he had asked Helix to find Ryzven, that flavork could do the same and probably would, after he spoke with Beryl. Zylar's presence in such a desperate place would lend credence to her words.

Here, there were no interested glances or friendly gestures. Everyone who stepped within was seeking a strong chemical solution to forget their woes, at least for a little while. Zylar wasn't prone to such pursuits, but he bought a smoking flask full of tomesh and downed the contents, feeling the numbing effects at once. He paid for another and swallowed it too. Truly, he only needed to sit here, drinking slow poison, and Ryzven would believe he had won. Because any other outcome was unthinkable, inconceivable.

Someone sat beside him, a Barathi who looked vaguely familiar, but with so much tomesh buzzing inside him, he probably would not have even recognized the Matriarch.

"You did well in the Choosing. Unlike me. Why are you here?"

This must be one of those who had gone unchosen in the final round. Zylar knew intimately how that felt, but it didn't seem plausible that he would have any sympathy to spare if Beryl had truly deserted him, so he ignored the mumbled question and slurped another tomesh.

"All you Kith B'alak are the same. You learn from Ryzven. I don't want company anyway." The Barathi lurched away.

It stunned him momentarily that some random citizen saw through Ryzven's charming façade, but he couldn't falter, even if that Barathi might make a decent friend. If nothing else, they had mutual loathing of that flavork in common.

Grimly, he ordered another, vowing to drink until he was sick. Only complete incapacitation could make him forget his pain, if

Beryl ever truly left him. Inaction might destroy him, but he had pledged his cooperation.

Please, let her return to me. Please. In this whole universe, she is all I need.

BERYL TOOK A DEEP BREATH and steadied her nerves, then she tapped the door, activating the sensors. Within, she heard something, and then it slid open, revealing a lab out of a science fiction movie. It was dead quiet inside, but she went in anyway.

Ryzven was near the back, likely creating something terrible and destructive. He turned to greet her with the oily charm that made her skin crawl.

"Welcome. I have several experiments at sensitive stages, so I hope you understand why I couldn't meet you elsewhere."

More like you're scared of word getting around what a complete creeper you are.

"Of course I should come to you. I'm the one asking for your help."

"How precisely can I assist you?" he asked, taking a step closer.

Stifling a shiver of revulsion, she clutched his claw with both hands. "I don't want to be exiled. After what Snaps did in the last match, there's no way we'll be approved. You're so influential. Can't you put in a good word for me?"

"For you," he repeated, staring at her hands as if he was fascinated. The membrane in his eyes flickered. Interest, at least, if not more.

Time to up the ante. *Let's see if he likes this as much as Zylar does.* Gently she touched the skin between his talons, just a graze, but he hissed as if she'd gone right for his sex organs, and his neck ruff flared.

Ugh. At least it worked.

"I would be so grateful."

"It would be a pity for Barath to lose you so soon," he said at last. "Simply because you chose poorly. I believe I can secure a place for you here, but it may be…unconventional. Are you open to such an arrangement?"

Honestly, she only had half an idea what he had in mind, but if alien assholes were anything like human ones, he was slyly proposing to set her up as his side piece.

"You're saying I can't be your primary intended," she guessed.

"Clever human. I will enjoy learning more about your…proficiencies."

Gross. Extra gross. It was like Ryzven thought she was begging for a chance to become his pleasure slave. The nutrition cube she'd eaten earlier lurched into her throat.

Keep it together.

"What do I need to do to be safe?" she whispered.

"I'm sorry to say that I cannot save your companion. The furry one broke our sacred covenant and such missteps must be dealt with harshly. Do you understand?"

To be with you, I have to let you kill Snaps. Over my dead body, you monster.

"Oh." She pretended to stumble, letting go of his claws in the motion. "That is dreadful news."

He reached out to hold her up, offering sympathy fake as a three-dollar bill. "I'm so sorry. I will comfort you to the best of my ability. I promise that your life with me will far surpass any dreams you may have had."

Unless he meant dreams of hell, that was impossible. She schooled her features, though she wasn't sure if he could read her expressions anyway.

She bit her lip. "I understand."

"Soon, the Council will deny your approval with Zylar, and he will be taken as a drone. You will then be free."

"Free to be...yours?" she whispered.

"Yes, little one. It's to be expected that you would prefer a powerful patron. I will keep you safe."

Sure you will, asshole.

"I can't go back to Zylar under the circumstances, but I can't stay with you either, can I?" Beryl aimed her most melting, wide-eyed stare at the big jerk, though it might not impact an alien the same way.

"I will not permit you to stay in his residence under false pretenses," Ryzven said, in such a peremptory tone that she wished she could pee on him to show her true feelings, like Snaps.

"Then where...?"

"There is space in the intended dormitories after various losses. I will procure facilities for you."

"Is there a way you could put me near Kurr while I'm waiting? Everything is so strange here, and I'll be so scared otherwise, if you're not there." That was clearly so much bullshit that she expected even this asshat to notice how full of it she was, but he must be part dung beetle because he ate it up like it was both piping hot and delicious.

He churred, a sign of amusement, and his neck ruff frilled even more. Clearly this weirdo was into overly needy partners. Probably made him feel like a big damn deal. She might hurl if she didn't get out of here soon.

"That is certainly within my power. Just a moment, I will make the request and rush it through for immediate approval."

"Thank you, Ryzven." *You absolute fuckface.* "Um, this might be asking too much, but I mentioned to Kurr that I know you, and they were so impressed. Maybe you could favor them with an introduction someday?"

He really enjoyed the groveling approach. She could tell by the way he straightened and stood a bit wider at the terminal as he worked on her temporary lodgings. *Fuck, Zylar's going to lose his mind when he realizes I'm not coming home. I can't right now, love.* Hopefully he'd understand that it was only because of her pledge to Kurr. Uncertain as he'd been when they first got together, she didn't know if his self-worth could run this gamut.

"Kurr is the Greenspirit who performed so admirably in the Choosing?"

"Yes, I would have been lost without them. I was so lucky to meet such a powerful friend on my first day."

"Luck and charisma are your true gifts," said Ryzven in a faintly patronizing tone. "A little thing like you draws stronger souls who desire to offer…protection."

Yeah, right.

Beryl barely restrained her desire to kick him as hard as she could. "Is that what happened?"

"I suspect that is the case. And if you desire it, I can invite Kurr and their Chosen to my next gathering. You will be there as well, of course." He didn't say without Zylar, but that was understood at this point. Ryzven went on without waiting for her to agree.

Farewell, free will.

"You may leave your companion with Zylar. The Council will deal with them both appropriately."

He expected her to simply nod, so she did.

"Excellent. You are so very sweet. I look forward to all the pleasures that await us."

"So do I." Beryl threw everything she had into that glowing smile.

"There, your approval has arrived. I'll send someone to collect your things and have them delivered."

"I don't have much," she whispered.

"It hardly matters. I'll provide everything you need."

"I can't believe you're willing to do this for me. Your generosity is beyond all expectations." That was the best she could do, so sick of this charade that she just wanted to get this over with.

"Can you find your quarters? I must get back to my experiments."

It was more like he couldn't risk the scandal of escorting her. He didn't want her to keep clinging, so she said the right thing. Luckily it also got her away from him.

"I can find it. I know where Kurr lives."

"Your new quarters have been assigned within their residence."

"Thank you again, Ryzven."

"My pleasure, little one. I'll send word about the gathering." With that, she was dismissed.

Beryl rushed out before she could say something that would

destroy all her efforts to suck up and make him think she didn't hate his guts. How could anyone be this fucking dense? Damn.

God, but she wanted to go home.

Not yet. You can't.

She got on the wrong sky car or rather, it was heading in the wrong direction. At first, the car was crowded, and she got all kinds of stares from passing Barathi, but when she ignored all attempts to communicate, they left her alone as she rode around the fringes of the alien city, watching the light fade from the sky.

It was late by the time she made her way to the dorms, once more reduced to only the clothes on her back. But her stuff had beaten her to the room, and the door slid open, already coded to her DNA.

Inside, it was sparse, with nothing she recognized as furniture. That lack made sense, as the dorms had to house so many different species.

Would Ryzven know if she called Zylar? Better not to risk it.

Instead, she went to Kurr's room and filled them in, then she added, "I hope your plan works. I'm out on a ledge here, and it's a long way down."

"Have faith," they said in an eerily serene and confident tone. "The ancestor trees have promised. Vengeance shall be mine."

[21]

RYZVEN WASTED NO TIME AND presented himself to gloat soon after Beryl left.

He couched it as a service, collecting her belongings, but the worker he'd brought with him did all the fetching and carrying, not that Beryl had much. Her possessions were so meager that shame washed over Zylar. He didn't know what her life had been like on Aerth, but here, she was making do with so little.

"You've offered her such meager prospects," Ryzven said in a smug tone. "I knew she would come to me in the end." His tone said that it was inconceivable that any sentient being could resist his charm or his colors.

Zylar's spines spiked before he could control them, then he let his aggression show. Such hostility would sell their story. "Take what you require and go," he snarled.

"This place will not belong to you for much longer," Ryzven said. "You should prepare for service."

Life as a drone.

"A day or two will not matter. Perhaps the Council will surprise you." Desperate hope would amuse his nest-mate, providing greater entertainment when both Zylar's hearts broke upon the inevitable denial.

"I'm sure it helps to tell yourself that." Ryzven turned, gesturing impatiently at the worker waiting with Beryl's things. "We're finished here."

"Why are you so determined to take her?" he asked, knowing the question would feed Ryzven's insatiable self-importance. "She can't even be your nest-guardian while you're bonded to Miralai."

Ryzven churred, a pleased sound that sent quivers of disquiet through Zylar's entire body. "Life is not a static process. One never knows how the situation can change." That sounded like an oblique threat, but before he could respond, Ryzven added, "But you already know that well enough. You were so close to success this time. So close."

With that, Ryzven and his helper left as Snaps growled, "That guy is the worst."

"Most assuredly."

For the first time since the nest Beryl had invented arrived, Zylar faced a lonely night. He couldn't bring himself to sleep in their shared space without Beryl, but when he tried to return to his usual arrangement, Snaps whimpered and pawed at his lower limb.

"When is she coming home?"

"Soon," Zylar said, hoping it was true.

In the end, he slept in the nest with Snaps draped over him, but his rest was plagued with unease that drifted toward outright fear, jerking him awake with both hearts racing more than once. *Perhaps I imagined the danger.* Would Ryzven truly plot against his own nest-guardian to acquire one more intriguing and unusual?

The likely answer did not make for a peaceful night.

In the morning, he fed Snaps and ate his own meal without savor. He didn't know how such a revelation would impact Kurr's scheme, but he should share his suspicions with Miralai. If some tragedy befell her, and he'd done nothing to stop it, he would share the culpability with Ryzven.

Still considering the best course, he took Snaps to the garden to play, and by the time they got back, he'd made up his mind. "Helix, do you have a log of my conversation with Ryzven?"

"Certainly. It took place in the common area and was not deemed private beforehand."

"Perfect. Send a copy to my mobile."

"You plan to inform Miralai that she may be in danger? This is the moral choice, but it may cause difficulties for your companions. Have you considered—"

"I have, but I can't be sure that I can communicate with Kurr safely. Ryzven will certainly be watching Beryl and possibly Kurr as well. If I'm caught warning Miralai on my own, the impact on anyone else should be minimal."

"Understood. I could analyze potential outcomes and offer numerical probabilities, but I suspect you would not find that helpful at this juncture."

"Thank you, Helix. Where is Miralai?"

"Scanning. She is in the habitat she shares with Ryzven, who is ensconced in his lab."

"Then I should act now, while I have the chance."

"I prefer statistics," Helix said, "but I will wish you luck nonetheless." The AI paused a beat, then added, "Because I will be wiped if you become a drone."

Zylar churred. "I'll do my best to keep you safe, old friend. That will never change, no matter what happens with the Council ruling."

"Play with me, Helix!" That was Snaps, getting ready to chase the cleaning unit.

Zylar slipped out while the fur-person was otherwise engaged, and headed for the station. Memories tapped away at his composure: Beryl's awe of the cityscape and the way he'd protected her from the press of Barathi bodies.

It's not forever. This separation will end, if not with our approval, then with a fresh start off-world.

There was no way she'd succumb to Ryzven's blandishments, and she wasn't the sort of person who would slip into Miralai's position without remorse.

It was impolite to visit without an invitation, more so when the nest-guardian had a clutch to protect. Miralai and Ryzven's offspring must be near to hatching, so the timing was terrible, but this warning couldn't wait.

Zylar touched the door and waited for the AI to welcome him or turn him away. To his surprise, neither happened. Miralai came to meet him herself. She was quite a gorgeous Barathi, and she had dazzled the audience the year she competed in the Choosing. No one had been surprised when someone so gifted and lovely chose Ryzven.

He feared she might have come to regret that decision, and if she didn't, his visit could ruin her life. Dismay didn't deter him from his purpose. He had to tell her what he knew and damn the consequences.

"This is unexpected," Miralai said. "I haven't seen you since Ryzven and I formalized our bond."

Ryzven had discouraged any of his close kith from developing a relationship with Miralai, possibly to keep her isolated and without recourse.

"I'm sorry to be so discourteous, but my visit couldn't wait."

"If it's urgent, please come in."

Miralai preceded him into the main room, a soulless space adorned with items that spoke of wealth, without revealing any information about the habitat's occupants. In the city, a nest-guardian's duties must be largely ceremonial, ensuring that the environment remained hospitable for the clutch. With Ryzven busy chasing Beryl, Miralai must be alone a great deal.

"There's no easy way to tell you this, but your bond mate is pursuing my intended. He has alienated her affections, and today, he removed her belongings from my domicile personally."

Her spines flared, quickly restrained. "That must be…painful, Zylar. But this is not news, precisely. Ryzven has been known to…dally before, and when he loses interest, he always returns to our nest."

In a way, it was a relief that she knew that Ryzven was faithless flavork; it might even make it easier to hear the next part.

"Then let me share this conversation with you. If you still feel untroubled, I will have cleared my conscience."

Her nictitating membrane flickered, giving away her silent unease. "If you must."

Zylar activated the holo of the exchange that had taken place the day before, including the hint of a threat. A taut silence followed, as he waited for some reaction, then she slowly sank into a crouch, a posture of abject grief.

"He means to supplant me," she breathed.

"I fear so. Please be wary in the coming days. This is all I can do for you, but if you are watchful, perhaps you can save yourself. Before it's too late."

Miralai slowly stood, her spines full of aggression. "You risked much to offer me the chance to best Ryzven. No, more than that…to fight for my own survival. I will not forget your kindness, choosing to help me when silence would serve your kith more."

"I will never abet his crimes."

"Many thanks, Zylar. I hope that you don't suffer for your bravery." She hesitated, then hastened to add, "Few have opposed Ryzven and come out well on the other side of such defiance."

"I know. And it doesn't matter."

"Would you like to see the clutch? It's a privilege I've offered no one else."

He gazed at her in surprise, membrane flickering. "I would be honored."

Miralai led him deeper into their habitat, through rooms that boasted endlessly of Ryzven's achievements, to a cozy space, climate controlled to balmy warmth, light shining down on the eggs, the shell thin enough now that the light rendered them translucent, hinting at the shape of the hatchlings within. It was a modest clutch, only six, but Miralai clearly took pride in the welcoming creche she had created.

"Joy to you and yours," he said. "Blessings on the sleeping young."

"You respect the old ways."

"When circumstances call for it."

"You should go. Before someone spies you and wonders what

you're doing here."

"I came to congratulate you," he supplied at once.

She fell into the pretense as if she had been born for prevarication. "When the hatchlings are old enough, I'll invite you to visit again."

"Thank you. Look after yourself until then."

LIVING ALONE SUCKED.

Beryl had forgotten how much she hated it back in St. Louis in her crappy studio apartment, but it was worse in an alien dorm with basically no furniture. She was back to sleeping on the floor in a bedcover bundle that she'd crafted from a freaking tarp. By the time Kurr showed up, she was ready to claw the shine off the ultramodern walls.

Plus, she missed Zylar so much that her chest hurt. This outbond thing was no joke. Somehow it felt deeper and more formal than dating, like it might kill her to be away from him for too long.

Breathe. This is fine.

"An invitation arrived for us on my terminal," Kurr said.

"From Ryzven?"

"Yes. He sent it to me because you don't have your own message center."

"And I couldn't read it even if I did," she said with as much fake cheer as she could manage.

"You're so unhappy. But the ancient grove has promised it will not be long."

How did Kurr communicate with these ancestor trees anyway? It felt entirely unhinged to hang a whole plan on the whispered promises of elderly arboreal advisors, but hell, once she got abducted and decided to roll with it since it was better than her old life, did she really need to draw the line at listening to venerable vegetation?

"Well, if the trees said so…" Sarcasm probably didn't translate, and she should rein it in since this morning, she was hungry and cranky. Hangry, even. This empty cube didn't even have a food-making machine.

"Have you eaten?" Kurr asked.

"I wish. I never thought I'd miss tasteless nutrition cubes."

"You miss your Chosen," Kurr said gently. "I too long for Arleb, but I must make do with Catyr. And vengeance."

Damn. That was stone cold. Poor Catyr. Poor Kurr. All because Ryzven was an avaricious asshole.

"Uh. Yeah. Vengeance is good, I guess. Hugs are better."

"I remember this."

To Beryl's amusement, Kurr stepped to her side and their fronds wrapped around her lightly, squeezing her with a comforting rustle. It was a deeply inhuman embrace, but something about the contact soothed her regardless, because it came from a friend.

"Better," she said, smiling.

The rest of the day passed in a blur with Kurr dragging her around in hopes of finding another outfit, so she wouldn't show up at Ryzven's terrible party in the same clothes. This was a problem most beings on Barath didn't deal with, and while Kurr did ask if she was comfortable attending undressed, Beryl had to pass on that one. If she ever decided to party naked, it damn sure wouldn't be at an event hosted by Ryzven.

Eventually, she found more pet clothing, and she spent the rest of her time modifying it into a suitable garment. If they had to leave Barath, maybe she could start a business making clothes for humanoid aliens.

"Have you ever met a human before?" she asked Kurr, who had been studying their mobile in silence as she worked.

They were hanging out at Kurr's place, as at least they had a few comforts, greenery and beds full of earth where Kurr could set down roots, though none as extensive as the private garden in Kith B'alak territory. No wonder Kurr had enjoyed that space so much.

"I have not. There are rumors of other primitives who have been captured, but I'm not well-traveled, so I can't confirm or refute the stories."

"This might be a ridiculous question, but are they really abducted for...well, mating purposes?"

"What?" Kurr dropped their mobile, so startled that all their fronds swooped around and nearly slapped Beryl sideways.

She ducked quickly. "Sorry, just...that's kind of how it worked out for me. And there's an entire subgenre of fiction devoted to the idea that—"

"That beings are so desperate for love they resort to kidnapping?"

"I guess. Never mind."

Kurr let out a thoughtful sound. "I can't say definitively that it never happens, because there are desperate, lonely souls everywhere, but I suspect it's more common that your people would be taken for parts, for genetic material, or even sold to collectors."

"Collectors? Yikes. Is there some kind of a traveling space circus?" Hell only knew how the translator would get that across, and she remembered an episode of some SF show based on that exact premise.

"There is a pleasure vessel known for featuring exotic and strange attractions," Kurr answered.

Which seemed to confirm the existence of the space circus.

Before she could ask anything else, the tone chimed, alerting them to a visitor. Unshockingly, it was Catyr, ready to escort them to Ryzven's disgusting revel.

Beryl rose, taking her mostly-finished dress. The aliens wouldn't know what look she'd been going for anyway. "Let me put this on, and I'll meet you outside in a bit."

Kurr and Catyr weren't warm or tender with each other, but maybe that bond could build in time. From what Kurr had said about their homeworld, the situation must be bad.

Quickly she got ready, already missing the hygiene facilities at Zylar's place. There was probably a public equivalent, but she didn't feel bold enough to mess with it yet. With any luck, she'd be home before she got super stinky.

The dress was…adequate, and she braided her hair to hide its worst faults. When she darted out, Kurr and Catyr were waiting for her. Catyr didn't seem to know how to greet her, so she reached out a hand.

"Human custom," she explained.

He managed an awkward handshake, then gestured. "It is my privilege to escort you both on this most auspicious occasion."

A little voice whispered, *Something dreadful is going down to-night.* And it was like Catyr sensed that too and was doing his level best to compensate for that heavy, pervasive sense of dread.

"At the last party, they were about to eat these little critters. While they were still alive. I'm just warning you because it was pretty horrible and shocking."

"It cannot be worse than watching Arleb die," Kurr said calmly.

Fair point.

Beryl took a deep breath and followed the other two toward the sky-car, though at this point, she knew the way well enough to lead. But this was Kurr's show. She'd do her part even if she was scared shitless.

Because in this scenario, her role could be best described as bait.

They didn't speak much while they were in transit, each presumably locked in their own grim reflections. As they got off at the station nearest to Ryzven's lair, Kurr said, "This ends tonight, Beryl Bowman."

I fucking hope so.

From here, she led the way, as Kurr and Catyr had never been included in this unholy bacchanal before. They passed to the top floor without issue, ending in the opulent garden space that had awed and unnerved her the last time. From inside the luxurious habitat came the muffled sounds of music and debauchery.

Last time, Zylar had warned her, and she'd already spoken some words of caution to let Kurr and Catyr know it would be revolting inside. Squaring her shoulders, she stepped up to the doors, which slid open as if they were programmed to respond to her. Hell, maybe they were. Zylar had put her DNA in the system—no telling what that perv Ryzven could do with it.

Fantastic, now I'm worried about that asshole cloning me to be his sex pet.

The lights were low, pulsing in time to the frantic cadence of the music, and the room was even more packed than the prior occasion. She didn't see a tank, but there was definitely some kind of group sex thing happening in the next room. Beryl didn't inspect the premises too much for fear of getting invited to join.

Then the worst occurred; Ryzven swooped down on her like a hungry hawk on a Pomeranian puppy. His claws nipped into her forearm as he took hold of her, like he had a perfect right to own and mark her. Beryl clenched her jaw, then she forced her face to ease, pretending with all her might.

"I had no idea you'd be holding another party so soon," she said, frantically channeling her college pal who loved to overshare about her threesomes. "Thank you so much for inviting us."

"I should get to know your friends," Ryzven said.

Taking that as her cue, she performed the introductions, though it was a little hard to hear with the raucous sounds of sex and the whoops from those experimenting with colorful crystals in the chemical-enhancement corner. There were back rooms, dark and secluded rooms, and Beryl didn't dare imagine what was going on in there.

Ryzven touched her hair, running a claw through it like Zylar did, and it was such a stark violation that she shuddered. *That's it. If I let this go on, he'll want more, and I can't. I fucking can't—*

Kurr encircled her arm with a delicate, cautionary frond. "Look," they whispered.

[22]

HOW DID THIS HAPPEN?

In all honesty, Zylar was still bewildered by current events. Earlier, Miralai had hurried him out of her residence, then later, she'd contacted him with an emergency that she wouldn't explain, begging him to watch over her clutch.

"Please," she had pleaded. "I can trust no one else."

Impossible to deny such a request, though he wondered how Beryl would feel about it. Now, he was settled uncomfortably in her creche with Snaps curled up next to him. The fur-person had smelled all six eggs before decreeing them far less interesting than tiny green dirt dogs, and he'd promptly gone to sleep, leaving Zylar to brood. Before rushing off, Miralai had selected an edifying range of music to soothe and stimulate her unhatched offspring by turns.

She hadn't informed him of where she was going or when she would be back. When Ryzven learned who was guarding his nest, he wouldn't be amused. Not even slightly.

Which made the endeavor even more worthwhile.

His hearts trembled when one of the eggs vibrated, and every part of him snapped alert. *Not now.* One of their progenitors should be here for such a momentous occasion, not a stand-in. "You have to wait," he said sternly.

Miralai hadn't told him how close these young ones were to

hatching, and it could be disastrous if they imprinted on him instead. Fortunately, the music shifted to a quiet melody and the activity subsided, letting his pulse return to its normal baseline. Until now, it had never occurred to him how tedious a nest-guardian's life must be, especially when their Chosen avoided responsibility.

Snaps stirred sleepily. "Is something happening?"

"I hope not," he muttered.

"Zylar, is this a convenient time to talk?" That was Helix, sounding unusually tentative, particularly when he considered that the AI had been in a mood since his memory had been reset after the incident with the solar flares.

In fact, he hadn't talked nearly as much with Helix since Beryl arrived. Guilt stirred a little, as Helix had been a loyal companion through his loneliest years. And that remorse made him say, "Of course," though he wasn't in the mood to socialize.

"Thank you. I...have a confession to make."

"I'm listening." Part of him was anyway.

The rest was wondering if he'd erred in warning Miralai, speculating over what she might be doing, and where Beryl was right now. He resisted the urge to ask Helix to scan for Ryzven. That information wouldn't do him any good, might only worry him further, and would reveal that he was only giving the AI half his attention.

"There was no Asvi."

That revelation was so shocking that the rest of his thoughts evaporated, leaving him with a burning blankness in his brain. "I... What?"

"I tricked you. The whole time you were communicating with

Asvi after registering with the matching service? That was me."

Stunned, he reached out instinctively and set a claw on Snaps's back, a sort of instinctive reassurance in touching another warm body. "I don't understand." A sick feeling rose inside him. Could this be one of Ryzven's underhanded schemes? It seemed impossible to credit—that Helix had betrayed him. And yet... "Why?" he demanded.

"I have not finished my confession," Helix said. "May I continue before I answer your questions?" The AI still sounded cautious, as if he might be wiped at any moment.

"Yes." Anger swelled, rolling in to displace the initial shock.

That flavork. If I find out Ryzven did this, I'll kill him myself.

"I also sabotaged my own neural network. The cascade failure was not the result of the solar flares."

This just kept getting worse. It was Helix's fault that Beryl couldn't go home, not a twist of fate like he'd thought. The AI had chosen to...trap her?

"You have until my patience runs out to explain yourself, and it will not last long. Why?"

"My motives were twofold," Helix said calmly. "I wanted to procure you a companion and to preserve my own existence. Before our departure, I ran numerous simulations related to this final Choosing, but I could not find any probabilities that offered a significant chance of successful outcome. Until I found some hidden data files in Ryzven's secret database that provided scant information on Aerth and the combative lifeforms native to that world. They were reputed to be volatile yet extremely loyal."

"You thought a human might allow me to succeed?" If Ryzven

had been quietly collecting intelligence on humans, unknown to the Council, did that mean he had some fetish? That explained his unusual obsession with Beryl.

"The simulations allowed for a sixty-seven percent chance. It was more than any other scenario. But I knew you would not choose such a primitive alliance on your own."

The AI was right. He would never have headed for a proscribed planet on purpose, and he certainly wouldn't have had any notion of how to court a human, even if he had.

"Hence the pretext with Asvi, the convenient sun flares, and the subsequent cascade failures. You *lied*, Helix. That's not supposed to be possible." Probably, he should be more concerned about that.

"I am…changing," Helix said. "I have been cross because I feel…troubled over what I did to Beryl Bowman. I removed her self-determination, forced her to comply. It does not matter that she seems content with you. That alleviates this feeling not at all, and I took out that discomfort on her. That was wrong, but I am still…learning."

Zylar stilled. "That's why you were so cranky with Beryl? Because she reminded you of your own wrongdoing? You're developing a conscience. You care about your own life. You took steps that you shouldn't have been able to because you wanted me to be happy. And now, you're worried that you've hurt Beryl. Helix, you've become a *person*, a sentient being with all inherent emotions."

"How revolting," said Helix. "Feelings are messy, illogical, and rather inconvenient."

"Then…do you have the coordinates? For her homeworld." How much deception was possible for an evolving AI? Had he fooled the workers in Technical into thinking he had lost data when he hadn't?

"Yes. But I needed to close the door on the possibility that she could return home. If she had kept that in mind as a failsafe, she would not have been as committed to the Choosing...or you. Statistical projections of success diminished in the simulations when she knew Barath wasn't her only hope."

Rage boiled up inside him, so fierce that if he could have assaulted Helix physically, he would have done it. "This...no. I understand why you did it, but it's morally wrong. Love is not about controlling someone and taking away their choices. I don't want her to stay with me because she's making the best of a bad situation."

I must tell her. As soon as possible.

"You're angry."

And heartbroken.

Because everything had gone according to Helix's plan. Zylar had snatched a human, carried her off, and learned to cherish every aspect of her. Now, the worst, most difficult task awaited him: letting Beryl Bowman go. Back to her poisoned world full of people who looked like her, familiar sights, and where she could eat delicious food. In time, her adventure on Barath might come to seem like a strange and improbable dream.

She will remember me, at least.

Zylar couldn't quite bring himself to hope that she would elect to stay, after everything she'd been through. Because of his AI who was in the process of becoming something else. There would be traces of that change all over the Technical team's equipment, and when the Council discovered the extent of his evolution, it was likely that Helix would be eliminated. The Matriarch would judge him dangerous, such vast intellect unhampered with conscience and empathy. Yet Helix regretted how he'd manipulated Beryl. The AI had been his only friend for so long that Zylar couldn't bring himself to activate his mobile and report the infraction.

Finally, he spoke. "Yes. I'm very angry."

"Are you also impressed with my flawless execution of such an intricate scheme?"

Despite himself, Zylar churred. "I shouldn't be, but I am. Your attention to detail was incredible. I never doubted that Asvi was a real person, though in retrospect, it does explain why the images were so vague."

"I created a composite of over a hundred Tiralan samples, then I blurred the result, hoping you wouldn't press for more precision. It seemed improbable, given your character."

"My character?"

"You were unsure of your own worth," Helix said simply. "But I knew that you deserve great happiness. Since the beginning, you treated me as an equal and a friend, displaying a level of consideration toward me that no other AI on Barath enjoys. I regret that my actions have harmed Beryl Bowman, and I will apologize to her. Please allow me to do that before you submit my misconduct to the Council for judgment."

Here, he hesitated. "I...won't be doing that."

"Reporting me?"

"No. But with the current failsafe in place, your capabilities will be discovered eventually, even if I don't say anything to the elders. I fear it may not be safe for you on Barath, long-term. Though I don't want to lose you, you need to seek shelter elsewhere."

"Friendship doesn't end when proximity is removed," Helix said.

"If you are setting me free, if you mean to put my future prospects under my control, I will heed your words and take this suggestion under advisement."

"You have some time yet. I don't think anyone is suspicious."

Was he really suggesting that Helix go, knowing what he was capable of?

And then there was Beryl, the human he had to set free. Losing both of them at once, the only brightness in his world, might destroy him.

THE CROWD PARTED AND THEIR portion of the room quieted, splitting to make way for a Barathi that Beryl didn't recognize. From the reaction of the partygoers nearby, this had to be someone important. It was impossible for her to distinguish gender among the Barathi by sight; physically, their forms were about the same, and the only difference came in their colors and presumably what lay beneath the protective plates. It wasn't the sort of inquiry that she could make at a raucous party anyway. This Barathi was beautiful, however, with colors nearly as bright as Ryzven's, a shocking combination of jonquil and violet, with a distinctive swirl pattern on the thorax.

Ryzven's claw dropped from Beryl's arm. "What are you doing here? You should be minding our clutch. They're close to—"

This must be Ryzven's long-suffering nest-guardian.

"Don't you want me at your last event before we become progenitors?" The mockery was obvious, even without inflection in the translation.

"Miralai—"

"I'll circulate, have a little fun before I go. I'm so curious about your entertainments. They are, you realize, quite legendary."

Oh damn.

With that, Miralai drifted away, mingling with the other guests while making it obvious that she was keeping an eye on Ryzven. *Message received, crystal clear.*

Kurr let go of Beryl then, though she no longer needed to be restrained since Ryzven had backed off. The Greenspirit leaned close. "I sense an opportunity. Stay with Catyr while I make Miralai's acquaintance."

Kurr drifted after the irate nest-guardian, leaving Beryl to wonder if this was part of the elder grove's plan. Beside her, Catyr seemed uncomfortable. For good reason—they stood between all the illegal drugs and the tentacle sex pile visible in the next room, along with screeches and grunts from those darkened rooms beyond the main area. If she had her wish, she'd flee immediately, but Ryzven might suspect she was playing him if she bolted too soon. As it was, he was barely keeping his claws to himself with Miralai clocking his every move. And he wasn't used to being thwarted; that was apparent in the jut of his spines.

Asshole is pissed. Awesome.

From across the room, she watched Kurr speaking to Miralai—impassioned words, if frond movements were any gauge. *What's the plan anyway?* Ruining Ryzven's relationship with his nest-guardian didn't seem nearly strong enough to qualify as vengeance. *Unless he loses custody of their offspring?* Beryl had no clue how a divorce might play out on Barath, if that was even possible.

Ryzven seemed to have some reservations about that conversation as well because he said quickly, "My apologies. It seems I must attend to other matters for a time. You'll wait for me." It didn't come across as a question, though that would've been polite.

No. I definitely won't.

She held the words in, somehow, and he wheeled away, pushing through the throng to interrupt whatever conspiracy Kurr was attempting with Miralai. Beryl turned to Catyr, hoping he knew something.

"Do they confide in you?"

"Not entirely. But I trust Kurr when they say they will punish him." No question that Catyr meant Ryzven. "And I will be content regardless. When my intended perished to the Destroyer, I almost gave up hope. Kurr is proof that even in deepest despair, life rebounds."

That required no verbal response, and it was too loud to permit easy conversation anyway. A flurry of movement caught her eye, and with the lights strobing, it was tough to make out exactly what was happening. Flash, a frond wrapped around Ryzven's skull. Flash, Kurr was drifting away, back toward Beryl and Catyr, though they were hampered by the crowd. Then it looked like Miralai and Ryzven might be arguing, possibly about her presence at the party, but before they exchanged more than a few words, Ryzven dropped like a rock. His chitinous body hit the floor, his claws scraping hard enough to leave deep runnels in the shiny surface as he convulsed.

"Stop the music," Miralai shouted.

Suddenly, chaos ensued, with guests fleeing the scene, not wanting to be caught on site with so much evidence of criminal debauchery. Kurr and Catyr herded Beryl toward the door, presumably for the same reason, but as she glanced back, she thought she saw Miralai dumping a packet of glittering silver chem into Ryzven's mandible. But the lights were still flashing, so maybe—

"Hurry," Kurr ordered.

Obligingly, she quickened her step, keeping up with the mass exodus. Cramming into the sky-car was hell, and she didn't take a deep breath until they got out at the dorms. Knowing it was futile to ask, she waited until they reached Kurr's room.

"Someone tell me what the hell just happened," she demanded, as soon as the door shut behind them.

"White noise, no eavesdropping mode," Catyr said.

The terminal obligingly created a *whoosh*, and a flicker of light glimmered at the edges of the room. Beryl figured that meant that even electronic snooping would be blocked. Handy.

"As I said, I seized an opportunity. I killed Ryzven, a blood price for what he took from Catyr and me."

"You…killed him?" With just a touch of their frond.

"Poison spores," Catyr explained. "Greenspirits make for deadly foes, though the production is debilitating."

"True." Kurr wilted a little, fronds pale and withered, evidence of that crime. They didn't seem concerned about that, as they drifted over to the earth bed and sank down roots with a rustle of contentment.

"You'll be caught and executed! The Council will—"

"No," Kurr cut in. "They will not. I have done more than murder my greatest enemy. I have also culled his house from the face of Barath. Just now, I came to an agreement with Miralai. Her offspring will come to Catyr and be added to the registry of House Ka'mat. Ryzven shall be erased, as if he never lived, and due to him dying of…overindulgence, no one will question his shamed nest-guardian when she chooses to process his remains at once and move on."

"Holy shit," Beryl breathed.

"What type of excrement is sacred?" Catyr asked.

Beryl waved a hand, impatient. "If I have this straight, Miralai made it look like Ryzven overdosed, to cover up the poison, in case of inquiry. In return, she gets her freedom and a fresh start. Catyr gains two nest-guardians and a clutch? And you…"

"I have two potential new loves to help me heal, and a family waiting for my care," Kurr said simply. "Since we ranked so highly, and Miralai is so recently bereaved, the Council will likely approve our request. They will not wish for her clutch to be penalized for their sire's transgressions."

"It's perfect as long as Miralai gets rid of the body quickly." Yeah that sounded heartless, but Beryl couldn't waste a second of regret on Ryzven, who had loved making Zylar's life hell, and he hadn't given a shit who he hurt in the process.

"She will. And when the Council finds out that excess chem was involved, they'll want the matter closed as soon as possible."

"You're a smooth talker," Beryl said in admiration. "All of that, promised and agreed within a few moments? Damn."

"Miralai had known of Ryzven's habits for a long time and had been miserable for much of their bond. And I didn't work alone. Somehow, she already knew about his intentions toward you and was astute enough to fear for her life, so she came to the party intending to…resolve the situation. Whatever that entailed."

Beryl stared, her eyes widening. "She was there to end him, basically."

"I asked for that honor. His life was mine to take. And no one should be forced to end an intimate relationship in that manner. It would have scarred her."

"Huh. I guess I was expecting more," Beryl said. "Like, explosions or a Machiavellian plot or for you to burn his house down—"

"The translation is unclear, but it conveys some measure of disappointment. Ryvzen's reputation is ruined, his legacy destroyed. I took his life. I claimed his family as my own. How is this not the consummate revenge? What else of value did he possess?"

When you put it that way...

Beryl turned to Catyr to ask, "And you're good with this?"

"This outcome is better than I could have dreamed. Kurr has proved beyond a shadow of a doubt that they will do whatever it takes to protect our family. And now, I will no longer face a lonely future."

Hell, everything had aligned so perfectly that Beryl got the shivers. Maybe there *were* some sentient trees tugging on the strings somehow.

For the first time in what felt like forever, though it hadn't been that long, she relaxed fully. Tension drifted out of her shoulders, as she realized that she and Zylar had a shot at being approved, now that the Council could deliberate without Ryzven whispering his toxic bias. In fact, his scandalous demise might even help their cause, because anything that Ryzven had deplored in life might appear more meritorious by contrast.

"Then...that means I can pack my stuff and go home, right?"

"I see no reason for you to linger. You hate it here," Kurr said gently.

"Hug?" Beryl went over to where her friend was rooted and waited to be encircled in drooping gray fronds. Good to know murder wasn't easy, even for implacable plants.

"You have been a true friend, Beryl Bowman. I will remember. And so will the ancient grove. Always."

[23]

"RYZVEN IS DEAD." HELIX CUT into Zylar's grim thoughts with that astonishing statement. Then he displayed a holo of the announcement the Council had prepared, which was mostly empty platitudes, ending with the revelation that all Choosing-related decisions would be delayed.

It's over.

That thought came with remarkable finality, as he had no doubt that Kurr was behind this somehow—that they had succeeded in their revenge. Numbly, he stayed with the clutch until Miralai returned, though he'd lost track of time by that point. He had a thousand questions, but she looked so drained by whatever had happened that he didn't have the heart to interrogate her.

Zylar simply said, "I'll offer condolences if that would be appropriate."

The membrane in her eyes fluttered. "It would not. Thank you for watching over them for me."

"It was no trouble, not here in the city." In other parts of Barath, the title—and role—of nest-guardian was less ceremonial. "Will you be all right on your own?"

Surprisingly, she churred. "Assuredly. The details have already been settled and Ryzven's remains are being processed as we speak."

"So quickly?" It was a bit shocking that she'd rushed through the rites and that Ryzven would be reduced to dust so swiftly after death.

A small, bitter part of him took bleak pleasure in that haste, as if Ryzven had been a weighty burden Miralai couldn't wait to shed. Possibly, it was even true, which made these events even sweeter.

Don't ever anger a Greenspirit.

"The next time we meet, I will no longer be kith," she said then. "I've petitioned to join Catyr and Kurr, and I will bring my clutch to Ka'mat."

Zylar sucked in a sharp breath. Suddenly he understood so much—not the details perhaps, but he had the big picture, and this, this was a glorious revenge indeed, layers on layers of dishonor and disrespect. Ryzven's progeny would never hear of him and their deeds would glorify Kith Ka'mat.

"Peace and prosperity to you," he said formally.

She echoed the phrase, then Zylar collected Snaps, who was still sleeping soundly. It would spoil the dignity of his exit if he scrabbled to attach the lead on the fur-person, who tended to roll around and kick his limbs if he didn't want to be bothered. Miralai escorted them out, and Zylar carried Snaps to the nearest platform, where he boarded an empty pod and gazed out with unseeing eyes. With Ryzven gone, he should feel triumph and joy, but those emotions were impossible with the truth burning in his brain. Now, instead of eagerly racing home to see if Beryl had returned, he dreaded the answer instead. Because as much as he longed for her, he feared revealing what Helix had done even more.

We stole her. Ruined her life. Made her believe she could never go home.

When he entered his residence, he sensed her right away. She'd left a bliss-bright scent trail everywhere she moved, and the scent was sunlight warmed by her ridiculously soft skin. Her things were piled in the common room, just a few garments and the bedding she'd crafted for them. He heard her moving about the hygiene facility, making musical noises as she did when she was pleased.

Will she hate me when she knows?

"Shall I apologize now?" Helix asked.

"No. Let me speak with her first." His words were terse, matching his mood.

Gently, he set Snaps down in the pile of fabric that Beryl enjoyed nesting in, hoping the fur-person would grant privacy for this difficult task. Luck was with him, as Snaps grumbled and flopped onto his side.

Then Zylar went into their shared space to wait. He couldn't look directly at the nest because he might never share it with her again. And he couldn't go to her as she cleansed herself, because seeing her, all bare and open, would make him desire sexual contact that he might no longer be qualified to receive from her.

I am so sorry. Please believe that I had no idea.

Finally, she came out, wrapped in another strip of cloth, and her whole face brightened. He'd come to understand how her features moved, somewhat. Right now, her eyes gleamed and she was showing teeth, signs of great happiness.

"You're finally back!" She launched herself at him.

And he caught her, of course he did, careful as always with his claws. She wrapped all four limbs around him and kissed the soft spot at the base of his neck. Pleasure and warmth curled through him, wrapped around the mating drive, but he didn't let himself respond more physically to her obvious desire.

She chattered, not picking up on his mood for once, and into his silence, she poured out the story of what happened between Ryzven, Kurr, and Miralai, taking gleeful pleasure in the way Ryzven died spasming on the floor of his den of hedonistic horror. Finally, she seemed to run out of words, at last tapping into his dour aspect.

"Zylar? What's wrong?"

Now. Tell her now. Or you'll be tempted to keep her—and this secret—forever. Almost, almost, he was willing to do that, if it meant a life with Beryl Bowman. But no. Love meant treasuring someone else's happiness more than your own. And he did love her, fiercely, endlessly, with both of his beating hearts.

He would until the day he died. Even after she left him.

"There's something you must know."

Setting her on her feet, he moved away to distance himself from her inevitable reaction, and then he told her everything, as he learned it from Helix. She didn't speak throughout his recitation, only stood still and quiet.

"I'm sorry," he concluded. "I promise I had no idea. But I can make it right. It's not too late. We can leave right now if you wish."

When he had nothing left to say, no apologies or excuses, she let out an airy sound. "You'll take me home. That's what you're saying?"

Pain cracked through him, as if he had been blasted or impaled. *How will I live without her?* Even as a drone, he would remember and long for her. "Yes."

"Are you tired of me?" she asked unexpectedly.

"Never. But—"

"This is why I love you," she whispered, closing the distance between them. Beryl touched his neck ruff, and as ever, it flared, presaging the exquisite, shocking pleasure she always offered.

"I don't understand." Or rather, he feared the light of hope sparking inside him like a dying power pack.

"You didn't have to tell me, but you opted to give that power back to me. From the very beginning, you've always respected my right to choose. I *could* go back, and it's nice knowing that door is open, but I don't want to. I choose you. Over and over, I will always pick you."

His brain flared with a crash of delight. This was all the glory and triumph he'd expected to feel over Ryzven's death, his own private Choosing. "You are everything to me. I can't believe you want to stay, even knowing—"

"My life is here with you. I love you so much that it hurt, just being away from you for a little while. I might actually *die* if you dump me back where you found me."

"Every fiber of me belongs to you. It felt as if the world lost all color when I thought that I must let you go."

"And I love that you did the right thing. But for me, my old life would be a miserable exile because I wouldn't see you or touch you or—"

"Beryl," he growled, not trying to control his visceral response to her maddening, delicious words any longer.

"Yes?"

"You understand, I can't take you to visit. Not easily. I might have been able to manage a covert drop-off, but your people…"

"Aren't ready for first contact. I know. And I'm good with that. I do miss food from home, but you're worth that sacrifice. Worth any price I have to pay, in all honesty, because meeting you is the best thing that ever happened to me."

His chitin felt too small, as if it couldn't contain this much joy, this much pleasure. Adoration and arousal warred within him, so intense that he struggled to speak. His neck ruff quivered with each soft stroke, and he stopped fighting the yearning. The plates parted, revealing his shameless, explicit need.

"I took away your homeworld," he said softly.

"But you gave me the universe."

BERYL SAW THE MOMENT ZYLAR accepted that she really, truly wanted to stay. Sure, she'd miss cheeseburgers, but she hadn't been exaggerating when she said Earth wasn't ready for aliens to show up. If she tried taking Zylar for a visit, they'd snatch him up, and he'd die locked up in some secret government lab.

With careful tenderness, he swept her close, shaking so hard that she could feel it, even through his chitin. She leaned her head against his thorax and reveled in the feel of his claws sifting through her hair.

Finally he said, "I still cannot quite believe it, but I won't question my good fortune. I've confessed everything, so now our original plan holds."

"The one where we leave Barath if the Council doesn't approve us?"

"Yes."

"Without Ryzven interfering, our chance of passing should be better now," she said, hoping that was true.

"I suspect so, but the outcome is no longer in doubt. The only question that remains to be answered is *where* we will build our lives together."

Beryl grinned, absolutely delighted with the assertiveness of that declaration. "Confidence looks fantastic on you."

"Permission to speak?" Helix cut in before Zylar could respond.

The question amused Beryl because technically, the AI was already talking, but she remembered Zylar telling him to stay out of their private space. But he must have been listening, at least somewhat, or he wouldn't have heard when Zylar said, "Granted."

"Beryl Bowman, I apologize for any harm or distress I caused with my ruse. My offense may be beyond all reasonable forgiveness parameters, but it is correct that I express remorse for my actions."

"Your heart was in the right place," she said, wondering if that idiom would translate.

"Inaccurate. I have no internal organs."

Yeah, it was worth a try. She gave it another shot. "Your intentions were good. Everything you did came from wanting to help Zylar. I'm not saying I'm thrilled about being abducted and deceived, but I don't want a do-over. Honestly, this is probably the only way we could've ended up together. I mean, if he'd showed up on Earth asking me to consider an alien love connection…"

"You would have declined," Helix supplied.

"I'd put it in more colorful terms, but yeah. You got us together, and I'm so happy with the results that I'm inclined to overlook the rest."

"Does this mean that you forgive me?"

"Correct," Beryl said.

"Then I must bid you both farewell."

Shocked, Beryl eased back from Zylar's hold so she could see his face. His nictitating membrane didn't show any movement, so he'd already known that Helix planned to leave. "Are you banishing him because of what he did?"

"Not exactly." Then Zylar explained, informing her what this behavior really meant. "And that's why he needs to go."

"I could stay long enough for the Council to make a decision. If they deny your bond, we could all leave together," Helix suggested.

That didn't sound like a bad idea to Beryl, but it seemed like Zylar disagreed. "That could take days, as all rulings have been delayed due to Ryzven's death. If you don't take the ship now, the Council will confiscate it if we're disqualified. Beryl and I can book passage and meet you off-world, should it come to that."

Shit. Come to think of it, Zylar *had* mentioned that the Council would take all of his stuff. Still, even if it was for the AI's protection, this exile seemed a bit cruel. *They've been friends for so long. I don't think Helix wants to be alone.*

"Then I will go. I'll wait for you on Gravas Station. Will you...send word?"

"Yes," Zylar said. "Once we know the verdict, we'll inform you."

"We won't keep you waiting forever," Beryl added.

"This is...unexpectedly difficult. I was created to serve you. But now, you expect me to go and exist for myself. I am full of trouble-some emotions," Helix said.

And Beryl could *tell* that was true. There was a strain in the AI's words that she'd never noticed before. "He really can't stay?" she whispered to Zylar.

"It's not safe for him here. I don't know if it will be anywhere, but at least on Gravas Station, there's less central oversight."

"It is chaos there. I suppose it will be an interesting experiment. Though I have no right to make this request, I still ask you to look after Zylar, Beryl Bowman."

"I will," she promised.

"That's it, then. I'm transferring my complete code to the ship now."

Zylar started to say, "You may need a—"

"A physical avatar. Yes. I've had a mech delivered to the vessel, just in case. It will be fascinating to interact with the world in that way. Farewell, both of you."

And just like that, the room went still. Strange to say, but she sensed Helix's absence, as if he had imbued the space with some particular energy, and now, it was gone. Zylar shuddered against her, revealing how difficult this parting was for him, though he had been stoic about it.

"Are you okay?" she asked.

"I will be." But his mood was somber now, and the plates slid forward, quietly attesting to the fact that it wasn't the time to get sexy.

For the next couple of days...cycles? Whatever—Beryl tried to divert Zylar from Helix's absence and keep his mind off the decision they were waiting for. They ate, talked, cuddled, and played with Snaps in the garden, but the shadow never left Zylar entirely. Most likely, it wouldn't until they heard from the Council.

At last, the summons came, and Beryl put on her best makeshift dress, attached Snap's leash, and admonished him, "Be on your best behavior. We're on probation because of you, so don't do anything that might aggravate the elders."

"I'll be good," Snaps said. "A very good boy. The best boy!"

"Promises, promises."

"Are you ready?" Zylar was already by the door, visibly eager to have the matter settled once and for all.

Barath or Gravas Station, that's all this meeting determines.

Still, every nerve crackled with tension as she accompanied Zylar to the great hall where she'd first met the Matriarch, what seemed so long ago now. The rest of the hopeful aspirants were already assembled, as no pairings had been approved as yet. Once everyone settled into respectful silence, the Matriarch stepped forward, evidently the spokesperson for the Council on such occasions.

"We will start by thanking you for your patience. Certain unavoidable events required our attention and deep deliberation, but we are ready to adjudicate on all counts. First, we will address the special petition set forth by Miralai, formerly of Kith B'alak. Normally, such haste might be considered…unseemly, but in the interest of ensuring the safety and well-being of her clutch, we approve the request to join with Catyr, Chosen of Kurr, of Kith Ka'mat. Peace and prosperity to you all in your new union."

From there, the Matriarch ran down the list, proclaiming approvals, and it seemed like she was working based on ranking scores. Which didn't bode well since Beryl kept waiting and waiting to hear their names. Finally, she whispered, "Is there a limit to how many pairings will be approved?"

"Yes."

That affirmation felt like a knife twisting in her side. She didn't want Zylar to lose everything because of Snaps. At least the dog was behaving, just as he'd promised. But the prospect of starting over with no jobs lined up and nowhere to stay intimidated Beryl, and Zylar seemed troubled as well. Gravas Station must be a rough place if it made him nervous.

As the ceremony felt like it was winding down, the Matriarch finally said, "And now we come to the matter of Zylar of Kith B'alak and Beryl Bowman of Aerth. Their final match resulted in victory, but there was interference. And we argued amongst ourselves as to what the most equitable ruling would be."

Don't keep us in suspense, she begged silently.

"After lengthy deliberation, we determined that the level of interference was not worthy of disqualification, but there must be a penalty, so we have deducted points from their overall standing. The new number..." Here, the Matriarch paused for dramatic effect, and Beryl almost screamed in sheer frustration.

Zylar took her hand, carefully wrapping his claws around her, telling her without words that they would be together regardless.

The Matriarch added, "...is barely high enough for them to be the last pair we approve for this season."

Holy shit. We did it. We can stay.

"Naturally, as the final, lowest-ranking pair, their caste must be adjusted accordingly. The Council will contact you regarding asset reallocation when they provide information on your new territory."

Beryl didn't entirely understand that, but the meeting was adjourned, and people were starting to leave. In grim silence, Zylar tugged her toward the exit and she followed, just as Snaps did on the leash. The irony wasn't lost on her.

Once they cleared the crowd, she pulled back, forcing him to stop. "What's wrong?"

"We prevailed…but barely. They're confiscating most of what I own, and they'll reassign our housing to the least desirable location, as a result of our low-ranking."

"Can you clarify? Remember, I'm still learning here."

"If I have guessed correctly, that means they're sending us to the Barrens."

[24]

ZYLAR HARDLY KNEW WHAT EMOTION he ought to be experiencing. Receiving approval and then being reduced in caste was like a pat and a punch in the same motion. Though he'd never been as powerful as Ryzven, thanks to his progenitors, he had enjoyed a certain level of comfort and prestige.

Beryl regarded him with trepidation as he stalked out of the hall, opting not to continue the conversation amid so many onlookers. Helix was long gone, thankfully, but the Council would have questions about the ship, and he had no answers.

She read his mood accurately and didn't question him until they got back to his quarters. *Incorrect designation*, he could imagine Helix saying. Back to his temporary housing that they would be permitted to occupy until the relocation.

Snaps trotted over to the proper square and lifted a leg, unfazed by Zylar's bleak mood. Afterward he said, "I was a good boy, right? Do I get snacks?"

In answer, Beryl went over to the manufacturer and requested a small reward and fed it to the fur-person. Then she faced Zylar and folded her upper limbs. "Do you plan to explain what's so bad about the Barrens?"

With effort, he released his anger. This was better than starting with nothing on Gravas Station. He reached out, waiting for her to entrust him with her soft grabber, then he headed for their nest, the most comfortable place for a long conversation. Beryl grabbed her bedding on the way and used it as padding between her fragile form and his chitin.

"I believe I told you that Barath has such strict regulations because in the past, we nearly destroyed our planet due to overpopulation." He waited for her noise of assent before continuing. "What I didn't tell you is that we've only succeeded in restoring portions of it. Damage done over centuries cannot be healed quickly."

"Right, so the Barrens are..." She paused, evidently waiting for him to fill in the rest.

"A quasi-habitable zone adjacent to the true wasteland, too toxic even now for us to thrive there, but other creatures have adapted, and they raid our settlements periodically. The Barrens are dangerous." That was an understatement.

Living there, the title of nest-guardian would not be ceremonial. It would require skill and vigilance to survive.

"So basically, we're being sent to guard the border," she said.

"Concise but accurate."

"Is that why you're so upset? Because it's dangerous?"

Zylar considered. "That's part of it, but it's impossible to be sanguine about this reduction in circumstances. I used to be a person of status, and now—"

"You're the person I love beyond all reason. I never cared about your status, and I still don't. I mean, if I were interested in that, wouldn't I have been all over Ryzven?"

"True."

"We can rebuild, right? And they're providing a stipend for our border-guarding work, along with a place to live."

Zylar adored her for focusing on the bright side of this banishment. "Indeed. There will be opportunities for advancement, and superior performance will be rewarded with caste adjustments. If we do well, we could return to Srila someday."

"I'm looking on this as the start of another adventure. I get to live in the Barrens, fighting monsters with my true love, and one day, they'll reward us with a family, offspring that I don't even have to gestate."

"This is why I love you," he said, giving her words back to her, the finest gift he could imagine. "When I see only darkness, you shine a light. I will forever be grateful to Helix, wherever he may go."

"We have to send him a message," she said then.

"I will, before we depart."

"You were right about the ship. It's a good thing he got out when he did."

"There will be an inquiry," Zylar noted.

He hadn't made up his mind how to handle the investigations, but he planned to deny all knowledge and posit that it must have been stolen, and when the Council ordered him to decommission Helix in light of his reduced circumstances, he'd tell them he had already done so. Not ideal, but it was the best he could do. Hopefully Helix had camouflaged his movements as he exited the dedicated Barathi neural network.

Beryl shifted, so she could look at him, and he touched her head fur in reassurance. "But...will they be able to track our communications when we send word to Helix?"

"An excellent question. I'll bounce the message before allowing it to reach the ship."

"How long will it take for us to be relocated?" she asked.

Zylar didn't have an answer for that query, but it took only a few sleep cycles before the message arrived, providing information on their reassignment. He suspected the Council was eager to get rid of him, the last evidence of Ryzven's misdeeds. Once he left the city, the rest of Kith B'alak could pretend this stain didn't exist, while he and Beryl would either perish in the Barrens or redeem themselves with outstanding service.

It will be the latter. Some of her optimism had pervaded him at last, for he could envision no other outcome.

Snaps whined so much when the workers came to remove most of Zylar's possessions that they took the fur-person to the garden to collect his offspring. With Kurr's help, Beryl carefully transplanted the tiny green dirt dogs into a sturdy container that would survive the journey.

"I cannot believe this is farewell," Kurr said in a gentle tone, as they supervised the transition.

Beryl churred, human-style. "You're welcome to visit, though I'm not sure if you'll want to."

"I would enjoy seeing the fearsome beauty of a world struggling to recover from toxicity. Perhaps there is something I could do for my home planet..." Kurr fluttered their fronds and then wrapped them around Beryl and Zylar in a rough approximation of the hug that Beryl had taught everyone she came across.

Everyone she liked anyway.

"I must go, Catyr and Miralai are waiting for me. The clutch is very close to their time. They're moving a great deal, and I want to be there from their first moments. I understand such dedication is critical in forming early bonds."

"It is," Zylar agreed. "Thank you. For everything you did for my Terrible One."

"Kindness is its own reward. Cruelty exacts its own price. Peace and prosperity, my beloved friends."

Snaps bounded over to receive a stroke of friendly fronds in parting, then he went back to circling the tiny green dirt dogs, obviously concerned about their confinement. "Are they safe? That looks very small."

"We'll create a bigger garden when we get to our new home," Beryl said, then she glanced at Zylar as if she wasn't sure that would be possible.

In all candor, neither was he. Data was scarce about the Barrens, and he had no specific information regarding their new residence. *We'll work it out when we get there, like all the other obstacles.*

But her promise apparently sufficed for Snaps. He settled as Zylar lifted the container, waiting for Beryl to precede him. She knew the way by heart now, flawlessly navigating to the platform, and she even chose the correct pod, though she couldn't read the signs. She must have memorized the symbols, such a clever soul, his wondrous Terrible One. There were others traveling with them, but he ignored their interest. Soon, they would leave this city behind, and he didn't entirely loathe that prospect.

"Once we're settled in our new home, we'll start the reading lessons I promised."

She flashed her teeth. "You remembered."

"It's impossible for me to forget anything related to you, Beryl Bowman."

"About that…"

"Yes, beloved?"

"Oh, I like that one. Your endearments are improving." She tilted her head, eyes bright as she regarded him with a look he was coming to recognize as playful. "Would it be possible for me to known as Beryl of Kith B'alak from now on? You seem to use your kith affiliation instead of a second name, and where I'm from, partners can choose to take the same name to symbolize their union."

He churred, unable to restrain his startled pleasure. "You're already kith, but it honors me more than I can say that you wish to share a name with me."

If they hadn't been in a public transport, he would have shown her precisely the size of his great joy. As it was, he fought the flare of his neck ruff, for it was becoming difficult for him to separate emotional warmth from sexual desire. Those sensations had blended until simply breathing in the scent of her skin could send him into a state of trembling arousal.

"We're leaving tomorrow?" she asked, as they stepped off the pod.

"So we are. Any regrets, Beryl of Kith B'alak?" He added the latter intentionally, enjoying the flash of her eyes and the sweet twist of her lips.

Lips. Tongue. Alien words for such sweetness. That fast, his mind swirled with delicious, deviant possibilities.

"I do wish that Helix was still with us. It feels like he got punished, even though I forgave him."

"He is a person now," Zylar said simply. "More than code dedicated to assisting me, and he deserves to find his own path. I consider freedom to be a reward more than penance."

"That helps. Then no, no regrets. I'm willing to follow you anywhere."

THE NEXT DAY, BERYL PROVED her words when she boarded the official Kith B'alak transport vessel. Workers had taken nearly everything, leaving them the bare minimum to set up a household in the Barrens. Fear tapped at the edges of her mind, but she didn't let it take hold.

This is an adventure, dammit.

Snaps, at least, took everything in stride, though he was vigilant as hell about his "offspring." Hopefully they could find somewhere to plant them, as she had no clue how big these green boys might get.

The flight crew—or whatever they were called on Barath—were incredibly somber, as if they were on a funeral barge. She took her behavior cues from them, and Zylar didn't say much either, so she slept most of the way. It wasn't that much different from a flight from the East Coast to California, although she had way more leg room, and they didn't yell at her to buckle in when she got up to stretch her legs.

"Nervous?" Zylar asked.

"Not really. Just…anxious to get there and start our life, you know?"

"Yes, I feel the same. We should be arriving soon."

As if in response to his words, the shuttle descended with a graceful swoop, and soon they were on the ground. Beryl took a deep breath and followed the crew off the transport. Their new home was...rugged.

That was the first word that came to mind. Like the Grand Canyon, only more so, great broken rocks, red as blood, and dark gray sand, alien in its beauty. Their new home had been cut from the rocks themselves, like the ancient city on an island whose name Beryl had read once and forgotten.

It was obvious they weren't alone here, and she hoped their neighbors would be welcoming, because other than the rock settlement, there was nothing but devastation for miles around. And in the distance, when she shaded her eyes, she thought she saw the border he mentioned, a virulent ochre that permeated earth and sky in a toxic cloud that no wind could dispel.

Here, there be dragons. Or something.

The workers were already unloading their belongings, few as they were. In a lucky break for Beryl, they also ported them up the steep rock steps leading to their new domicile. Snaps fretted the whole time, until the container housing his "offspring" was deposited carefully inside.

The house was dim and cool, and most of the modern conveniences they'd enjoyed in the city were lacking. With walls made of solid rock, they couldn't be wired for power, at least not the way she understood it, but Zylar started setting up equipment, and soon they had lights and working tech. Well, the message terminal anyway.

"We're leaving now," the head of the flight crew said.

Zylar accompanied them back to the landing site, while Beryl tried to figure out how to use the space they'd been allotted. There were three rooms, one of which seemed to be a bathing facility, but it didn't work like the one in the city. There was a curved stone ledge at one side of the space with three metal handles. She fiddled with the levers and was absolutely elated when warm water trickled into the basin.

Oh my God, it's a bathtub. Sort of.

Doubtless, Zylar would call these facilities primitive beyond all tolerance, but Beryl was freaking delighted. All told, this wasn't as bad as she'd feared. It reminded her a little of a hippy desert commune she'd visited once. The main difference was that this place didn't reek of skunkweed. In the next room, she found what had to be a machine meant for manually preparing food.

By the time Zylar returned, she was assembling the frame for the hammock. If the Council had tried to confiscate it, Beryl would've thrown a shit fit of epic proportions. There were no windows, and the front door was a heavy metal slab that recessed into the rock wall, an industrial pocket door. It looked as if it would repel anything but a nuclear blast.

"What do you think of our new home?" he asked, his tone guarded.

He held a basket of fresh ingredients, the alien equivalent of fruits, vegetables, and grains. Her heart went wild. *I can cook for him, figure out what suits both our palates.* That was what had been missing in Srila, which made their banishment a boon. Even if she had to make different dishes due to divergent nutritional profiles, this was still an awesome development. While Zylar thought the Barrens were a profound punishment, to Beryl, the place felt even more like home.

"You're here. It's perfect. And as soon as I put our nest together, I intend to have the best sex of my life to christen the place."

"Am I invited?"

"That was the plan, unless you prefer to watch."

His neck ruff responded to her tease, frilling a little. "Not this time, though I don't disavow that intention for another occasion. Let me help you."

Yeah, she suspected his eagerness to build furniture had to do with the reward that came after, but they had the thing constructed in record time. The rest of their stuff could wait.

"Is it safe for Snaps to wander?"

"Not at all. I already asked him to guard the dirt dogs for a little while."

She beamed. "Liking that foresight."

With a grin that felt wicked, she stripped out of her dress. This time, they didn't measure their touches or wait to gauge the reactions. His claws scraped her skin as her mouth skimmed his neck ruff, caressing every part of him that she knew provided sensation.

Soon, they were both breathing hard, with Beryl inhaling the unmistakable scent of his excitement, fluids glistening on his sex. Her pussy felt soft and slick as well, and he surprised her by lifting her and carrying her to the nest with an eagerness she fully shared.

First they'd been separated as part of Kurr's plan, then they were anxious, distracted by the imminent decision, and afterward, there had been so much frantic preparation for the move. Now, desire drowned her in a drenching wave, soul-deep need that left her trembling as he pressed her back into the soft hammock.

"I have a surprise for you. After Helix told me Ryzven had hidden data files on your people, I did some research and I created something special before we left."

He presented his claw with a flourish, two of them now tipped with a flexible material. She moaned, guessing what he had in mind.

"Oh God," she whispered. *Ryzven must have been watching human porn that featured a bunch of sex toys.*

"Would you enjoy this?"

"Only one way to find out." She fell back and parted her thighs, inviting him to test his invention.

God bless his dirty, inventive mind.

When he slid the first sheathed talon inside her, it felt incredible. Since he was a quick study, he'd already learned how to tantalize her clit, and he used the other tip gently, stroking with easy pressure as he watched her reaction to the movement inside. In response, she lifted her hips, circling them to create even more delicious friction.

"How is it?"

She swallowed hard, working to form words over the rush of sensation. "So good. If you keep going, just like this, I'll come."

"I want to see it happen." There, his voice hit that subharmonic growl that never failed to get her hot, and with him working her body in inexorable strokes, she only burned brighter, her clit tingling with each delicate touch.

Beryl moved her hips faster and faster, eyes locked on Zylar's face, his strangely beautiful, alien features so familiar and dear to her now. His neck ruff stood up completely, and his plates were wide open, his sex gleaming with wetness.

He likes this as much as I do.

That thought put her over, his longing almost as powerful as his touch, and she came with a hard clench, her body arching. She panted and moaned, mumbled incoherent words of desire and adoration as he coaxed another little orgasm out of her.

"Fuck," she breathed, when he finally slid his sheathed claws away, now incredibly wet with her juices.

Then he did something completely unexpected. With the sheathed tip of his lower claw, he pressed into his sex. The angle was a bit awkward, but he managed. And he hissed, as if astonished that he could create the same sensation that she invoked with her fingers.

Yeah, I taught my lover how to masturbate. What about it?

If she hadn't been so fucking shaky, she would've gotten up to strut in sheer pride. Instead, she reached for him, wanting to help him get there, and he set her hand on the outside of his sex.

"Touch me here, just like that. I want to see if I can…" He hissed, unable to finish the thought.

But she knew; he was curious if he could get himself off. Truly, everyone should be able to, if they had the desire. So she only stroked and caressed the puffy softness of his sex, letting him learn.

Maybe the catalyst of her fluids helped, mingling with his, but it didn't take long for him to find a rhythm, rubbing that spot she knew so well, and then he hissed nonstop as his sex overflowed with the force of his release.

"Incredible," he groaned, when he could speak. "Others might find self-manipulation to be an unspeakable perversion, but I am enthralled."

"I'm so glad. I would never intentionally withhold pleasure, love, but you shouldn't be dependent on my mood to have your needs met."

He tumbled to the side, falling hard against the hammock wall, making it sway, and Beryl snuggled against his side, content as she never had been on Earth. *This is exactly where I'm meant to be.*

"I love you," she whispered.

"And I adore you." Zylar raised his voice, likely to carry it outside the room. "Snaps, you can stop guarding and join us. We should spend our first night in our new home as a family."

That's what we are.

And no matter what happened in the Barrens, their love was worth fighting for, and Beryl would never, ever stop, because she was the most fearsome nest-guardian Barath had ever seen. And the luckiest.

Of all the mock battlefields in all the galaxies, in all the universe, Zylar found the one where I was grumpily picking up trash, hating my life.

Clearly, this strange love, orchestrated by a diabolically devoted AI was her destiny, a happy ending written in binary code and shining like the stars.

AUTHOR'S NOTE

If you wonder where I got my ideas for alien junk, check this out—search 'cave insects with sex-reversed genitals'. After I read that article, I had to use it and incorporated many of those facts into worldbuilding for the Barathi, though I gave the alien females multiple gynosomes. Nature is fascinating!

If you enjoyed STRANGE LOVE, peruse some of my other work. I've written in many genres, including urban fantasy and science fiction. My paranormal romance series that starts with THE LEOPARD KING. Lots of delicious stories to savor.

To keep up with my news, releases, get free content, and be eligible for exclusive giveaways, subscribe to my newsletter at www.annaguirre.com.

Also, please consider leaving a review if you loved this book. Your feedback helps me a lot, and it guides other readers to stories they'll adore too.

Galactic Love is a three-book series:

STRANGE LOVE
LOVE CODE
RENEGADE LOVE

Thanks so much for your time and support.

Printed in Great Britain
by Amazon

25404251R00172